AF266744

Foxglove and Felonies

A Bunny Sparks Cozy Mystery

Pru Scott

Holy Crow Publishing

holycrowpublishing.com

FOXGLOVE AND FELONIES

A BUNNY SPARKS COZY MYSTERY

Copyright © 2026 by Pru Scott.

All rights reserved.

ISBNs:

Paperback: 978-1-971170-00-8

eBook: 978-1-971170-01-5

Hardcover: 978-1-971170-02-2

Audiobook: 978-1-971170-03-9

This book is a work of fiction. Any references to historical events, real people or places are used fictitiously. Other names, characters, places, and events are products of the author's imagination, and any resemblance to actual events or places or persons, living or dead, is entirely coincidental.

This book is a product of the author's own work and was not generated by artificial intelligence.

No portion of this book may be reproduced in any form without written permission from the publisher or author, except as permitted by U.S. copyright law, and may not be used or reproduced for the purpose of training AI models.

Published by Holy Crow Publishing
P.O. Box 90411
Burton, MI 48509
holycrowpublishing.com

Cover Design: 100Covers

Contents

To my Appalachian granny, whose wit and wisdom infuse these pages.

Chapter One

B y the time Bunny filled the hole she'd dug with earth, daylight was fading fast. Twilight was falling earlier than expected, but that often happened when she was in the garden. She straightened, one fist pressed into her lower back as she steadied herself on the shovel with the other, and squinted at the hills. The old cemetery in the woodlands to the north would already be swallowed by darkness. A chill ran up her spine, not altogether unwelcome in the August heat.

Determined not to leave the disturbed ground bare and obvious, she pushed nearby mulch and leaf litter over it, using her foot to spare her sore back. Brushing a stray streak of white hair from her face, her only concession to time, Bunny smiled, taking in the work she'd done that day. *Not bad for an old timer*, she chuckled to herself, mentally patting her own back, something she rarely allowed. Time for a sit-down and a cup of tea. She'd choose rose hips and hibiscus in honor of Venus and the roses she'd planted that day. It was Friday, after all.

Wiping sweat from the back of her neck with the hem of her apron, she made a mental note to visit Leo soon for more rose hips. Visions of ice dancing in her tea glass teased her imagination. She looked back toward the enchanting cottage, now her home, and felt proud of the progress made since she'd arrived. The once-rough and rickety porch steps, where over fifty years ago she sat with her sisters helping their granny shell peas or shuck corn, were now smooth and level. The cedar still smelled sweet and wrapped around three sides of the cottage.

Victor, a neighbor across the road and over the hill to the south, had done a fine job and charged a reasonable price. He'd been doing odd jobs since arriving in the valley five years earlier, he'd said. She was happy to have the help. Refreshing the paint and cleaning were easily done, but woodwork wasn't in her wheelhouse. Not like her papaw, who had whittled the most delightful creatures and carved them into posts and beams. Bunny remembered the stories he told by firelight, when she was little. The creatures seemed to move and dance in the shadows, and he assured her they were there to keep her and her sisters safe. No monsters under *those* beds.

Caught in the reverie, she caught sight of the little lights in the dormer windows flicker on as the sun slipped behind the hills, now a soft velvet purple. She told herself that one day she would figure out how those candle lights worked. There was no electric line, no bill, no solar panel. Her granny always said it was a kind of magic. "Don't tell anyone," she'd say, with a wink. "Let 'em all think we're primitive. It's best to be underestimated."

The lights flickered in the windows, dimming then brightening. Bunny had seen the rise of plastic LED candles in recent years, but these weren't plastic and had no batteries. They had been there as long as she could remember.

Tamping the soil around the base of the rose one last time, she jumped when she saw movement in the foxglove.

What are you doing here?

She watched as the unusually large toad scrambled over smooth stones near the mailbox. Another chill crept over her arms. This time, she paid attention.

To Bunny, Toad's appearance would often carry a message. Though, it could also mean Granny Didima needed something. She glanced toward the hills beyond the cemetery, no longer needing to squint, as violet darkness blanketed the holler.

No white smoke.

Soon it would be pitch black. A shiver ran through Bunny, and she wished she'd waited until morning to plant her latest propagated roses in the front flower bed. It's not as if the women in the study group she hoped to start would notice.

She'd hosted plenty of groups back in her old life. Whether it was herbal study, foraging hikes, or monthly moon gossip, she knew the chatter would be the focus. They probably wouldn't even notice the ghastly ceramic rabbit she'd received from someone. She'd placed it between the weathered-gray barn and the path to the centuries-old graveyard. She had hopes the sender might acknowledge the gift if they saw it displayed so prominently, tucked just under the stand of pines.

She looked back toward where she had seen Toad. It was too dark now, or he'd already hopped away, but she could see the spire of a purple foxglove leaning dramatically to one side. Rather than fetch a lantern and investigate what looked like damage, Bunny chose to check it in the morning. The darkness, the toad, and a growing sense of dread pressed at her back, ushering her quickly onto the porch and into a house that felt too dark.

Inside, she lit the lanterns in the kitchen, breakfast nook, and hallway, then grabbed the last of Papaw's moonshine from the cupboard. She'd been saving it for a special occasion, but plain iced tea no longer held much appeal. She poured a finger of firewater and the last of the ice into her glass, silently thanking Granny for her foresight. The cold box. The lights. The rotary phone. She still had them all.

She made a mental note to visit the caves in the morning, after checking on the foxglove. She'd dig some saltpeter for Granny Didima and check in. If she had run out, she couldn't as easily make her signal smoke. She didn't use it often, but it was usually important when she did.

With her chin, Bunny cradled the heavy black receiver on her shoulder and dialed her sister, who lived up north, several states away. As she waited, her eyes wandered over the familiar kitchen. The wood stove in the corner. The handmade table Papaw built with his own hands. It was almost tempting to get sentimental.

She took a breath, twisting the phone cord around her index finger as the third ring echoed in her ear. She thought about whether badgers ate things that burrowed under foxglove. She wouldn't mention that she felt alone. Or that she was more than a little scared.

Rose answered on the third ring. "Hey, Sis. I was just thinking about you."

Bunny took another breath before she spoke, then another. "How are you?" she asked, hoping for words that might lift the weight of dread she felt.

Without hesitation, Rose asked, "What's wrong?"

"Nothing," Bunny lied. "I was just thinking about you, too, and I haven't talked to you in a while."

Rose said, "That's true! It *has* been a while. Are you all settled in?"

When Bunny moved into their grandmother Gene's cottage, Rose was still on sabbatical and drove down to help. They spent two weeks cleaning and airing rooms in the main house, which was all but boarded up after Granny Gene died the previous year. That was in May.

"I'm getting there," she said. "I finally got the barn tidied up, thanks to a helpful neighbor. Victor Tew. Remember him? He built the shelves in the barn basement, where we found so many bottles of Gigi's homemade medicines."

"Potions," Rose said. "Yeah, I remember meeting him. Always had one of those flat pencils tucked behind his ear. Did you do an inventory when he was finished to make sure all Gigi's potions were still there? I thought I remembered him having a drinking issue."

The sisters called Granny Gene "Gigi" since they were small. All three of them, Bunny, Rose and Dotty, who now lived in Colorado and worked as an architect, spent summers helping her collect flora from the hills and forests behind the homestead. Listening to Gigi wax poetic about the way flowers could ease sadness or an aching joint, and were once used to send messages of love or warning, made evenings better than *Wagon Train* or *My Favorite Martian* ever could.

Bunny laughed. "Okay, 'potions.' And he's sober now. Proud of his sobriety, in fact. Wears a button and everything. I think it says 20 years, but it may have been more. Anyway, his wife, Gloryanne, remember her? She's interested in joining the study group. I'm just starting to put it together... just meeting once a month, maybe, to learn something new. And we can use the barn as our meeting place."

"I'm surprised! You're finally starting to branch out and make friends in the valley?"

"Holler," Bunny said. "I keep saying 'valley' and every time I say it, someone is correcting me. But, yeah, I'm starting to make acquaintances here and there in the valley now."

"Holler," Rose corrected.

"Holler," Bunny continued "and, anyway, I've been keeping busy with the gardens and trying to sort things out in the house. I still haven't found Gigi's manuscripts or any of her recipes."

"That's crazy. She had so many! A whole room, right?"

"I remember a pretty extensive library, but it's only in my memory, apparently."

"Maybe it's in one of the hidden rooms. Your study group can help rap on all the walls and pull on sconces to find it!" Rose laughed.

"I haven't met many of the people in town yet. So far, those I have are really quite lovely, but I can't see inviting them over to look for secret passages."

"Have you met any lovely people of the opposite persuasion?" Rose asked, feigning innocence. "I remember Big Jake asked if you were married that first week in the parking lot at Hoodoo's little store!"

Bunny swallowed and closed her eyes. When she opened her eyelids and looked through the window at the darkened sky, she caught the movement of storm clouds rolling in.

"A storm is coming," she said.

"Beatrice, that's not what I asked," Rose teased.

"Big Jake asked *you* right after he asked me. Anyway, he didn't even wait for my answer when he saw you get out of the truck," Bunny reminded her.

"Nevermind. No one would argue that you need time." Rose's voice was softer now. "So, this study group... I'm happy to hear that you're planning one already! I really thought you were going to stop peopling altogether. I know how introverted you are. If you aren't going to have them do a scavenger hunt, what do you think you'll start studying first?"

Happy for a reprieve from any insinuations about her love life, Bunny put her glass down and started closing windows. Stretching the phone cord to its limit, she said, "Cilla from the bookstore said she could give a lesson on basic astrology. Several women she knows have already expressed interest."

"I'm surprised, actually," Rose said.

"Me, too."

And she *had* been surprised, but the number of people in the valley who expressed interest in seeing what Bunny inherited seemed to grow monthly. She suspected that some of the women who responded to Priscilla's idea were only after a peek at Granny Gene's laboratory beneath the barn, or to get confirmation about stories they'd heard about spirits roaming the land, especially up at the old graveyard. It could also be the intrigue of the gadgets providing power here and hot water there without connections to the local utilities.

"How are you getting along without electronics?" Rose asked.

"I miss *Golden Girls* reruns... and vacuums... and having a dryer to fluff up towels. I have no idea how Gigi did it in the winter," Bunny said. "When I figure out whether I can power these things, I'll start looking for a dryer, at least. In a weird way, I miss text messages. Can't get a signal anywhere in the valley because of the observatory rules. But, the quiet has been really good for me."

"Well, I think you are brave. I remember having fun as kids, but at my age I prefer quick texts and fluffy towels after a shower." Rose's tone changed slightly. "How are your own classes going?"

"I haven't started any." Bunny felt her cheeks flush as she said this.

"What? Why not? I thought that was your plan... Gigi's garden is already there!"

"I just don't know why anyone would want to learn about herbs from an old woman who just moved here?" Bunny was finally forgetting about her previous anxiety, though its replacement wasn't pleasant either.

"Bunny, you are *not* old." Rose laughed. "Otherwise, I'm old. I'm only two years younger than you, and I'm certainly not old. You're having normal self-doubt. Besides, how many wanted to learn from Gigi when she was still around? Every time she held a talk, people came out of the trees like bees to honeysuckle."

Bunny nodded, though she knew Rose couldn't see her through the phone. "I don't know anyone here."

At this, Rose snorted. "You practically know everyone! We virtually grew up there. Now get that flyer I mailed to you copied and posted at the library, the bookstore, the tea shop, and let people know you're going to teach a class! It's already August."

"We were only here summers when mom dropped us off. I haven't been back here in years. I'm just going to do the study group first and see if there's any real interest," Bunny said.

"I can print off another and mail it to you." Rose's voice took on the sound of a scolding mother. "I can sneak time at the printer in the back office and print the whole lot for you, if I have to."

"I'll think about it," Bunny nodded again. "Really. Thank you, Rosie. I have it here somewhere and I'll consider it, now that I've moved the rose garden. That's what I did today. Because it's Friday."

There was a pause in the line.

"Are you there?" Bunny asked.

"Yes. I'm just trying to figure out why Friday has anything to do with moving roses."

"Well, Friday was named for Freya, the goddess of love. Rose is the flower of love," Bunny explained. "Has to do with the planet Venus and the five-petaled pattern it makes as it moves through the heavens."

"Ah," Rose said, "how did I not know that? And how do *you* know that?"

"Might be from Cornelius Agrippa... or maybe Galen." Bunny tapped her cheek with a finger, trying to remember why she knew that.

"See? You need to teach a class!"

Bunny could feel warmth creeping up into her cheeks again. "Like I said, I promise to think about it."

Rose changed her tone again. "Okay. Good. Now tell me why you called."

Bunny knew it was pointless to make more small talk with her little sister. She wasn't sure why she ever tried. "Creepy feelings tonight. I saw Toad."

"Why did seeing a toad creep you out?"

"I didn't see a toad. I saw Toad." Bunny stressed. "The one that G. Didi told me I should keep an eye out for because he brings messages."

"G. Didi? Do you mean Granny Didima? That old lady who lives in the shack just past the graveyard?"

"She's an elder. She lives in a cute little cabin, if a little primitive."

"Primeval, more like. Like the little shanties people call their 'cabins' up here. Funny that you call her G. Didi. Reminds me of a rapper or something," Rose chuckled. "So, did it bring a message tonight?"

"What?"

"The toad."

"Oh. I don't know."

"Are you sure it's the same toad? How can you tell?"

"Well, I get a feeling, and if I look toward G.Didi's cottage, sometimes there's a signal. But there was no smoke tonight."

"It's August," Rose said. "It's too hot for a fire, isn't it?"

"Not smoke from heating," Bunny said. "The white smoke from burning saltpeter. It usually means she needs something or wants to tell me something."

"Where in the world does she get saltpeter?"

Bunny contemplated whether she wanted to spend time talking about the caves in the hills behind the property, her visits to dig and deliver the saltpeter to G. Didi, or the many ways G. Didi had to color smoke. White was a general request for a visit, red meant something was urgent. Bunny was relieved she hadn't yet seen red smoke. She didn't have to address that question, however, as another question immediately followed.

"So, is this Toad like your familiar now? Shouldn't it be more like a black cat or something?"

Bunny laughed. "Oh, no. Not you, too! I get enough teasing because I work with plants."

Rose chuckled." I remember. Anyway, what will you do in the winter, when Toad is hibernating?"

"Oh, I don't know. I'm sure G. Didi has more than one messenger. I just haven't met them all yet." Bunny contemplated. "Anyway, I know you've studied the animal spirits and their meanings far more than I have, so I was wondering if you could tell me a little about Badger Medicine."

Both Rose and Bunny had worked at a university up north, where Bunny lived until she moved to Cranberry Creek. She and Rose, with the blessing of Dot, agreed Granny Gene's house should not be left vacant after she died. Too many rumors were getting back to them that speculators were eyeing the property even while she was still alive. The decision came at the perfect time, really. Bunny had been hoping to retire for years, but the research office kept tempting her with a raise here and more comp time there. The extra time and money did make Bunny's love of plants easier to nurture, and she spent a lot of her off hours on herb walks with a field guide in one hand and a journal in the other so that notes and drawings could be recorded.

The bureaucracy of her job was stifling though, and more than a few co-workers made her working life bothersome enough that when the suggestion was made that she should be the one to preserve Granny Gene's homestead, she jumped at the chance.

Rose was still there, working as an adjunct professor in Physics. Rose found her own job interesting and it nurtured her love of mysticism. The many years she spent studying, blending spiritual insights with scientific curiosity, and her natural love of animals, practically made her an expert. She would never say such a thing, however.

"What is it that you'd like to know?" asked Rose. "I'll do my best."

"Do they ever dig under foxglove? Eat their roots?"

Rose paused for a moment. "They are the keeper of root medicine, yes. Eating roots, like foxglove, no. Why are you asking?"

"I'm not sure. Just something that popped into my head. Maybe it was Toad."

"You mean, the message from Toad was about badgers?"

Bunny thought a moment. "Maybe. What else can you tell me?"

It sounded like Rose was pouring herself a drink, so Bunny waited and took a sip of her own. With ice tinkling in her glass, Rose said, "Badger Medicine is stomach medicine. Like Bear Medicine, really."

"Oh, yes... Badger is called 'Little Bear.'" Bunny remembered having read that somewhere.

"Right," Rose continued. "They are fiercely loyal... and just plain fierce."

Bunny swirled what remained of the ice in her own glass. "So, what is the message, I wonder."

"Gut instincts? Follow your gut?" Rose wondered aloud. "Watch for disloyalty? Maybe you should ask Granny Didima. G. Didi, I mean. Did you say this was her area of expertise?"

"I don't think I did," Bunny said, "but I may ask her. I plan to head over there tomorrow."

"Well, be careful. It's a long hike up that hill."

"I'll take the Willys," Bunny said. "I'm not young anymore."

"No, but you're not old either, Sis. But that Jeepster sure is. It's older than both of us! What'd Gigi call it?"

"The Keely. I still don't know why."

"That's what we'll call it then. When you take the time to dig through all her secrets, I can't wait to hear what you find!"

They both laughed and said their good-byes. Bunny felt better. She usually did when she talked to her sister. With her new plan to ask G.Didi about badger messages and Toad's visit, she blew out the lanterns and headed for bed. As she made her way up the staircase to the room she once slept in as a child, she heard the clap of thunder and the ping of rain against the metal roof. She'd been so focused on moving Gigi's roses she failed to see the many trees speaking of the coming rain, lifting the silver underbelly of their leaves toward the sky.

She smiled in the darkness. It was good that the new transplants were being watered. She'd been preoccupied by Toad, and the abnormally tilted foxglove, and so forgot this important step. She cringed at the thought of causing harm to roses whose origins began with the settling of her ancestors in the valley.

When the thunder clapped again, it followed close on the heels of a lightning flash that illuminated the open window and the rain now pouring onto the windowsill. Perspiration beaded on Bunny's forehead at the thought of sleeping in the August heat in a stuffy room. Setting the lantern down, she closed the sash, peeled off her skirt and used it to mop up the water. She stripped down to her white cotton shift, now damp with sweat, and grabbed a feather pillow from the bed. At least one side of the wrap-around porch would be dry, judging by the direction of the rain. She'd find the driest spot and make a nest, after closing the rest of the windows.

On the porch, she found only one area that felt dry enough to settle down for the night and pulled the chaise lounge into that corner, under a window on the northwest side of the house. The wicker creaked and groaned as she shifted her weight, pulled the wet cushions out from under her, and set them against the wall. She wasn't sure she could sleep this way but was determined to try. She drifted off remembering Gigi perched on the edge of the chair, on the once bright and colorful pillows, shelling peas and humming a tune Bunny couldn't quite remember.

She was jolted awake with a crash of thunder so loud it shook the windows, including the one above Bunny's head. She sat up straight, blinking in the dark, wondering how long she'd been asleep. From this part of the porch, she could just make out the clearing that was the garden. The scarecrow she named Mr. Darcy was just a dark silhouette, but recognizable. What was not recognizable was the large figure moving through the row of carrots, stumbling over cabbages, and cursing in the dark.

The impulse to cry out "Who's there?" lasted less than half a second before Bunny felt her throat tighten and her heart beat in her ears. She had no idea what time it might be, but she was sure it must be after midnight. Frozen in place, she watched the lumbering shadow make its way from between the tomato plants to the path that led behind the house, through a stand of pines, and toward the barn. By the time the hulking figure was at the barn door, Bunny regained some movement in her limbs and clambered out of the chair.

Following the porch around the front of the house to a vantage point on the other side that gave her a view of that part of the property, she stayed in the shadows, watching. She had just made the decision to go inside and call the sheriff when a brilliant flash of lightning sparked across the sky. *Holy crocus, is that Gloryanne Tew?* She blinked into the sheet of rain as it blew onto the porch.

"Gloryanne? Is that you?" Her attempt was drowned out by a boom of thunder. *What in the world is she doing?*

Stepping out into the rain, Bunny made her way toward the barn. She could make out Gloryanne yanking on the curved handle of the door in a way that seemed almost frantic. As one hand slipped off the latch, an acrylic nail flew into the mud and a string of curses flew from her mouth.

"Gloryanne?"

Gloryanne jumped and let out a yell. "You scared me, dang you!"

"What are you doing here?" Bunny had to raise her voice, as the wind picked up and blew the rain sideways.

Gloryanne's hair was fast escaping an updo, a sparkly purple hair comb threatened to slide down her back as surely as one set of false lashes was poised to slip down a cheek. Adjusting an equally slippery spaghetti strap on what Bunny could only presume was a now-ruined evening gown, Gloryanne straightened her plump frame up to its full height and sputtered, "I thought you would be asleep! I was looking for the little ol' Jeepster thingy your granny drove. I was just going to walk but then this started, and everything else." She pointed a bright red, heavily lacquered nail toward the sky. "Your granny always let me borrow it when I needed it at night, and everything else."

Bunny stared at her, one hand covering her eyes in an effort to see through the downpour. "The Keely is on the other side, in the open stall." She jerked a thumb toward the back of the barn, hoping to indicate where she meant. She didn't think it would be necessary to inform her about all the work she'd been doing on the barn that meant most of it had been rearranged. "I don't keep the key in it, though."

"I forgot. You ain't from the country."

Considering this, Bunny could only stare back at her once more. She also didn't think it a good time to remind Gloryanne that she'd lived here with Granny Gene every summer of every year of her life before she was twenty-one, but she might not remember that.

Bunny met Gloryanne again soon after Granny Gene died. She remembered the day, in fact. She and Rose spent that morning moving boxes, sweeping cobwebs, and learning how to use the hand-crank washer on the porch. Gloryanne teetered up the steps while they worked, one kitten heel, then the other, catching on each stair as it dangled precariously from her fleshy toes, her bright purple dress rustling with each step. Both sisters stopped in mid-crank and marveled as she plodded up to the porch, one hand holding a plastic tupperware dish filled with something hugely curried, the other smoothing her coppery, newly-hennaed hair.

"Yoohoo!" she had called out, in a high-pitched sort of squeal. "I've come to welcome the long-lost grandchildren of the late, great Genie Sparks!"

Bunny remembered she and Rose looked at each other with eyebrows raised.

Gloryanne laughed. "Oops," she'd said, with a sort of giggle. "I meant Gene. We only called her Genie because of her potions and everything else."

"Maybe that explains the pile of little brass magic lamps out behind the garden shed," Rose said to Bunny, under her breath.

"You mean the charred remains," Bunny added, also in a low voice. "I thought she might be working on a new smelting hobby we didn't know about."

Gloryanne looked from one to the other and back again, her smile revealing a smear of bright fuchsia on teeth that had seen too much coffee. "You have your granny's button nose," she said to Rose, "and you have your granny's pretty auburn hair and everything else," she said to Bunny. "Right down to the long braid and the white bits in your bangs."

Looking at each other, Rose rubbed her nose and Bunny combed her bangs back off her forehead with her fingers.

As Bunny stood in the rain with Gloryanne, whose one meaty hand still gripped the door latch to the barn, she remembered how insistent she was to be shown around that day. She was eager to see inside the house, the contents of the barn, the way to the cemetery up over the hill past the cluster of pine trees marking the path. "I always wanted to learn about the plants, and the remedies, and everything else," she said.

That was the day she volunteered her husband, Victor, to help with any carpentry that needed doing. "He ain't had a job since he got here." She shifted to one side so dramatically to see around them and through the screen door they thought she would fall. "But he's real good with a hammer and he ain't had a drink since I've known him."

Bunny took this to mean he was reliable, and he had been. He arrived on time each day he agreed to work and he completed each task to exceed Bunny's expectations. She paid him each day before he went home, as was customary in the valley, and he had been polite and gentlemanly.

"Victor didn't tell you the barn was renovated?" Bunny yelled into the rain. She didn't think this was the best time to ask this, but wasn't sure what else to say.

"Oh, he's about as..." Gloryanne seemed to bite her lip, but it was hard to tell in the dark. She yanked her hand from the door handle and tried to smooth the hair away from her face. "We ain't talkin' right now," she said.

Her eyes darted to look toward the road that led past Bunny's and toward the hill on the other side. If one traveled as the crow flew, it was a straight shot over the hill to the farmhouse where Gloryanne and Victor made their home. "Oh, my hickory stick!" Gloryanne's eyes widened as she sputtered, then screamed, "Fire!"

Chapter Two

Bunny's eyes followed the slow descent of the false eyelash as it finally gave way and slid down Gloryanne's plump cheek, then turned to see what had captured her attention. Smoke was billowing above the hill across the road and the rain clouds were now shades of orange and red.

"Oh my criminy, that's my house!" Gloryanne shrieked.

Bunny squinted at the bright sky above the hill. "And Leo lives across from you!" she said, more to herself than to Gloryanne, who was now jumping from one foot to the next in a puddle, flapping her hands.

Gloryanne grabbed the barn door latch again, yanking with all her might. She was emitting a shrill sound Bunny tried to decipher, but all she could hear was a high-pitched squawk. She made out what might have been the word "wheel" and turned back to see Gloryanne pulling on the handle with both hands, one foot now braced against the door frame. "The Keely isn't in there," Bunny shouted, "I need to call the fire department! Leo or Victor might be in trouble."

"We don't have a fire department in the holler!" Gloryanne shrieked.

Bunny was already running back toward the house, bare feet slipping in the mud. Once inside, as water pooled beneath her, Bunny flipped through the yellowed rolodex by the rotary phone. She had no time to remember sending that to Gigi more than thirty years ago, when the switchboard in town disappeared and progress quietly forgot the people deeper in the hills.

There was only one card in the "F" section and on it was written "far" in Gigi's beautiful scrawl. On any other occasion, Bunny would have smiled and thought about her granny's way of being both proud of her roots while also poking fun at herself in a loving way. With the receiver pressed to her ear, Bunny looked upward and thanked her granny for putting that Rolodex to good use and leaving it near the phone. She also crossed her fingers that the numbers were still in service.

As she waited for an answer, she pulled the cord taut and leaned over to look out the window. No one was answering and she wasn't sure if she could still see Gloryanne by the barn. She flipped through the rolo looking for a secondary number she could try when the sound of a siren, faint but definite, could be heard growing closer. Relieved, she put the handset back on its cradle and tried to peer through the rain outside the window. The road wasn't visible from the house. Gigi had made sure the plantings of lilacs, spruce and juniper were decorative, but her main goal must have been protection from prying eyes.

At least help was on its way.

Outside, another lightning flash illuminated Gloryanne, who was now headed toward the road. One hand held the hem of her dress up out of the mud and the other waved about wildly for balance as she stumbled around puddles and rocks in the drive.

Bunny grabbed the set of keys from the hook by the door, pushed her wet feet into her garden clogs, threw a wrap-around apron over her head, and was off the porch and to the barn as fast as she was able. She would think about her aching joints and tired bones tomorrow.

When she reached Gloryanne, Bunny honked the little horn on the old Keely. Gloryanne jerked her head toward the sound, but continued toward the fork in the road that would lead around the hill. Bunny wasn't sure how she might get her into the cab, but she honked again and shouted, "Gloryanne! I'll drive you... can you get in?"

Gloryanne stopped, turned to look into the cab, then back toward what remained of the daunting journey she would surely have in those heels. Frowning, she said, "Okay." It was barely audible, but Bunny thought that was what she heard.

The Keely lurched as Gloryanne maneuvered her frame up onto the seat, holding her dress tightly with one hand. As Bunny waited for her to settle, two pickup trucks tore past, light bars flashing and sirens screaming, before turning at the fork ahead.

Gloryanne shouted, "Hurry!"

Bunny popped the old vehicle in gear and pulled onto the road, following the volunteers, their taillights already gone.

Gloryanne pulled at her dress, smoothing wet wrinkles and feeling about as if to make sure she hadn't lost anything. "My flower!" She spit these words as much as said them aloud. "Hickory sticks!"

"What did you lose?" Bunny glanced over at her, then quickly back to the road. It was difficult enough to see, even leaning over the steering wheel, her face close to the windshield.

"The flower that Da—" She clamped her mouth shut and patted the top of her dress with her free hand.

"What?" Bunny glanced over again. "Do we need to stop?"

"No, it was just a flower picked for me. It's fine. Hurry. Let's just get there!"

When they crested the hill and the blaze was in full view, Bunny could see Leo's little cottage was still there, up the drive to their right, every bit of the decorative carving he'd done himself untouched.

"My house! My house! Oh, no! My house!" Gloryanne scrambled down from her perch on the seat.

Ahead of them, the hose from the volunteer fire truck was pulled taut, the first attempt at dousing the flames just beginning. Of the people holding it, Bunny recognized only Leo.

She hopped out and went after Gloryanne.

Gloryanne had gone stock still in front of the flaming little house she shared with Victor. Her eyes were wide and fixed. Her mouth open.

Victor! Bunny scanned the men moving through the chaos, searching faces she mostly didn't know. Leo was already bracing the hose from the water tank. A battered Chevy truck roared past her and skidded to a stop behind the fire rig. She recognized it by the hand-painted sign on the door before she saw the driver. When the lanky man with the bandanna jumped down from the cab, she knew it was Hoodoo himself. Several young men piled out of the truck bed, faces unfamiliar, carrying buckets toward the shared well. Bunny searched them anyway, but she couldn't tell if Victor was among them.

Patting Gloryanne's bare shoulder, Bunny felt her clammy skin. "Gloryanne, we need to move out of the way."

Gloryanne stood fixed and unmoving. Bunny startled as Sheriff Greenwood shouted right behind her, "Let's get her out of the way!"

She wasn't sure to whom he was directing this order, but this was the one way she felt sure she could help.

"Gloryanne!" She patted her shoulder harder this time and took her by the elbow. "Come on. Leo will let us watch safely from his porch. There isn't anything we can do here."

Tugging at her arm, Bunny led her across the short, muddy expanse to Leo's and gently guided her into one of the rocking chairs. The porch was dry enough, and at least they were out of the rain.

When the screen door popped open, only Bunny looked up.

"Y'all alright?"

A woman in a wheelchair pushed the screen door further open with the footrest.

Bunny didn't recognize her. "I'm sorry. We didn't know anyone was here."

"Oh, I'm just visitin', Bunny," the woman said.

Bunny frowned, trying to place her.

"You don't remember me? Jerlene. We used to pick weeds for your granny over your summer visits."

Gloryanne still sat, transfixed, staring toward the now dwindling fire.

"Yes. I remember. Leo's your uncle." Bunny's gaze dropped to the wheelchair, its shiny metal rims catching a faint orange reflection from across the road. "But, I don't remember your being… injured."

She pulled the door further open to make room for Jerlene to push her chair onto the porch.

"Oh, I wasn't injured. I have MS." Jerlene smiled up at her. "I was diagnosed a few years ago now."

Once she was able to push the door closed, Bunny sat in the other rocker on the porch so she could be at eye level. "I'm so sorry," she said.

"Oh, heck fire. You don't need to be sorry." Jerlene smiled wider. "I make the most of it."

Bunny tried to smile back, but the situation was feeling a little surreal. She looked at the men working feverishly to squelch the flames. They were making progress and looked as if they were going to save most of Gloryanne's house. *The rain surely helped*, Bunny thought.

She looked back to Gloryanne. No change.

"I didn't know you lived here." Bunny looked into the room beyond the screen door. She could see only a small area illuminated by a green camp lantern. Leo's single rocker sat by the dark wood stove and the portable radio he left on top when the stove wasn't in use. Looking back to the porch, she noticed there was no ramp.

"Oh, I don't live here. I just got here a little bit ago. Like I said, I'm just visitin'. I do that when my husband is out of town on business."

"Where do you live now?" Bunny asked. She shifted in the seat, pulling the wet apron further around her bare legs, and hoped this would be over soon.

"Dave and I,... Dave, that's my husband, we live near the lake, over on Azalea. Do you know the area?"

"Not really."

Gloryanne may have moved a bit in the rocker, and Jerlene looked her over as she went on.

"It's newer, maybe that's why. It's a real nice area. We have all the comforts."

"That's nice, Jerlene." Bunny continued to look from the volunteer firefighters to Gloryanne, and back to Jerlene. Her attempts to be polite and cordial were as strained as the situation. *How could Jerlene just keep talking, like everything was normal?*

"It *is* nice. I don't know how y'all do it over here on this side of the holler with no electricity. When you going to move into the 20th century?"

"21st?" Bunny corrected, without thinking.

"21st. Whatever. You can't be happy, coming from the city and all, with no TV and no running water."

Bunny was answering mindlessly, no longer looking at Jerlene. "My granny had a little windmill built and connected to the spring. I have running water, and having no television means I get a lot more done." She would not mention the devices that seemed to run on their own.

"A windmill!" Jerlene squealed. "I didn't even know those things were real. They actually work?" She didn't wait for an answer. "But, oh right... I remember. She not only had running water, but a fancy copper contraption that heated it up as if by magic. Fancy. It must be sure somethin', though, banging around in that big ol' house of your granny's all by your lonesome."

"Big ol' house?" Bunny looked at Jerlene for what felt like the first time tonight. Though the light from the fire was almost completely extinguished, the reflection on Jerlene's thick glasses gave Bunny a chill.

"Well, yeah." Jerlene's smile lingered. "Your granny's house must be the biggest and fanciest in the whole of Cranberry Creek. This side of the lake, anyway. Maybe 'cause your papaw and Uncle Leo built it. I don't know why your granny pretended to be poor in that fancy house. I mean, hangin' out bedclothes and shellin' peas on the porch? Heck fire, there's more finery in that house than the governor's mansion. I hear there's original art from some Southwest painter and first-edition books signed by the authors. Is that true?"

Bunny stared at her. She was unsure why they were discussing the house she lived in while Gloryanne was watching the destruction of her own right before their eyes.

"Jerlene," Bunny interrupted, "my granny's home—*my* home—is comfortable, not extravagant."

Jerlene rolled on. "Your granny musta thought herself the queen of the holler with that big ol' house. A whole third story and wrap-around porch. Who else has a wrap-around porch in Cranberry Creek? And all those gardens... vegetable, herbal, roses, and all kinds of flowering things. And my, oh my, she must have had stock in a wax company. She burned more candles than anyone 'round here could ever afford."

Now Bunny was really confused. "Jerlene, my granny hardly thought of herself as queen of the holler. She was a good woman, who was good to her neighbors, including you and your uncle."

Jerlene seemed unfazed. "Oh, my bad. Bad, Jer!" She lightly smacked the back of her own hand. "There were rumors, though, your granny was a witch and made love potions and cursed people for money, and that's how she got such nice things."

Bunny's voice sharpened. "My granny never cursed a single soul in her life."

"What about the love potions, though?" Jerlene leaned forward, hands gripping the wheels of her chair. "Think that's true?"

Gloryanne bolted upright, her weight jerking the rocking chair forward, and almost catapulted herself onto the floorboards.

"Oscar," she squeaked.

Jerlene and Bunny both looked at her. In unison, they said, "What?"

"Oscar Wildecat!" she repeated, this time with force, if not a hint of hysteria. "Oh my! Oh no! Oscar Wildecat!"

"Oh, that's her cat," Jerlene said. "He's around here somewhere. Don't you worry, hon."

"Have you seen him?" Gloryanne pulled herself up from the chair, trying not to take it with her as she did. Her eyes scanned the darkness, flitting from one shrub-shaped shadow to another.

"Yeah, I think Uncle Leo fed him some leftover giblets earlier, before heading off to Hoodoo's." She motioned toward the porch steps. "He likes that cat. You'd think it lives over here. Probably 'cause it has company over here. So, he feeds it."

Bunny wondered if that was an insult or simply an observation.

"We'll find him," Bunny said. "You and Victor can look in the morning, when the sun's up."

Jerlene shifted in her chair. Gloryanne sat back down in hers.

"Gloryanne, do you see Victor?" Bunny scanned the scene at Gloryanne's house beyond the water tank. The men were setting buckets down and gathering around the black and gaping hole from which white smoke was now rising. She looked back to Gloryanne and tried to smile. "Looks like most of your house has been saved."

Gloryanne blinked a few times and shook her head, as if coming out of a fog. "Oscar!" She jumped up, the arms of the rocker hugging her ample hips. She struggled for just a moment, freeing herself, and stepped off the porch. "Oscar Wildecat!"

Bunny watched her scoop up a big, gray tomcat and hug it tightly to her chest.

"I was so worried," she rasped into his fur as he squirmed in her arms.

To Bunny, the men seemed somber as they put away their tools. *It's late*, she thought. *They're tired.*

It was more than that.

Sheriff Greenwood broke away from the group and made his way across the road toward the three women. Bunny couldn't make out his expression in the darkness. At the foot of the porch, he straightened his tall frame and removed his hat. "Ladies," he said.

Gloryanne put the big tom down and he leaped up onto the porch, rubbing his wet and matted fur on the legs of Bunny's rocker.

"Sheriff!" Gloryanne gushed. "I didn't know you were over there with that rowdy bunch."

Bunny looked at Gloryanne and gaped. The woman sounded like she'd just bumped into him at a cocktail party.

Jerlene beamed at him, too. "Why, Sheriff, you must be tired and thirsty after all that work. Can I get you some iced tea? It's still mighty hot and you look like you could use a cold drink."

"No, thank you, Mrs. Bittle-Baer."

"I brought plenty of soda pop with me, too. I can get you one of those out of the cooler. They're all diet, but they're cold."

He shook his head.

Bunny stood up and walked to the edge of the porch. "Sheriff Greenwood, we haven't met yet. I'm Bunny Sparks." She stepped down from the porch to shake his hand, thankful the rain had stopped. "I live over the hill. Gene Spark's granddaughter."

The sheriff took Bunny's hand and gave it a firm yet gentle shake.

"Nice to meet you, ma'am," he said. "I was fixin' to come over and introduce myself one of these days. Nice to see some life on that property. It's been a while."

Gloryanne and Jerlene were still beaming at him, eyes as wide as their smiles.

"Sheriff, have you seen Victor?" Bunny asked. "I don't think we know where he is."

Sheriff Greenwood dropped his head and turned toward Gloryanne. "That's what I came to talk about, ma'am."

Gloryanne's smile faltered and her eyebrows furrowed. "You want to talk about Vic?" she asked.

"Yes, ma'am." The sheriff looked up at her, then back to Bunny. "My deputy has already radio'd Doc Fisher. We just want to be sure."

"Sure of what?" Gloryanne's voice was taking on a shrillness Bunny remembered from earlier at the barn.

"We'll let you know, Gloryanne," he said, his voice low and calm. "You might want to see if Leo can put you up for the night, or until we can know more. And..." He turned his hat in his fingers. "...take some time off the next few days. We'll ask Fern or Jerlene here to come in to the office this next week to help out."

"Jerlene?!" Gloryanne sputtered. "She ain't been near the files since I took over, and Fern only fills in now and then, and everything else."

"We'll get by," he said, his voice low and steady.

Jerlene pushed her chair forward and back, just a few inches, and chimed in, "I did that job before Fern. It really ain't all that difficult. I could do it, instead of Fern. She has her sister's tea shop and all."

Gloryanne puffed herself up even more, if that were possible, and huffed.

Bunny cleared her throat. "The sheriff must have a good reason and is looking out for you, Gloryanne."

At this, Gloryanne softened and smiled at him.

"Jerlene," Bunny continued, "does Leo have any space to put Gloryanne up for the night?"

This time, Jerlene puffed up. "*I'm* staying in the spare room. Why don't *you* take her home, Bunny? You have that big ol' house. Gloryanne can pamper herself in the clawfoot. You still have that hot water contraption, don't you? She can take a bubble bath… *if* she can fit in the tub."

Bunny waited for Gloryanne to spit back at Jerlene, but she was still smiling at Sheriff Greenwood, who was waiting patiently for the answer.

Jaws tight, muscles aching, Bunny was losing steam. "Gloryanne? What do you say? I can put you up in the guest room."

"Ooh, see how fancy?" Jerlene cooed. "A *guest* room. 'Round here, y'all."

Ignoring her, Bunny said, "I need to be up and out early,… at least, I planned to be. I'll give you a ride back over here to Leo's in the morning so you can find out what's happening."

The sheriff looked back at the group of men, still huddled together. Some of them looking back to the sheriff, some speaking in low voices to each other.

Bunny watched as Gloryanne and Jerlene followed his gaze as though invisible strings tied their focus directly to his.

"Where's Big Jake?" Gloryanne wondered allowed. "Has he ever missed a fire?"

Jerlene shook her head. "I'll bet he never has. Most on-call volunteer in the holler."

"Well, can I go collect my toiletries, Sheriff?" Gloryanne looked up at him without a smile this time. Her dress clung to her, soaked through, revealing even more of her corpulent figure than usual.

Sheriff Greenwood looked down at her, his eyes held a kind sadness. "I'll have to escort you, Gloryanne. A good portion of the house is untouched, but I need to keep things as they are as much as possible."

Gloryanne allowed herself to be led across the road, the kitten heels she'd been wearing still on Leo's porch. Bunny watched as Sheriff Greenwood politely offered his elbow as he guided her around puddles and rocks, and she rubbed her own elbows as she wondered how long the wait would be.

"I hope the bed springs in that guest room are solid," Jerlene said, no longer watching them herself. She turned her chair and opened the screen door. Bunny stepped onto the porch to hold the door as Jerlene maneuvered her chair into the house.

"It was nice seeing you again, Bunny. Maybe you can tell me about your granny's love potions next time I see you. Gloryanne was trying to teach me some things she learned about plants from your granny, but I'd rather hear about the potions. G'night."

Standing alone on the porch, Bunny tried to see through the screen to catch sight of a clock, but couldn't see one. She settled for not knowing rather than asking Jerlene, and decided to get the Keely in position to make it easier to leave when Gloryanne was ready.

Driving in a loop behind Leo's little cottage, Bunny wondered if he ever meant to build a ramp to the back door, and how long Jerlene planned to stay. As she rounded the far side of the house, Doc Fisher was easing up the road in his old Ford Bronco.

Gloryanne and Sheriff Greenwood stepped out of the Tew front door as Doc parked as close as he could manage. Bunny pulled in behind him, hoping Gloryanne would notice she was waiting.

When there was nothing more she could do, Bunny tipped her face toward the clearing sky. The clouds were breaking apart, the moon riding high but already drifting west. By its position, she guessed it was close to three. She sighed. It would be a beautiful day, if she managed any sleep at all.

At last, Gloryanne spotted her and climbed in. Without a word, Bunny eased the car back onto the road and headed home.

By the time she finished putting fresh sheets on the bed in the first-floor guest room, Gloryanne came padding in from the bathroom.

"Ah, thank you for that wonderful handmade soap, Bunny. It was delish."

"I hope you didn't eat it." Bunny was exhausted. It was close to four, and Gloryanne's nonstop chatter since arriving was beginning to wear her down.

"Of course, I didn't *eat* it, silly," she kept going. "I love the smell, though. What is that? Pine trees? Sort of smells like a forest and everything else."

Bunny smiled at her, but found it difficult to maintain the expression.

"Oh, I just love this room. It's so bohemian. Like a Home Magazine page from the '70s. Did they have a Home Magazine then? I don't know. But, I could see it if there was one. This could be a spread. You know, a photo-spread. Like the home of someone famous. Well, your granny was pretty famous. Around here, anyway. Wasn't she? Granny Genie. I mean, Gene. We only called her Genie 'cause we loved her, is all. And she had that way with people. People and plants. She had a lot of respect in the holler, you know. We called her that 'cause we loved her and everything else." Gloryanne prattled on as she walked around inspecting the rugs, the art, the curtains, and the bedding as she towel-dried her hair.

"I was wondering if you would have shelves in here. You know, like Vic made for your granny's barn. I mean *your* barn. It's *your* place now. Of course. But, Vic was good with shelves and stuff. Carpentry, really. About all he *was* good for. Is, I mean. I tried to get him to do more, but he only liked to hammer things and cut pieces of wood out there in his workshop listenin' to the Beatles. He listened to a lot of those Beatles songs. Over and over. Said it made him feel young. I thought Leo was gonna kill him one of these days. He'd give us the ol' stink eye for awhile and then finally he'd shake his cane in the air and yell 'Turn that blasted stuff off! I can't hear myself think.' But I don't think he could hear all that well anyway. Nothing to do with music keeping him from hearing. I'd talk to him every time I seen him... 'Yoohoo!' I'd say, and I would wave and he would just keep working or walking or whatever he was doin' and never once heard me calling." She stopped and looked at herself in the mirror above the dresser, pressing the towel through her hair.

Bunny winced as she watched the transfer of dark henna bleed onto what was once a pristine and blemish-free guest towel.

"Leo is a little crazy anyway. He said the Beatles were a Tavistock creation. I don't even know what that is, but it sounds made up," Gloryanne continued as she dabbed. "And your towels... they are really soft and absorbent, and everything else. They don't smell like any towels I have."

"I don't use commercial soaps and detergents. I hope you'll be comfortable."

"You know me, Bunny, I can make myself comfortable any ol' place. Don't you think Sheriff Greenwood is handsome? He's very professional. But, you shouldn't be interested in dating him or anything. He won't date any women in the holler. It's his rule. He's handsome, though, ain't he? Sometimes hard to work for because of that." She wrapped the towel, turban-style, around her head. "Vic don't look nothing like him. He isn't all that professional neither. Good at building. Not much else. Least he was 'til he got hurt on a construction project. They fought him over his workmen's comp claim and everything else. But, the money's coming. Should be in the bank any day now, he said."

"Speaking of Victor," Bunny began.

Gloryanne cut her off. "Oh, Sheriff Greenwood said he was being evaluated by Doc Fisher."

"Evaluated?"

"Yeah, Doc Fisher was going to come and check him over."

Bunny bit her lip. "Gloryanne, are you sure Vic is just being checked over? That nothing worse happened?"

"Like what?"

Bunny stared at her. Maybe now was not the time to address it. In fact, it probably wasn't her business to address at *any* time.

Bunny was ready to step out of the room when Gloryanne asked, "You don't use commercial stuff? What do you use? Do you make your own? Do you buy it somewhere? Is it expensive?"

"I'll tell you tomorrow... I mean later today. I do need to get up soon and visit a friend."

"Do you want me to get up and make breakfast? I make a mean curried scrambled egg, and everything else."

Bunny shuddered. "Let's just see how we feel when we get up. Good night."

She stepped quickly out of the room and closed the door behind her. With a sigh, she made her way around the house opening windows to let in the cool morning air, then finally up to her bed. She decided against setting an alarm, and hoped she'd have enough stamina to be up before it was too late in the morning.

Chapter Three

When the sun streamed in through the window that morning, the comfort of Bunny's bed and the ache in her body seemed to form an ionic bond. It took all her might to roll over and open an eyelid to the clock next to the bed.

Seven o'clock.

This was late for her. However tired she was, though, she'd made a promise to Granny Didima. This was the day she would deliver vegetables from her garden and a bucket of saltpeter from the old mine. There was no text or email that could be sent to beg off for another day. She stretched. Twinges of dull pain tugged at the muscles in her limbs, even deeper in her back. "This is going to be a Meadwort kind of day," she said aloud.

She made a plan to find a tincture of this in the herb cabinet promptly. An efficient analgesic, it would do the trick quite nicely, and maybe a little mullein root for her back pain specifically.

Gathering her will, she rolled out of bed and stood before the open window to breathe in the morning air. It was cool and clean, as it often was the day after a good rain, and the smells of honey-scented woodbine and moist humus wafted in the window. She plucked a modest sundress from its hanger in the armoire and made her way to the bathroom for a quick, cool shower.

Getting up and about helped. She opened more windows throughout the cottage on her way to the kitchen. The events of the night before felt far away in the clear light of the morning.

She quickly sliced and set out a variety of the fruit that was in season - watermelon, cantaloupe, honeydew, and the last of the blueberries. She had gathered these from the garden early the day before, prior to moving roses, and placed the slices ornately on a platter with a note to Gloryanne to find her in the garden if she woke before Bunny returned to collect her. Grabbing a soft pear for herself, she picked up the garden trug and headed out to harvest something for Granny Didima.

After hanging wet things from the night before, including the pillow and wet cushions she'd left on the porch, she headed for the vegetable patch. She was torn between laughing and cursing after seeing the soil bestrewn with puddles that distinctly resembled large feet. Some of the tomato cages were bent wildly and stalks of sweet corn that had yet to be picked leaned into the path. She told herself she could come back later, though every instinct urged her to fix it now. Today, it would have to wait. She stood quietly among the basil and breathed. This was going to be a long day. She needed a few moments to slow down, as hurrying usually meant more mistakes. She gathered chard, cucumbers, scallions, and snapped off several garlic scapes, holding them up to her nose to enjoy the scent.

The sun was bright and the morning felt serene. Soon, it would feel less so, but for now the smell of fresh earth, pungent scapes, and the songs of indigo buntings and far-off crows were luxurious.

Bunny looked toward the hills, north of her cottage. She filled the rest of the trug with bright orange carrots, a variety of lettuces, and ears of sweet corn that were plump and ready. She would straighten and fortify the downed stalks with fresh soil when she returned later that day, which she hoped would be sooner rather than later. She snipped and tucked basil and parsley sprigs into the trug on one side, and filled the remaining spaces with yarrow and wormwood. Inhaling deeply, she relished the aroma of the freshly cut herbs.

She yearned to stay here all morning, but it wouldn't be long before the day became hot and sticky. She needed to move more quickly now. Making her way to the front flower beds, she gathered a bouquet of bright blue cornflowers, deep scarlet dahlias, and some large white blooms of the Casa Blanca Oriental Lily. She snipped the stamens from the lily blooms before slipping them in among the other flowers. No need to stain everything indelibly.

As she looked to see if there were any other blooms that might be willing to join the bouquet, she remembered the foxglove. There it was, near the mailbox post, drastically uprooted and more horizontal than she remembered seeing it last night. She set down the loaded trug and bent at the waist to inspect the area, rubbing her knees as she scanned the ground for clues. She'd been trying to avoid being self-critical, but in times like these she wished her joints were more cooperative.

She did her best to set the foxglove, a pretty *Digitalis mertonensis*, aright. Or was it a different variety?

Sometimes it was difficult to tell plants apart.

Just as she was pushing mulch around the base, being careful not to brush the leaves or exposed roots with her bare hands, Gloryanne appeared on the porch. Bunny couldn't see her as much as *sense* her, the stand of arborvitae between the house and the mailbox blocked the view.

"Yoohoo!"

Bunny grimaced and straightened, arching her back a bit to stretch out the new kinks.

"I'm here by the mailbox, Gloryanne."

Gloryanne thundered down the steps and announced, "Isn't it a beautiful morning? Listen to them birds just a singin'. Your hair is so long! I had no idea. It's all the way down your back." She flipped her own shoulder-length hair, shining copper in the morning sun. "Whatcha doin' in there? Pickin' flowers?"

Bunny forced a smile as Gloryanne rounded the backdrop of trees, pushing what Bunny guessed was the last of the melon in her mouth.

"I'm gathering things for G... for Granny Didima. I told her I would visit her today."

"Granny Didima? She still alive up there?" Gloryanne turned to look toward the hills behind the house, her bright purple dress shimmering as she swung back to look at Bunny. "I don't think I've ever seen her. Only heard about her, and everything else. She and your granny would get together and make magic on the full moons. I heard that, anyway. Kids around here were scared of her. Shoot, we *all* were scared of her. I heard she sends critters after you if you make her mad. Jerlene said she was bit by a bunch of spiders in her bed one night after she teased you for being a tourist. Your granny musta overheard her telling you that. Do you remember that? I think we were about ten years old."

Bunny squinted at her. The shimmer in the garish dress was painfully electric in the bright morning sun. "The Grannies would not have needed to 'send critters' to punish Jerlene. She slept in Leo's old hunting cabin. It's *filled* with spiders, snakes, and mice. It's a wonder she wasn't bitten more often."

"I didn't even know that weren't a dirty word until I was older. Tourist. Sounded like a bad thing the way she said it. You know, Jerlene didn't like your granny none, but I loved coming over here and listenin' to your granny do her talks, and everything else, so I would drag her over here with me anyways. Do you remember that? She told me that pretty purple plant right there is called ..." She scrunched her nose. "It was called something like a fox, maybe... or a fairy... do you know what that plant is, Bunny?"

"Foxglove." Bunny stooped to pick up her trug and tried not to grunt as she straightened. "Gigi called them Fairy's Gloves."

"Foxgloves! That's it! You know that grows everywhere! I see it all along the side of the road, all the way down to Hoodoo's and beyond. It's so pretty that I am always tempted to pick some, but your granny said it's poisonous. She also said they use it for medicine, so I don't know how that can be. Digital something."

Bunny strained to smile at her. "*Digitalis*. I might do some talks of my own one day. I'll try to talk about *that* when I do."

"Heart attacks, she said. I mean, it makes medicine for heart attacks."

"Well, the compounds are used in heart medication. It helps the heart beat better for the people who need that." Bunny knew this was a rudimentary explanation, but didn't have the strength to expound on the topic.

Gloryanne's smile widened, revealing smudges of fuchsia across her front teeth.

Resisting the urge to tell her, Bunny said, "And I'll point out the fireweed that grows along the road to Hoodoo's. It's similar, but different. I need to get on over to G... Granny Didima's now, so can I drop you off at Leo's?"

The sound of an approaching vehicle caught their attention, and Gloryanne adjusted a spaghetti strap with one hand and pulled at the tight fabric around her middle when a patrol car pulled into the drive. Sheriff Greenwood turned off the ignition, grabbed his hat, and got out of the cruiser. He didn't return the smile Gloryanne was beaming at him.

"Miss Sparks," he said, offering a polite nod.

"Hi Sheriff. Any news?"

"There is. That's why I'm here. Miss Gloryanne, we need you down at the station for a bit. Doc Fisher needs to talk to you."

Her smile faltered. "Why does Doc Fisher need to talk to me?"

Bunny looked between the sheriff and Gloryanne. Sheriff Greenwood pressed his lips tightly together. Bunny thought the shadows under his eyes were even darker than they were the night before, actually *in* the dark. She was contemplating the irony when he shifted from one foot to the other, pushing a bit of gravel and dirt with his boot, then shifted back. The sweat stains down the front of his shirt and under the arms, coupled with the distinct smell of smoke, and Bunny wondered if he'd been to bed at all.

"Can I get you a glass of water, Sheriff?"

He looked at Bunny. The expression in his eyes was soft, but he kept his lips pursed. He shook his head, only slightly.

"Could I get you anything else?" She turned to Gloryanne. "Is there any melon left?"

Gloryanne swayed in place, gently flapping the hem of her dress to and fro in front of her, staring at Sheriff Greenwood.

Again, he shook his head. "Miss Gloryanne, please collect your things and I'll give you a ride to the station. We have a fire inspector who made the trip all the way from Morgan City on account of the... er... special circumstances. There are some details we need to go over and we need your help."

Bunny watched her spring to action at the words "need your help."

"Oh! Of course. Why, I just need to go grab my things, and everything else. I can be back in two shakes, Sheriff. Bunny, you don't mind if I keep that herbal soap I used, do you? I mean, I used it and all. No one else would want to use it now, I don't think. Do you think?"

"Of course, you can keep it." Bunny made a quick scan of the trees to check for the Candid Camera crew, just to be sure she wasn't missing something. She breathed a sigh of relief as Gloryanne practically skipped back to the cottage. It wouldn't be long before she would be untangled from this particular drama.

When she was out of earshot, Bunny looked back at the tall, lanky, and obviously exhausted man standing somberly at the edge of the flower bed. The silver at his temples stood out against the curls of his dark hair.

"Is it bad?"

"It is, ma'am."

"Is it Victor?"

"I'm afraid so."

Bunny looked at the ground and bit her lip. She took a deep breath, only to find it catch in her throat. "He was a good man. I wonder what Gloryanne is going to do."

Sheriff Greenwood shifted from one foot to the other, again pushing gravel and dirt with a boot.

"Would you like to sit down, Sheriff?" Bunny walked to the edge of the arborvitae and motioned toward the porch. "I don't know how long Gloryanne takes to get ready."

"No, thank you, ma'am. If I sit down, I might not make it back up for a while. There is a lot to do today, so I need to keep going."

Bunny hiked the overflowing garden trug up onto one hip and said, "I'll just go check on her then. See if I can't help move her along."

"Much obliged," he said, shifting his weight again.

Bunny wondered if his feet hurt or if this was his way of indicating impatience. Climbing the porch steps, she could hear Gloryanne's heavy footfalls. They reached the screened door at the same time, and Gloryanne waited for Bunny to hold the door for her.

"Thanks for everything," Gloryanne gushed. "It was real fun being in Granny Genie's house and seeing all the potions and gadgets, and having a real mini spa party for myself, and everything else. I was peeking in the closet, don't mind me, and under the bed. I just know there's spooky things in there."

Bunny held the door wide so Gloryanne could make it through with her bags. She wasn't sure what to make of the "spooky" comment, so only said, "Good luck today, Gloryanne."

She watched as Sheriff Greenwood held the door to his patrol car open and stood silently as Gloryanne put her things in the back seat. He waved to her and called out, "I may need to talk with you, too, Miss Sparks. I'll be in touch."

Bunny waved back.

She filled the back of the Keely with the garden trug, a bucket and spade, a basket of sourdough bread she'd baked earlier in the week, jars of homemade mustard, and a bottle of mead. Seeing her pair of thick, rubber boots were still on the porch by the door, she decided to step inside and also grab a good pair of socks and a jacket, in case the cave was cold.

The air was fresh, the sun bright, and the blue sky was pristine. These were the sort of days Bunny relished. There were no such mornings in the life she left before coming here. She slowly drove up the path that would take her into the forest, through the hemlock and pine. It was always cool here, no matter the temperature or time of day. Delicate fern and cushions of dark moss blanketed the forest floor. There were times when Bunny would stop driving and just sit, breathing in the rich aroma and soaking up the deep ancestral healing that came from these trees.

The journey always brought her to the Y in the road near the old cemetery, a historic family plot that held untold generations. The wrought iron enclosure that surrounded the site was still standing strong, and the periwinkle that covered the ground among the markers was vibrant with pink flowers and lustrous leaves. Bunny stopped to visit there often on her way to the caves or Granny Didima's. The space was comforting to her and her curiosity about the relatives buried there led her to study a new headstone or two each time. She studied the engravings that were still visible, noting the names, dates, and symbols. There were many curious markings, such as the bat carved on one stone, or the ouroboros on another. She couldn't make out the names on either one. Several were adorned with poppies. Granny Didima told her this meant they died in the Civil War. Some markers had been there so long they were on their sides, some face down. Bunny planned to properly reset these, but needed the help of someone with more muscle than she had. The newest grave was, of course, Gigi's.

Unlike the majority of markers, Gigi's was a white marble that she, Rose and Dot picked out together from the main cemetery's memorialist. They agreed to a simple epitaph and a carving that depicted a sprig of herbs atop a closed book. To them, this honored her knowledge. She was not sure why the gravestone that was delivered was shaped like a truncated obelisk, topped with a crystal orb, but they liked it well enough and it hadn't affected the cost.

She didn't have time to stop there today, so she turned to the left and followed the path that sloped down and around into the old-growth red spruce. The caves were hidden throughout the forest and, fortunately, the cave where she gathered saltpeter for Granny Didima was the closest. The ice caves were further on.

Gathering saltpeter wasn't a difficult job. She slipped on her socks and rubber boots, grabbed the bucket and spade, and picked up the long stick she kept by the entrance to the cave to remove any spiderwebs constructed since her last visit. There were always a few. Bunny hated destroying them, but hated more having them end up in her face and hair.

Just inside, she scraped the mineral crust loose with relative ease, and filled her bucket. The scent of metal striking flint was familiar now and not unpleasant. She ignored the strain on already spent muscles, loaded the bucket into the Keely, and made her way back to the fork in the path near the cemetery. She continued in the other direction, following the path that rose up over a steep hill. Bunny had to slow to a crawl many times to safely circumnavigate the jagged outcroppings that could easily mar or permanently damage something on the undercarriage.

It was a long walk. She drove carefully.

When the trees opened and Granny Didima's cottage came into view, Bunny eased the Keely to a stop and cut the engine. The sudden quiet rang in her ears. She sat for a moment, hands resting on the wheel, then climbed out and stretched the stiffness from her back.

As she passed, she peeked into the contents simmering in the large copper pot on the fire pit some twenty feet before the cottage. "Smells like lavender, lemon balm and old socks," Bunny laughed.

Granny Didima puffed away on her pipe, slowly pitching back and forth in her rocking chair on the covered porch. In the shawl draped across her lap was a sleepy tortoiseshell cat. "Valerian root smells like ground-up walnut shells," she said. "Smoke inhalation and lack of sleep has vitiated your sense of smell."

"Vitiate? That's a word I'm not familiar with."

"It means to corrupt, essentially. Websters New International Dictionary. 1911. I'm at 'v' now."

"Ah, I don't have that version." Bunny smiled and began unloading her cargo. "Vitiate," she repeated. "I'll try to remember."

Moving to sit on the steps of the porch, the two women pulled vegetables and herbs from the garden trug. Granny Didima put each one to her nose and made little noises of satisfaction, then placed each carefully in the shawl on her lap. Her torti saved her seat on the rocker. "Hildegarde had her babes." Granny pointed to the mother goat and two little kids bounding around her. The bell around her neck clang softly as Hildegarde sauntered over to see what goodies might be for her.

When Granny Didima wrapped a long bit of wormwood around a smaller ear of corn and tossed it to her, Bunny asked, "Worming?"

"Best to stay on top of it."

"I would imagine so. I'll bring more the next time I visit."

"I have plenty dried, chil', but I'm happy to have your visit no matter. You want to talk about the fire?"

Bunny nodded. "I *thought* you must have seen it. You mentioned smoke inhalation. *Did* you see it?"

"I saw. Didn't last long. The menfolk are fast in the holler."

"It was Gloryanne and Victor Tew's home. Sheriff Greenwood came to take Gloryanne into town this morning. It sounds like Victor didn't make it." Bunny looked at the little goats chasing each other while keeping close to their mother. On another day, she would find their antics delightful. Not today.

Granny Didima was silent.

The torti jumped down from the chair and came to bump her head against Bunny's arm.

"Who is this one, then?" Bunny reached down and scratched the fur behind the little cat's ear.

"Gertrude." Granny clicked her pipe in her teeth. "After Saint Gertrude."

"Ah. Patron saint of cats." Bunny nodded.

"Among other things, yes."

"Who is the patron saint of toads, I wonder."

Granny Didima tapped a knobby finger against the side of her head. Bunny sat patiently, admiring the silky white hair that hung down the old woman's back in a braid so long the bottom of it lay behind her some ten inches on the porch. Her dark eyes looked into the distance, as she squinted. The lines that scored her tanned face were deep and copious. She adjusted her slight frame on the edge of the porch step and, with more agility than even Bunny could muster, stepped off in a bit of a twirl and gave a musical laugh. "Wilgefortis!"

"Wilge...?"

"The bearded lady saint. Wilgefortis." Pleased with herself, she stepped over to the kettle with a little jig and stirred the pot. "Wilgefortis," she repeated, her little pipe held in a toothy grin. She stroked her chin and, holding her long braid out of the way, leaned over the pot, allowing the steam to envelop her face. She breathed deeply. "Ground up walnut shells," she said conclusively.

She set the ladle back, stretched, and turned to look at Bunny. "Toad pay you a visit?"

"Last night," Bunny nodded. "It was almost dark and I couldn't tell what the message was."

"Sometimes Toad has a message of his own. I didn't send him."

Bunny watched the little goat kids leaping over and around each other. Envious of their energy, Bunny sighed. Sleeplessness was catching up with her and the desire to lie down right there on the porch and close her eyes was a seductive lure. She stood and attempted to stifle a yawn. "The thing is," she reflected, "I need a big sign, I think. Billboard big. I'm not very good at subtlety. I over think and over analyze."

"This, chil', is the problem."

Picking up her long skirt, Granny moved to the porch and said, "Come. We'll have a nip and find your message."

"I'm not sure I can manage a 'nip' this early, G.Didi."

"Ain't talking 'bout firewater, missy. Come on inside and bring those garden treasures or Hildegarde will eat 'em. She is voracious."

"Another good 'v' word. I know that one."

Once inside, Granny Didima began lighting candles on the long oak table in the middle of the room. The space inside was much larger than it appeared from the outside. It rather resembled an old apothecary with floor-to-ceiling shelves filled with brown bottles and specimens of all sorts. The smell was faintly floral, heightened by the many dried herbs and flowers hanging from almost every rafter. Atop the table was an array of hand-dipped tapers aflame in wrought iron candlesticks of varying heights, mortars and pestles filled with ingredients in various stages of trituration, and a variety of dried mushrooms. Two empty cups sat waiting, one a thick mug with a hefty handle and a dark glaze, the other a dainty bone china teacup with a pastel rose decoration and matching saucer.

Bunny waited to see where she would be directed to sit, but was motioned to sit anywhere. She chose the spot before the thick mug and lowered herself gingerly into the chair.

Granny Didima pointed to the bright tea kettle, steaming on the table, and asked Bunny to pour for them both. Bunny had long since stopped asking how things like tea kettles and lanterns worked by themselves here.

"Tell me about last night, chil'," Granny directed. She was sprinkling powder over a black bowl of what appeared to be water.

"Gloryanne showed up at the barn sometime after midnight. It was too hot and rainy to sleep inside with the windows closed, so I was on the porch when I saw her. She said Gigi always let her use the Keely and she was there to get it, but I keep the door locked and I've moved things around in the barn, besides. I was trying to tell her that when we saw the fire."

"Your granny was generous, yes. But, she didn't let anyone use her vehicles and she didn't have that little sport you are driving around until just before she left us here alone." Granny Didima shook a fist in the air and looked up at the ceiling as she said this. She stirred the powder into the liquid and continued, "It's a 1940-something military machine. Ask

Hoodoo about it. Anyway, she had Topaz, the golden mare, before that. She wouldn't have loaned her to anyone either."

"Oh, yes. Topaz," Bunny mused. "What happened to her?"

"She was old, like me. But she left us before her time, the way your granny left us before hers." She shook her fist again at the ceiling. "No, your granny was generous, helped a lot of folk in the holler, but very few came up to the house. She gave her talks near the road. Remember? She would hang a pretty red scarf on the mailbox the night before those days she planned to give one of them talks, and everyone knew to be there right at ten in the mornin'. Word spread like wildfire and sometimes she'd have pert-near thirty hill-folk awaitin'."

"Speaking of fire," Bunny continued, "when we saw it, I heard a siren and Gloryanne was going to head over the hill on foot, so I drove her. It was *her* house on fire and the men were already showing up to put it out. It didn't get very far, luckily, but it must have been far enough because Victor didn't make it."

"But you didn't know that 'til this mornin'?"

"Right. When Sheriff Greenwood came to pick up Gloryanne, he told me. He must have been up all night. He looked worn out, and his clothes were the same. Still smelled like smoke."

"So she stayed with you last night?" She stirred the water, inspecting it closely.

"Yes. I asked Jerlene if she could stay at Leo's, but Jerlene said *she* was staying there. I didn't know she did that. I didn't know Jerlene was in a wheelchair either. Did you know that?"

"Leo mentioned it." She stirred. "He visits. Brings me rose hips and garlic. Best garlic in the holler, next to yours, of course."

"I'm glad he stops by. I worry sometimes that he might be lonely."

"Since Susie died, you mean? He keeps busy. We trade things, like his garlic and Hildegarde's butter."

Bunny watched her stir. "Gloryanne said something about her that I thought was funny. She said Jerlene was afraid that you and Gigi put curses on the children."

"She was a vile little thing, that Jerlene Bittle was. Pulled cats' whiskers and lopped the heads off flowers for fun. If any child were curse-worthy, it might've been her. But no child deserves to be cursed. She needed more attention. I suspect she still does."

"She *was* mean, alright. She used to make up rhymes about us three girls and Gigi being hillbillies. 'Barefoot, black soot, your granny is a substitute.' I never understood what she meant by that, but the way she said it felt like she meant it to be hurtful."

"She was calling your granny a substitute mother."

"Oh. She made up rhymes about our not having a father, too, but mostly she just called us 'orphans,' so I guess that makes sense. She seems to think I live in the governor's mansion now and that Gigi thought of herself as a queen."

"Your granny was good to all the children in the holler. Rescued a fair few of 'em. Animals, too. Even the mean ones. But that child ain't never even been inside that house. I know that for certain. Gloryanne neither. Prolly just heard about it from her uncle. He and your papaw did a fair amount of fine carpentry work together."

"Well, Gloryanne slept in the guest room downstairs this morning. Had a bath. Treated it like a spa day and admitted to poking around. It was like she didn't have a care in the world, once she found her cat."

Granny Didima frowned into the water. "Why did you ask about Toad?"

"He startled me. It was just before I went in for the evening. I thought you might have sent him, but I didn't see the smoke."

"I didn't send him. What was he doin'?"

"He was just sitting there. I didn't see him until he hopped by a foxglove that was leaning over oddly."

"Foxgloves can lean."

"Well, all the spires were upright and beautiful the last time I looked at them, which was the day before, I guess. I was focused on getting the roses moved. Anyway, this one was really leaning. Like something knocked it over."

"What came into your mind when you saw Toad?"

"Badgers. I don't know why. I called Rosie and asked her about Badger Medicine. She said something about loyalty and fierceness. I don't know what it means."

"Then we're ready to begin."

Granny Didima blew out all the candles, save one, and moved it close to the bowl. Bunny stifled a gasp.

Chapter Four

The reflection of the candle flame undulated on the surface of the liquid. Though the surface was still and calm, the image it reflected was not. The scene depicted in the bowl was that of men battling flames. Smoke rose into a black sky, fractured with streaks of lightning.

Granny Didima's voice was low and soft. "What do you see, chil'?"

"Fire," Bunny answered, her eyes fixed to the moving picture in the bowl. "Don't you see it?"

"What I see is unimportant. This message is for *you*. Drink your brew and clear your mind."

Bunny dutifully picked up her mug and placed it carefully to her lips, unsure of the temperature and not wanting to burn herself. The flavor was acrid and singed her throat as she swallowed, but it was not heat that seared. She grimaced and wiped her mouth with the back of her hand.

"What do you see, chil'?" Granny asked again.

Bunny began to feel heat rising, starting in her feet and traveling up her legs.

"I see fire and my legs want to move." Bunny wasn't sure what else she was supposed to say.

"Tell me about your legs."

"They feel as if fire ants are stinging me. I want to run." Then, "Oh! There's Toad," she said, as she watched Toad hop into the picture in the bowl. "He's in the fireweed. That's not foxglove." Bunny was straining to see more clearly. "He's gone. Now a badger... Wait. *Is* that a badger? I don't know now. It was too quick. More flames. Fire. Water in buckets. I see the fire reflected on the surface of the water in the buckets."

"Firewater," Granny said. "Fireweed."

"And badger?" Bunny asked. "I asked Rose about Badger Medicine. I called her."

"What did she say about Badger Medicine?"

"Fierce. Loyal."

"Faithful?" Granny added.

"Yes, loyal. Faithful."

Granny waited until she saw Bunny sit back in her chair and close her eyes, then she stirred the water in the bowl and blew out the candle. They sat, quietly, for some time. All was still apart from the soft sound of Hildegarde's bell as she moved about outside.

The spell was broken when Granny said, "I suppose I will need to jump to "f" in the dictionary now."

Bunny opened her eyes wide and said, "I didn't think anything could be funny right now, but that's funny."

"Another "f" word," Granny said, a twinkle in her eye. "How fortuitous."

They both giggled together like tickled children until tears rolled down their cheeks.

As the laughter began to wane, Bunny realized she was crying. She wept softly, her hands over her eyes, for just a few moments. "Victor was a quiet man who kept mostly to himself. You could tell he carried some heavy weight on his shoulders... shadows from his past, I suppose. I heard he might've had a record, though I never caught the full story. Gloryanne never had a kind word for him, but from what I saw, he seemed to be working hard to build something here." She wiped away somber tears and sighed.

Granny Didima was serious now, too. "Leo didn't like him."

"What? I didn't know that."

"Said he wasn't friendly unless he wanted something. And he was always playin' music from his garage and it was always too loud. Couldn't hear himself think. It was strange sitar music or something. Leo didn't like it."

"I heard it was the Beatles. Maybe it was from their Maharishi Yogi days."

"Leo said it made his apples bitter."

"Is that a metaphor, or did he mean his literal apples having a bitter taste?"

Granny Didima frowned. "Hard to say. I know that speaking ill of the dead is verboten—'v'—but I'm talking about Leo, so that's different."

"I didn't think you were speaking ill... of either Victor *or* Leo."

"Good. Now, chil', it's time for you to rest a spell. I can see in your field there's very little sparkle."

"I really should get back and fix my plants. They may not make it if I don't tend to them."

"I'm insistin'," Granny said.

"...and the sheriff said he may want to talk to me later." Bunny yawned.

Granny stood and moved around the table to Bunny's chair. "I'll red up here and you go on an' lie down." She motioned to the twin bed tucked behind a large bookcase, only the ornately carved foot of it visible from where Bunny was sitting. "When you wake up, we'll have us some beans an' cornbread with some Hildy butter."

Bunny found she could not resist the offer. Or was it a command? In either case, she obediently shuffled across the floor, around the bookcase and to the bed. She lacked the energy to exclaim how beautiful the little sleeping nook was, but through sleepy eyes she admired the red and white quilts that hung around the bed frame and covered the feather bed. Sinking into the plump pillows, she drifted off to sleep before she could decide if the designs were Scandinavian or Dutch.

She dreamed of fire, and badgers, and statues of patron saints with beards.

Bunny stretched her legs and arms before opening her eyes. Her limbs felt leaden. She considered staying in G.Didi's bed for a while longer until she heard noises from the other side of the bookcase. Scraping of metal on metal. The smell of cornbread wafted to her nose and Bunny imagined the sound was a spatula slipping under a scrumptious slice in a cast iron skillet. Willing herself to roll over and push herself out of bed became easier knowing this feast awaited her.

As she shuffled over to a chair, Granny set her bowl of beans, hot from the beanpot, on the table. "Smells delicious." She smiled and rubbed her eyes.

"Just like when you was a child, chil'," Granny said, ladling up a portion for herself.

"I remember," Bunny said. Her mouth watered and her stomach growled.

Granny heaped a dollop on her own slice and pushed a mortar filled with coarse white grains across the table to Bunny. "Prolly need some salt."

They sat in silence, enjoying the meal. A familiar comfort settled over Bunny as she remembered sitting at this same table as a young girl with her sisters while G.Didi served up whatever delectable fare she prepared from her garden. She served stories and lessons, too, always with a little stern tenderness that only the Grannies could provide.

She remembered each year at the end of the summer, when her mother would return to collect them, she and her sisters were heartbroken to leave, never knowing to what new town they were headed and with what new "uncle." The idea of starting another school year in another unknown school with children that would examine them like exotic bugs was terrifying. Each time, they would try making new friends, only to face the heartbreak of leaving *them* when the school year was over. In the end, it hurt less to keep to themselves, despite being scattered across different grades.

They played alone, together, at whatever corner of the playground was least occupied, and moved along quickly if it appeared that bullies threatened to encroach. At the end of the day, Bunny would gather her sisters and they would choose a different route home than the one the day before, often going out of their way for more than a mile to avoid running into any little tyrant determined to harass them. Walking as fast as their little feet would carry them, they stopped only to collect nuts from the ground or fruit hanging low from branches shading the road.

Winter brought different challenges, depending on where they were that year. In the South, little changed. In the North, they simply hurried home, heads down against the cold.

Bunny considered herself fortunate, hardships and all. Still, she relished the comfort of her most cherished memories, like those made at this very table.

Granny Didima patted her shoulder. "Find comfort where you can, chil'," she said. "And keep your eyes on what's ahead. Lookin' back is how we lose our footing."

Bunny nodded, though she wasn't entirely sure what to make of the advice. She gathered her things, including a crock of freshly churned Hildegarde butter, and carried those words with her to the Keely.

Waving good-bye, she carefully eased her way back down the rocky track toward home, savoring the cool, dappled shade the forest trail provided. At the fork in the road, she was again tempted to stop at the old cemetery, but was determined to get back to her garden in hopes of repairing the damage done the night before. She waved to her relatives, and those unknown to her, as she passed and kept going. The path would be easier now and she could go a little faster, but she still took her time. She knew that, once out of the forest, the afternoon air would be thick with heat and humidity.

When she arrived at the cottage, she was relieved to see all was much the same as when she left. She parked close to the porch, hurried to put things away, and headed to the garden. She was happy to see it wasn't as bad as she expected. She mounded fresh compost around the stalks of corn and staked them in place, doing the same with the tomatoes. She then surveyed the rest of the beds, following the path of deep depressions Gloryanne's kitten heels had left and filling them with mulch. She pulled some onions and carrots for Leo, snipped more basil, and placed all in the trug to deliver.

For a moment, however fleeting, she held a tiny regret that she hadn't set up the old answering machine. Then again, no one on this side of the holler had such devices. No one felt the need for them. "If it's that important, they'll call back or come over," Leo would say.

She felt fidgety. Determined not to focus on yet another 'f' word, she decided to head over the hill without calling. If Leo was home, she would ask him for any updates he might know. If he wasn't, she would leave the veggies and a note for him. The antsy feeling she had meant she didn't want to wait to find out what happened if someone might be able to tell her now.

When the old Keely neared the turnoff to Leo's cottage, Bunny stopped to look across the way at the damage to the Tew house. In the daylight, and from the road, the blackened hole that marred the side of the house was actually smaller than Bunny thought it would be. It appeared to be where the side door once was. She could see yellow "Do Not Cross" tape draped across the opening, and over the front door as well.

Turning down the drive to Leo's, she could see Leo and Gloryanne on the porch. Both were seated in rockers. Gloryanne seemed to be struggling to keep Oscar Wildecat on her lap.

"Come on, Oscar," she cooed, sharply. "Why don't you wanna sit with momma? Oh, hi, Bunny!"

Leo frowned at the cat struggling to get down. "Cats don't like to be forced to do nothin', Gloryanne. Why don't you just put the poor thing down and let it do what it wants to do? Bunny, I'm glad to see you."

Gloryanne's mouth made a wide "o" and she glared at him. "I just lost my husband and everything else, Leo. I can't have a soothin' from my cat? He's *my* cat, you know. Bunny, you know he's my cat, don't you? I mean, I'm the one who found him and I'm the one who feeds him real cat food, special from Hoodoo's."

"I know," Leo murmured. "Sorry, Gloryanne."

Bunny could hear there was something unsaid in that apology, but wouldn't dare ask at a time like this. "I brought something from the garden for you, Leo." She pulled the trug out of the back of the Keely and set it on the porch. "Any news?"

"They won't let me in my house. That's one thing." Gloryanne sniffed. "Sheriff said they have more investigating to do, and... Oh!" She almost seemed to brighten. "He said he needs to talk some more about those plants that you have. Remember, the fox plants? The digital."

"*Digitalis?*"

"Well, Jerlene told him there was *digitalis* all over the ground near the house. She said it was important that he pay attention to it and everything else."

Bunny looked toward Gloryanne's house. From where they were, it could be seen easily and, if there were flowerbeds, they were neither well-tended nor featured cottage garden flowers. Looking back at Gloryanne, Bunny asked, "What does she mean?"

"I don't know. Sheriff Greenwood just wants to talk about it, is all. I'm waiting here for him. He said when he has more information, he'll let me know if I can go back in my house. Jerlene met him at the office saying she could help even before he came to get me. I guess she ran over his foot a few times with her chair. You'd think she'd know how to use it by now. Poor Sheriff."

"How would Jerlene be able to help? Did she *see* anything?" Bunny looked at Leo.

"I was at Hoodoo's last night, so I ain't sure what she saw. Fridays is poker at Hoodoo's. Good thing, too, so we could get here fast when Jerlene called. We didn't have to scramble from all over the holler and yonder."

"Where *is* Jerlene?" Bunny looked over to where her minivan had been parked the night before, along the side of Leo's cottage. Deep ruts in the mud where she'd driven could still be seen, puddles shining in the sunlight.

Leo pointed a weathered finger to the west. "She headed to the sheriff's early this morning and said she would head home after she talked to him. Said she needed to get some real sleep and wanted to see if Dave's home."

"Dave is her husband?" Bunny couldn't remember from the conversation during the tumult.

Leo clucked his tongue. "I guess you could call him that."

Gloryanne shifted in her chair, jerking forward hard enough that she had to release the cat to catch herself from falling out. Oscar Wildecat catapulted himself off the porch steps and, with his tail twitching haughtily, trotted away from the three of them. "Dang it!" she muttered.

Sheriff Greenwood's cruiser finally made its way up the hill as the sun reached the west mountain. It hadn't sunk behind the hills yet, but it wouldn't be long.

"Sheriff." Leo stood and stepped down the steps to greet him. Gloryanne rocked away in her chair, watching closely. No smile this time, Bunny noted.

"Leo. Miss Gloryanne." Sheriff Greenwood tipped his hat to both of them in turn, then looked at Bunny. "Ms. Sparks, I'm glad to see you here. I was hoping you'd tell me some things."

"I'll do what I can, Sheriff."

"Let's take a walk then," he said. His voice was low and steady.

He waited for Bunny to join him and then they walked together down the drive, across the dirt road, and toward Gloryanne's.

"Ms. Sparks, Jerlene Bittle-Baer tells me you know all about plants. Things that can help a person or kill them."

"Well..." Bunny looked at him as they stopped before the blackened hole that was once a door. "I know some things. I'm not an expert in botany or anything."

"She said you should know what this is." He pointed to the ground where a large number of wilted flowers were scattered. All were flattened, including leaves and stems, mashed into the earth.

"It's difficult to tell." Bunny bent at the waist to get a better look.

Sheriff Greenwood pulled out a pocketknife, squatted on his haunches and used the knife blade to lift a stem from the mud.

Bunny looked closely at the specimen the sheriff held up. "It'd be easier if it wasn't crushed and muddy."

"Probably the men working to put the fire out."

She straightened and looked around to see if there was at least one that hadn't been crushed underfoot. "I'm really not sure, Sheriff. These are not the best samples."

He stood, a dangling stem still balanced on the blade of his pocketknife. "Mrs. Bittle-Baer said it's digital. I don't know what she means."

Bunny felt a laugh begin to bubble up, then admonished herself. Why would she laugh at a time like this? Perhaps because she wanted to answer that all plants were analog, as far as she knew. Instead, she straightened and took a breath. "I think she meant *digitalis*. Gloryanne called it 'digital' this morning, too. Why are you asking, Sheriff? What would these have to do with a fire?"

"I don't know. Maybe nothing. But, the fire looks like a cover. Doc said Victor may have been poisoned."

"Poisoned?" Bunny looked toward the gaping hole. "How?"

"We're still looking into that, ma'am. Maybe too much heart medication." His eyes were sharp and steely green, but Bunny could see the lack of sleep pulling at the edges and the shadow of stubble on his strong chin. The gray just appearing at his temples seemed slightly more prominent in his dark hair, and the smell of smoke still permeated his work shirt and trousers.

"Please, Sheriff, call me Bunny. Only pimply-faced waiters and clerks at the grocery store call me 'ma'am.'"

"Well, ma—Bunny, I'd appreciate it if you didn't mention this to Miss Gloryanne. We're still investigating."

Bunny looked back toward Leo's porch where he and Gloryanne were watching from their rockers. "I didn't know Victor was taking heart medication."

"Gloryanne said he doesn't. Do you know anyone who does?"

"I don't." Bunny looked back to the trampled remains of plants on the ground around them.

"This plant, digital... *digitalis*, though... Mrs. Bittle-Baer said it can cause poisoning, like taking too much heart medicine. The medicine comes from this plant."

Bunny looked up at him. "Originally, yes. It did," she said. "A plant can't be patented, though, so it was synthesized. But, I don't know that this is the same plant. I don't think it is."

"You said you couldn't tell."

"Well, these are crushed and wilted, not to mention muddy. If it were foxglove... *digitalis*... the flowers would be different. If the leaves were intact, it would be much easier. These are probably fireweed. It's a local plant we see all along the roadside. People get them confused. Jerlene is one of them."

The sheriff looked sternly at her. "Would you swear this is *not digitalis*?"

"I would swear that's what I think. Couldn't you get it tested?"

"We're working on that," he said.

When the sheriff drove away, slowly, he gave a solemn wave to Leo and Gloryanne, which they returned just as solemnly. As Bunny approached Leo's porch, Gloryanne stopped rocking in her chair. "Those flowers are digital, aren't they?"

Was she curious or accusing? Bunny couldn't tell.

"I am not sure, Gloryanne. I think they might be fireweed. It's hard to tell with the state they're in." Bunny looked back toward the Tew house and shook her head.

Leo continued rocking slowly in his chair, silent and stone-faced.

"So you don't know?" Gloryanne chirped. "The granddaughter of the Holler Witch don't know?"

Bunny felt the sting of accusation in her voice.

Leo stopped his chair abruptly and spit off the side of the porch before turning to Gloryanne. "Never talk about Gene Sparks that way, missy, and never talk like that to Bunny if you want to be welcome here."

Gloryanne extracted herself from the rocking chair and stomped into Leo's cottage, letting the screen door slam behind her.

"I'm sorry about that, Bunny." Leo started the forward and backward motion of his chair again. "She may be upset, and she has every right to be, but she has no right to talk about your granny that way and insult you, to boot."

"Thank you, Leo." Bunny smiled, if wanly. "I should be getting back anyway."

Leo only nodded and continued rocking.

"Is Gloryanne going to stay with you, then?" Bunny asked.

"For the time bein', I reckon. She's in the extra room 'til she can get back in her own house. Sheriff said he'll let us know."

"Thanks, Leo... again."

He nodded once more and said, "Don't you worry, hon. Susie taught me how to deal with Gloryanne before she went home and left us."

Bunny remembered Leo's late wife and her no-nonsense manner. Suzanne Bittle was as loving as her own Gigi, but quick to snap an errant child into good behavior, sometimes with just a look.

Bunny hopped in the Keely and maneuvered it down the dirt drive. The summer shadows that stretched out behind the trees were growing longer. It was hard to make out the sound of crickets and birds over the little engine, but she was looking forward to hearing them and the quiet of the evening. It was a solitary life and she had come to cherish it. She wasn't sure how everything could suddenly be so turbulent.

When she pulled into the stall at the barn's rear and turned off the engine, blissful quiet followed.

"Home." She sighed a little burst of air and gathered the tools and containers in the back of the Keely, patting it as a 'thank you' before closing the barn door. The air was calm in that pre-twilight stillness when sounds seemed to carry furthest in the valley. She made out the far-off sound of a dog barking. The faint caws of crows having a heated conversation made her smile. Then the crunch of gravel under car tires. Close. Too close.

She stepped out from behind the barn and her momentary reverie to see a dark-green and gray Subaru pulling slowly up the drive.

Chapter Five

Bunny watched the car pull in, the driver's eyes fixed on the front door of the cottage. When the car pulled to a stop in front of the porch, Bunny hoisted the trug full of tools up on her hip, then bent to see if the driver might be visible, but it was impossible to tell in the dimming light. She walked to the porch, keeping her steps light and quiet, when the engine switched off and the dome light in the car illuminated the face of a woman Bunny wasn't sure she knew.

The short reddish hair and bright green-rimmed glasses of Fern Booher jerked back when she caught sight of Bunny walking up the porch steps. "Oh!" Fern exclaimed, pulling her car keys up to her chest. "I didn't see you there!"

"I didn't mean to scare you," Bunny said. "Are you lost?"

Fern opened the car door and stepped out, grasping the door frame as if for balance. "I'm Fern. Fern Booher. Ivy Tichner is my sister."

"I'm sorry. I don't know who that is." Bunny hoped to sound pleasant, rather than tired and put-upon.

"She owns Tickety-Boo Tea Shoppe in town. It's right next to The Gilded Owl, Cilla's bookstore?"

"Oh, yes. I heard it's a lovely shop. I've been meaning to visit."

"I'm the Boo part of Tickety-Boo." She smiled, dabbing her forehead. "This humidity is really something, isn't it? With last night's rain and all, it's a bit stifling."

"I was about to go in and make myself some iced tea," Bunny said. "Can I offer you some?"

"My goodness, yes. That would be marvelous." Fern closed her car door and walked around to the porch steps. "It's nice to finally meet you," she said, offering her hand. "In person, I mean. I've heard about you, of course."

Bunny shook Fern's hand and tilted her head. "You've heard about me?"

Fern smiled again. "It's a small town. Everybody knows everybody, right? At least, in theory. But, even if they didn't, your grandmother was practically a legend in the holler. My sister opened her tea shop hoping to sell some of the famous Gene Sparks' herbal blends to tourists and the occasional academic that avoids caffeine. They were working out the details when she..."

Not waiting to hear the rest, Bunny turned to open the screen door and set down the trug.

"I'm sorry." Fern reached out and held the screen door open while Bunny flipped through her keys.

"Thank you." Bunny unlocked the door and let it swing open. "Let me just freshen up and I'll make the tea."

Fern nodded and stood in the entryway, staring around the interior of the cottage as if she'd never seen one before.

Bunny caught a glimpse of her mouth drop open as the candle-lights in the windows began to flicker on. "Unless you're tired of tea," Bunny said. "You work in a tea shop, after all. You must have your fill of all the tea you can stand."

Fern gathered herself and turned to look at Bunny as if she'd just noticed her for the first time. "I'm sorry. It's just that your home is so beautiful. It smells heavenly, too. And all these carvings and gorgeous woodwork..."

"My papaw did that when he built the house," Bunny said, admiring the pillar Fern was petting like a soft animal.

She stopped, mid-stroke, and said, "Oh, please. I would love to have some of your tea. I only work at the tea shop part-time and I don't actually drink very much. I would like to try yours. It's the primary reason I came to see you, actually. My sister would like her shop to sell *your* blends, if you make them. She likes to use local herbs as much as she can, and since your grandmother..." She pressed her lips together and looked down at the floor.

"That's an interesting proposition," Bunny said. "Are you Tickety-Boo's purchasing manager?"

Fern laughed and looked up. "No, just my sister's grunt, really. I only help with the kitchen and serving, but I'll be spending more time there. I'd love to learn more about herbs and things."

Bunny pulled several amber apothecary jars filled with herbs out of a large, ornate armoire and placed them on the counter. "I would have thought that having your name on the shingle might mean you had half ownership or something. Is there any particular flavor you prefer for your tea?"

Fern's eyes brightened as she scanned the ornate labels. "It was really my sister's way of luring me here after my divorce. She has big plans for us. I think she sees us growing old together with a house filled with cats, except she'd never settle for a stray cat hair ending up in her tea, so I'm not sure how that's going to work." She picked up one of the jars and brushed her fingers over the glass. "Are these all from your garden?"

"And the woods beyond, yes."

"Ivy *told* me she'd heard that you took after your grandmother. How wonderful!"

Smiling, Bunny opened one jar, then another, passing them under her nose and inhaling the aroma of their contents. "So, you never met my granny?"

"Sadly, no. I didn't move here until after, well, until after she was gone." She looked around the room again, studying the bunches of dried herbs suspended from beams over the kitchen, her eyes settling on a vase full of roses. "I moved here after my sister bought her tea shop and talked me into coming to visit. She said the valley is magical, and she's right. It's beautiful here. The Appalachian mountains are special. So, I got a job at the sheriff's office part time. Then the research facility part time. You know, the one just across the lake that does all the sensitive work with the observatory?"

Bunny pulled a handful of ornate silver spoons from a drawer in the armoire and began scooping fragrant herbs, a little from this jar, a little from that, into a strainer nestled in a large burnished teapot.

"Yes, I've heard about it. The one that requires residents to agree not to install wifi. The reason there are no cell towers within miles."

Fern shifted slightly and frowned.

"Oh, don't get me wrong," Bunny continued. "I love it. It's quiet. Birds and insects love it, too, and I also love that." She plucked another jar from the armoire, this one filled with star anise. "So, you're a researcher?"

"Not really. I worked *for* the researchers, mostly editing grant submissions and putting together the packages for funding requests. It was all very clerkish. Not that exciting, really."

"And you quit because it was boring?"

"The funding for my position ran out, which is ironic considering the sole purpose of my position was to help the researchers pull in more funding." She leaned over and inhaled the perfumed steam rising from the teapot, then stepped back and chortled, removing her glasses to wipe away the veneer of fresh fog that covered the lenses. "They are forever battling closures and bureaucracy that seems determined to shut down their research. Imagine how many developers and communications companies that could claim a monopoly in the valley."

"What kind of research are we talking?" Bunny asked.

"Oh, acoustical types of things. They look for all sorts of things in space. Black holes. Quarks. Interesting anomalies."

"Sounds fascinating." Bunny opened the cold box and removed several trays filled with ice, dropping several cubes into a glass pitcher.

Fern looked around her at the cold box. "So, you have electricity! I thought this whole stretch of the valley was without it."

"Nothing is connected to the grid on this side of the holler." Bunny closed the door to the cold box.

"So, you have solar panels? Wind turbines?"

"To be honest, I'm not entirely sure how it works. Gigi, my grandmother, had a lot of tinkerer friends. She called them that. I'm guessing they were inventors based on raw schematics I've found here and there. I'll do some serious searching when the snow flies. I haven't even looked in all the rooms yet."

"You haven't been in all the rooms yet?" Fern's eyes widened as she repeated the words.

Bunny blushed and shook her head. "Felt a little like I was invading privacy."

"But, this is *your* home, right? You inherited it."

"I know. What's odd is that *you* know."

"Small towns, remember?" Fern grinned sheepishly.

Bunny handed her a glass filled with an elixir the color of pale lilacs. "Let me know what you think. It's one of my favorite summer blends."

Fern stuck her nose into the glass, took a tiny sip, and smiled broadly. "It's delicious," she said. "What's in it?"

Bunny smiled and began placing jars back into their respective places in the armoire. "A blend of garden sage, lavender buds, and shaved licorice root."

"My sister will be excited to hear I got to try this."

After a few minutes of silence, punctuated by the sound of sips and sighs, Fern said, "I heard about what happened to Victor, of course. Gloryanne came into the shop today and let us in on the dreadful news."

"It's a terrible thing. I still can't believe it." Bunny shook her head.

"She told us she was with you when it happened. You two have been friends a long time. It's nice she had someone to help her through such a tragedy."

"We aren't really friends, just neighbors."

"Oh! She made it sound like you two grew up together and that your grandmother was like a second mother to her."

"Really?" Bunny could feel the space between her eyebrows pinch together. "That's news to me."

"You didn't grow up together?"

"I was only here during the summers. I knew her, but I wouldn't say we were friends. She and Jerlene used to tease us from the road, mostly."

"You and your grandmother?"

"No, my sisters and I."

"But, she was with you during the trauma, she said."

"I only gave her a ride over the hill after we saw it. I still don't know why she was here at all." Bunny picked up Fern's empty glass and moved it to the sink. "I'm still quite exhausted. Can I walk you out?"

Fern's eyes widened once more. "I've overstayed my welcome. I apologize. I'll get out of your hair."

"It was a nice visit. I appreciate getting to know you. It's just been a long couple of days."

Fern nodded and forced a smile.

Bunny didn't want to just push her out the door, but then again.

As they stepped out into the night air, Fern stopped and turned to look at Bunny. "Maybe I should tell you what else she said."

"Who?" Bunny asked, softly pulling the screen door closed behind her.

"Gloryanne. It's just that she was insistent you two were such good friends and that she learned all about herbs from your grandmother, so it surprised her that you didn't know what flowers were all over the ground. She made a big deal about it for some reason."

"You mean the muddy, trampled plant parts on the ground the day after the fire? Did *she* know what they were?"

"She said it was something digital. And she mentioned that it was suspicious you didn't know."

"Suspicious?" Bunny stood for a moment, gathering her thoughts, then sat down in the wicker chair near the door.

"It just feels like you should know. These kinds of insinuations... well, they could lead to all sorts of speculation that isn't true. You know small towns. They're wonderful when they're wonderful. But, they can also be cruel. People jump to conclusions. Especially about those they haven't taken the time to get to know, or who haven't taken the time to get to know *them*."

Bunny gripped her stomach. "I—"

"Oh, I didn't mean anything against you personally," Fern said. "I just meant that when people don't really know each other, they tend to make assumptions. I've heard enough gossip about my sister and I to fill the holler. I've heard crazy gossip about you, too. Probably because you seem to keep to yourself up here. Out of sight isn't exactly out of mind in a town like this. If there's nothing to talk about, they'll talk about *you*. And if they don't know what you're actually doing, they just make stuff up."

"So, people in town are making things up about me beyond being good friends with Gloryanne?" Bunny put air quotes around the words "good friends," slumped down further in the chair, and looked out at the stars growing brighter in the clear night sky.

For several minutes, the cheerful chirping of crickets was the only sound.

Fern pulled the other wicker chair from across the porch and sat down. "I can only presume that what some people say is made up." She leaned over and put one hand on Bunny's knee. "I've heard about you being in the garden naked in the moonlight conspiring with forest creatures, conjuring spirits in the graveyard, making potions with starlight, and all manner of silliness."

Bunny looked down at the hand on her knee.

Fern straightened, then stood up. "I don't want you to get the wrong idea, Bunny," she said. "I didn't stop by to sling mud. But, I don't want to lie to you, either. I think you should know, especially now, because if there was finger pointing going on before, who knows how much worse it will get after what's happened?"

"I appreciate that, Fern. I do. And I'm not sure I should say this, really, but if I were going to talk about 'suspicious' I might wonder why Gloryanne was more interested in the soaps in the guest bathroom and the paintings hanging on the walls in my home than what happened to her poor husband."

"Well, maybe because Sheriff Greenwood is heading the investigation."

"Why would that matter?"

"I might just be spreading gossip if I hadn't seen it myself, but she practically glows when he's around. She and Jerlene both get a little possessive about him. I've been told on more than one occasion that

I need to keep my sights set somewhere else because he doesn't date women in the holler. It's a rule."

"He told you that?"

"No, Gloryanne. She has told me, my sister, and just about any woman under the age of 70 at least three times."

"Does she think you have your sights set on him?"

"I think it's just fair warning to anyone who might be competition."

Bunny stood up and took a breath. "This is too strange. What competition? She's married."

"I know. *Was* married, anyway. Though, I never heard her utter a nice word about Victor to save her life. Frankly, I've had enough drama with my own husband… ex-husband… to ever want to date again, no matter how handsome or gallant he might be. But, watch out, she'll be sure to tell you all about it, too."

"I think she may have already. But, she can stop worrying. Like you, I've had enough drama for a lifetime before moving back to the holler. I just want to make a life here. A quiet, peaceful one, growing a garden and maybe learning some things about my granny's life that I didn't know before. I'm not looking for a relationship with anyone. But, from the sounds of it, I need to make a point to quell the gossip."

Fern smiled and stepped down the stairs to her car. "I just thought you should be aware. Let me know when you can come in and meet with my sister, if you decide you're interested."

As the bright glow of taillights grew more and more faint down the gravel road, Bunny made her way to the clothesline to collect the pillow and linens she'd hung out to dry. A light breeze kicked up, carrying the scent of roses and the promise of a reprieve from the stifling heat and humidity. "Please," she whispered to the slight movement in the air. "One good night of sleep?"

She was just latching the screen door behind her when she heard the crunch of gravel under hard soles. She contemplated ignoring it and heading up to bed when a high-pitched whine called out her name.

"Bunny! Yoohoo! Bunn-eeeee...?"

"Ugh," Bunny said out loud, unable to stop herself. "Gloryanne, I'm headed to bed. It's late."

"Oh, I know. I'm sorry and everything else." She clopped up the porch stairs, holding the skirt of her bright purple sundress to keep from stepping on the hem. "I just came by to tell you 'sorry'... for calling your Granny Genie... Gene, I mean... Granny Gene... I'm sorry I called your granny a 'holler witch' and everything else. I was just upset."

"Forget about it, Gloryanne. You've just suffered a terrible tragedy. No one will hold it against you."

"Oh, that's all I wanted... I just don't want you to think I have anything against your granny. She was a mentor and a friend. You know that, right?"

Only, Bunny did not know that. She'd never heard that, and didn't believe it was even remotely true. Now was not the time, however. She leaned closer to the screen that separated them and whispered, "Goodnight, Gloryanne."

"Oh, okay. Goodnight, Bunny."

Bunny softly swung the front door closed and listened to the clop-clop-clop down the porch steps and the crunch-crunch-crunch across the gravel drive until she could no longer make out the sounds. Hugging her clean linens to her chest, she locked the bolt and turned to will herself up the stairs to bed, when she heard the crunch-crunch-crunch.

Was she coming back? Bunny sighed and again considered ignoring the sound.

Clop-clop-clop.

Gloryanne's heels sounded up the porch steps and back to the door. "Bunny? You still there?"

Bunny rolled her eyes to the ceiling and whispered, "Give me strength."

"Bunny, I want to tell you something else, too."

"What is it, Gloryanne? I'm exhausted. Can't it wait?"

"I want to tell you why I was here. In the middle of the night."

"You can tell me tomorrow, Gloryanne."

"I did something... have been doing something... I have been for a while now."

Bunny sighed. "I am headed to bed, Gloryanne. We both need sleep. Honestly, you don't have to confess anything to me right now."

"No, but I do need to tell you. Your granny gave me a good talking to once. Told me if I didn't listen and stop what I was doing that it was gonna bite me. I didn't listen. Now my house has a big black hole on one side and Vic is gone."

Bunny, still clutching the bed linens to her chest, opened the door a sliver and looked at Gloryanne. For a moment, compassion overtook exhaustion seeing the streaks of mascara that ran down each side of Gloryanne's face in rivulets. Even in the dim light streaming through the screen door, Bunny could see blackened tears collecting at the curve of her round chin before spilling onto and staining the elastic bodice of a dress stretched to its limit.

"She wouldn't sell me a potion, your granny. When I asked. She wouldn't sell me one." Bright fuschia lipstick glistened as Gloryanne's bottom lip protruded, quivering. "She told me it would bite me and it did."

"Gigi never cursed anyone, Gloryanne, if that's what you are implying."

"No, no, no. I ain't saying she cursed anybody. I'm saying I should have listened. And now…" A sob strangled the last sentence before she could finish it.

Eyes straining from fatigue, Bunny said, "Gloryanne, you have a place to go to tonight, right?"

Gloryanne sniffed and pulled the hem of her dress up to wipe her nose, bending at an angle Bunny imagined was meant to keep her from seeing. "I'm staying at Leo's tonight. In the room Jerlene uses when she visits."

Bunny crossed her fingers, took a deep breath, and asked, "Do you need a ride?"

"No, thanks, Bunny. The walk'll do me good."

Bunny blew out a breath and said, "Okay, then. Goodnight."

Without another word, Gloryanne turned and clop-clop-clopped down the porch steps and crunch-crunch-crunched her way toward the road. Bunny didn't wait to hear the sound fade this time.

Cranberry Creek's downtown area was a flourishing collection of shops and boutiques, thanks to the nearby research institute that drew students and fellows year-round. Bunny only remembered ever visiting the little library or the one tiny ice cream shop across from the pharmacy on rare occasions when she was younger. Now, there was a new-and-used bookstore, a yarn emporium, and a fish and tackle store. That was all on Main Street. Nestled among these were the post office, the CranBank, and the Tickety-Boo Tea Shoppe Fern's sister had opened.

To keep from losing her bearings, Bunny noted the library and ice cream shop —"Now with fat-free yogurt!"— were still where she remembered them. She also noted they were smaller than she recollected, and now seemed set off by themselves. Doubtful that every shop would be open early on a Monday morning, she was certain the library definitely would be. At least, if Mrs. Kettel, the librarian, was still there.

Bunny took the flyer Rose had sent her and set off for the library first. If she made 25 copies, that would be more than enough.

Mrs. Kettel looked up from behind the counter and smiled broadly as Bunny walked in. "Why, Bunny Sparks! Is that you?" She pushed her reading glasses up into the wispy white hair over her forehead and shuffled around a book trolley, frail arms spread wide.

Bunny hugged her gingerly.

Mrs. Kettel had shrunk considerably since Bunny had last seen her. An exaggerated bend in her back hunched her forward to such a degree she must have lost a foot in height. She stepped back, holding Bunny by the shoulders. "You look just like your granny did when she was your age." Her eyes twinkled with tears as she looked up at her. "Just as pretty as ever."

"You're too kind, Mrs. Kettel." Bunny blushed. "It's been too long, I know. I should have made an effort to stop in before now."

"Fiddlesticks!" She gave a wave with one gnarled hand while retrieving the glasses from her head with the other. Putting them on, she looked more closely at Bunny through the lenses, her pale eyes now magnified. "Leo's been keepin' me updated on the progress you've been making with the homestead. He says you've been busy making repairs and the gardens are bountiful. He saves some of the garden produce you share and brings it for me every week."

"I should have been doing that myself, Mrs. Kettel." Bunny could feel more color rise in her cheeks.

"Fiddlesticks!" Mrs. Kettel swatted the air in front of her. "You just keep Leo's poke full and he'll share what he can't use, plus all the goosefat, too!"

"Goose fat?" Bunny asked.

"Oh, that's just what I call the gossip he brings me from up the holler. Mostly, he hears juicy bits from Hoodoo and passes them along to me. He's one of this ol' lonely woman's lifelines, these days."

Bunny smiled wanly and made an internal note to stop in more often and bring Mrs. Kettel some flowers, too. She looked around and saw not much had changed. The long, sturdy oak table still stood to the left, its grain worn smooth with time, accompanied by an equally long oak card catalog. Two clunky computer monitors sat atop the cabinet, a pastel green cursor blinking faintly in the corner of one screen. Behind her, the front door creaked open and she turned to see a woman in her thirties, smartly dressed in a taupe linen shift and white cardigan tied loosely around her shoulders.

Attempting to straighten, Mrs. Kettel cleared her throat and put on her librarian demeanor. "So, Bunny, what can I do for you today?"

"Is that Bunny Sparks?" The young woman, dark hair tucked up neatly in a hair clip, breezed into the room holding what looked like a ceramic statue of a saint. It was too small to tell which one.

"I thought you were picking up pastries for us," Mrs. Kettel scolded, eyeing the statue.

"I'm sorry, Memaw. I stopped in to the antique place on the way and plum forgot."

"I see that."

Bunny looked from the statue, to the woman, to Mrs. Kettel, then held out her hand. "I'm Bunny Sparks. It's a pleasure to meet you."

The woman looked down at Bunny's outstretched hand, then looked down at her own hands grasping the statue. She blushed profusely and swallowed.

Mrs. Kettel stared at her quizzically, then said, "Are manners farren to you, child?"

There was a little gasp as the woman quickly turned on her heels and walked away, holding up the statue and saying, "I'm so sorry. I just need to put St. Joseph away with the others before I drop him. You know how I am, Memaw. I'll be right back."

Mrs. Kettel puffed out a breath and said, "That's my granddaughter Misti. I'm training her to run things around here, and I guess she's lost her manners."

From another room, Bunny could hear water running and the echoic voice of Misti as she called out, "That's not fair, Memaw. And, no, manners aren't foreign to me. I just had to put the statue away in case I might break it. I just got it and you never know who else might need one."

The acoustics of the building hadn't changed. Sound reverberated clearly from one room to the other. Remembering why she was visiting, Bunny turned to Mrs. Kettel and offered the flyer. "I actually stopped by because I need to make some copies. I'm going to start a study group, I think, and want to spread the word. See if there's any interest."

Misti rounded the corner and said, "Oh! You're a plant whisperer, too, then?"

"Well, an herbalist, yes. I don't know about plant whisperer." Bunny smiled. "Though that sounds fascinating."

"I love the idea and I'd be interested in doing your study group! Memaw says your granny was a legend in the holler and I always wished I could have learned from her," Misti said. She came around the counter and stopped in front of Bunny, holding out a hand.

Bunny looked down and stopped herself from declining the gesture. She looked up into blue eyes that reminded her of a younger Mrs. Kettel and delicately grasped the white cotton glove now donning the hand Misti presented. She wasn't sure if it was appropriate to ask if it was a phobia or a physical affliction, so she said nothing.

Misti held out the other hand, also gloved, and said, "I'll make those copies for you, Bunny. How many do you need?"

"Just twenty, I think."

"I'll make twenty-one, so I can have one, too. Is that okay?" She smiled up at Bunny, color still in her cheeks.

"Yes, of course."

"We'll put that extra flyer on the Community Bulletin Board," Mrs. Kettel said.

As Misti walked back behind the counter to the large copier, she said, "You should see the color we can produce now with this new copier!"

"It's not new," Mrs. Kettel corrected.

"Well, it's new to *us*." Misti busied herself with fitting the paper just so in the feeder and pressing buttons. "And it was nice of the research place to donate it to us."

"It's a write-off for them," Mrs. Kettel huffed. "But, true. They could have thrown it away. Like the computers." She waved a hand toward the card cabinet.

"They didn't throw those away, Memaw. They donated those, too. It was nice to finally have computers in here, even if they are a little outdated. We have DVDs now, too." She turned back to the copier and pulled the finished pile from the tray. Tapping them together on the counter to straighten them, she looked over at the case with two shelves stacked with DVDs and nodded. "And Vic, Victor, I mean, Mr. Tew, he built the display for us. He was going to build more, but..."

She quickly looked away.

"I don't have a DVD player," Bunny said, "or a television, for that matter, but I'll have to remember that in case I ever get one." She took the stack and reached into a pocket, pulling out several dollars. "How much do I owe you?"

Misti opened a little drawer behind the counter, then looked up at Mrs. Kettel, who shook her head and waved a hand. "You don't owe anything, Bunny." She pushed on the drawer without fully closing it. "It's on the house, I guess."

"I can't do that. I owe you for the paper and toner cost, at least." Bunny put five dollars on the counter. "I insist."

Mrs. Kettel shuffled closer to the counter and picked up the bills. "We heard about what happened with Victor Tew. Gloryanne was in to tell us and she told us all about how you saved her. If she hadn't been with you all night, she may have died in that fire, too."

Bunny stepped back as Mrs. Kettel held the money out to her with a tremulous hand.

"I have to be honest, Mrs. Kettel, we were not together all night. What happened is horrible. I don't know what I would do if I were in her shoes. But, I only gave her a ride, which may have saved her a blister, but I didn't save her life."

"I know you're being modest, like your Granny Gene always was," Mrs. Kettel said. "Gloryanne's car being in the shop and all, of course you gave her a ride. And she told us all about how you let her sleep in the big guest room downstairs, and gave her some beautiful herbal soap. How was she? I mean, last night. Did she know?"

"I was only with her a short time," Bunny recalled. "I think she was mostly in shock."

Misti nodded. "I'm sure. Shock. Not today though." She gave her grandmother a sideways glance.

"What do you mean?" Bunny was beginning to realize she missed out on a lot of what went on in the valley by keeping to herself so much.

"I think what Misti is saying is that Gloryanne might be a little happy to have the attention directed at *her* for a change, even if it means somethin' awful." Mrs. Kettel frowned at her granddaughter.

"Everyone usually pays attention to Jerlene." Misti ignored the look her grandmother was giving her.

Bunny looked back and forth between them. "Do you mean because of Jerlene's MS?"

Misti bit her lip. "She *says*. Doc Fisher thinks it's psychosomatic. Besides, she seems to get around fine when no one's looking."

Mrs. Kettel narrowed her eyes and clucked her tongue. "Did you tell me it was unethical to talk about what you overhear in Doc Fisher's office when you work there or did you not, child?"

"Two days a week isn't often enough to hear everything I hear." She rolled her eyes. "Vic, Mr. Tew, told me that Dave told him that he actually polishes her wheels every morning before heading to the shop. He said they are always sparkling clean when he gets home. How's that possible?"

"Clean floors?" Bunny offered.

Misti smirked. "You haven't seen her house, I take it."

Mrs. Kettel shook her head. "We don't need to be spreading more goosefat." She reached over and pushed the bills into Bunny's hand. "You keep this, hon. Misti may be sending us to the poor house going through our supplies..." She looked down at the archival gloves. "...but you keep it."

Misti closed the drawer with a snap and smiled a tight smile. Turning away from the register, she leaned across the counter and pulled a tall jar toward her. "Besides, you will want to save your funds for your move. Unless you would like to donate it? I did start a collection for Gloryanne. After what happened..."

Bunny noticed there was money in the bottom of the jar, just a few wrinkled bills. She looked from Mrs. Kettel to Misti and back again. "I'm happy to donate, of course. But, what move are you talking about?"

"Gloryanne said she heard from Mr. Reiter that you were moving." Misti seemed to look at Mrs. Kettel for confirmation.

Mrs. Kettel only frowned back at her.

Bunny could feel her jaw tense. "Who is Mr. Reiter?"

"He's the owner of Reiter's Antiques and Rare Treasures. It's a block southwest of here, same street as the sheriff's office. I picked up the statue there today on my way to get scones for memaw and me." She looked sheepishly at Mrs. Kettel, who was still frowning.

"I'm surprised he was open," Mrs. Kettel said. "He's never open."

"Where in the world would he get the idea that I'm moving? I've never even met him." Bunny looked at the ceiling, feeling the weight of the last few days starting to creep back, and took a deep breath. "If gossip is goose fat, then I would say this kind is rancid."

Misti let out a little nervous laugh.

"Rancid goosefat," Mrs. Kettel nodded. "What did he tell *you* about Bunny moving, child?"

Misti blushed and reached down behind the counter. "I almost forgot! He told me that I should give you this card. His wife is a real estate agent. She has her ear to all the gossip about properties in the county."

"She must need a hearing aid because her ear could not have heard that I was looking to sell." Bunny shifted her weight from one foot to the other and put one hand on her hip. "I've never met *her*, either."

Misti offered the card to Bunny who only stared at it. When the moment became awkward, she took it and turned it over, inspecting both sides.

"I tried to stop by early Friday morning to give it to you, but you didn't seem to be at home," Misti offered. She looked down at her hands, rubbing one gloved finger over another as if the material were irritating. "I was going to stick it in the mailbox, the card, but decided I'd try to stop by another time so I could talk to you in person." She looked down at her gloves again and the pink in her cheeks deepened by degrees. "And I brought a statue for you to bury at your mailbox."

"Well, that was nice of you." Bunny handed the card back to her. "Wait. What? You brought a statue for me to bury?"

"Yes, well, when I heard you wanted to sell, I wanted to help. Vic, I mean Mr. Tew, mentioned he was helping you fix up the place to put it on the market. Mr. Reiter told me that if you bury a statue of St. Joseph, upside down, you see, somewhere in the yard… by a mailbox works best, he said… then it brings the seller luck. So, I brought one for you. But, I didn't see you, so…"

"I was moving roses all day on Friday, so I was probably back behind the barn."

Bunny straightened the flyers in her hand, trying to smooth out the creases she'd just made from gripping them too tightly. Forcing a smile, she said, "It was really nice to meet you, Misti. And, Mrs. Kettel, I promise to bring some produce out to you personally the next time I have something good. The sweet corn is coming in now." She held up the stack of flyers. "Thank you again for the discount."

Mrs. Kettel patted her arm. "Don't be a stranger, missy!"

The air was beginning to feel stifling. As Bunny stepped out into the morning sunlight and pulled the library door behind her, she breathed deeply and decided she would stop in to meet this Mr. Reiter before the day was through. She wasn't sure where anyone got the idea that she was moving, least of all a man she'd never met. If Victor Tew had planted the idea around town, maybe he could give her a clue about why.

Chapter Six

T he hands on the big town clock over CranBank told Bunny she'd been in the library just over half an hour. It had felt infinitely longer. She stood at the intersection and looked toward the sleepy downtown just starting to stir and decided to check in at the tea shop first. She was sure a flyer would be welcome there, and she had been personally invited to stop by.

Tickety-Boo was easy to spot by the large, black teapot sign. It was ornately lettered in gold and hung from a thick iron rod that jutted out over the sidewalk facing the front door.

The shopkeeper's bell clanged musically as Bunny pushed the door open and stepped into antiquity. The room took her breath away. Rows and rows of shelves lined the walls. Each displayed various tools and accessories related to making or keeping tea. Tea caddies. Tea pots. Teacups and cozies. Fine china and rustic stoneware. Tea strainers and ornate spoons. They looked to be from all over the world. Some gleamed with newness, others bore the patina of age.

Throughout the room, the labyrinthine path wound through vignettes of small tables set with tea trays that suggested they were waiting just for you to seat yourself and pick up your cup. Along the back wall was a glass case filled with little desserts, behind which stood a tall apothecary cabinet filled with jars of leaves and colorful boxes.

Bunny bent to see the array of confectionery goods on display. Lemon truffles, blueberry scones, and shortbread cookies dipped in chocolate filled the top row. Before she could discover the wonders on the bottom shelf, she heard the soft rattling of wood baubles and looked up to see a slight woman in a beautiful bohemian outfit coming through a beaded curtain. Suspended above her kerchiefed head, an elegant sign announced:

Tea Leaf Readings by appointment.

"Welcome!" she said, her large smile lighting her eyes.

"Good morning, how are you?" Bunny smiled back. "You must be Ivy? Your shop is just beautiful."

"Why, thank you!" Her smile grew even wider and she gave a small bow. "What can I help you with this morning?"

"I'm Bunny Sparks. Your sister came to visit me last night and told me you were interested in local herbs for your tea blends. She said you'd been talking with my grandmother?"

"Oh, yes! I should have recognized you! You look so much like her. She was beautiful, wasn't she?"

Bunny felt her face warming. "*I* thought so." She cleared her throat. "Fern said that you were still interested and wondered if I might want to partner with you, in a way."

Ivy glided around the counter, her lacy skirts sweeping to and fro about her as she walked, and lifted a slender arm dripping with bangles to point at the apothecary cabinet. "Oh, yes! As you can see, the bins are almost empty. Some have been empty for months. I've had to purchase herbs from a company on the west coast, and their prices and shipping are excruciating."

"But their herbs are good?"

"Oh, yes, they're good. But, they come from such a long way. So hard on the planet. Not to mention the age of the material... the dried plants,

I mean. Local is always better for most things, isn't it?" She nodded as she said this.

Bunny found herself nodding with her in response.

"Anyway," she continued, "if you are anything like your grandmother, there will be magic in your herbs and that can only bring us both joy."

"And a bit of income, which would also be good." Bunny smiled.

"There is *that*," Ivy said. "It's nice to keep the lights on!" She laughed when she said this, a melodic lilting sound. "I was talking to someone who mentioned she was a student of your grandmother's and insisted that *she* could carry on providing herbs, but she hasn't been in since our conversation. That was last month. I think she is one of your neighbors. She said she's a master herbalist. Do you know her?"

Bunny bit her tongue. "Do you mean Gloryanne Tew?"

"Yes, that's her! You *do* know her!"

Nodding, Bunny took in a breath and focused her attention on a stack of golden desserts in the glass case. "Mm hmm, I know her."

"It must be amazing to have someone close by who speaks your language, so to speak. Would you like to sample the lemon truffles?" She breezed back around the counter and slid on a clear glove.

Bunny stepped back from the counter and took in a wider view. "I would love to try a lemon truffle," she said, "and that's the first I'm hearing that Gloryanne is a 'master herbalist.' I'm wondering where she earned that title."

Ivy stopped, mid-reach, and said, "Really? She didn't get that from your grandmother?"

Bunny shook her head. "Gloryanne is going through a really hard time right now... but my granny didn't offer titles like that. She never thought plant medicine was something one could master. Personally, neither do I."

"No?" Ivy lifted a luscious amber square and placed it delicately in the center of a patterned paper napkin. Offering it to Bunny, she said, "Maybe it was the one-day class she took in Morgan City. I know she brought in a certificate to prove she knew her stuff."

Bunny laughed. "I wish I could learn a life-time mastery of something by taking a one-day class!"

Ivy laughed, too. "Come to think of it, so do I!"

Bunny carefully bit into the treat and couldn't help but let out a murmur of delight.

"Do you like it?" Ivy stood, eyebrows raised, smiling.

"I love it," Bunny said. "The only thing that could make it even more divine would be a little sprinkle of lavender."

"Ooh!" Ivy cooed. "That *does* sound divine! I'll make a special batch, just as soon as I have some lavender to use." She waggled her eyebrows dramatically and they both laughed.

"I'll get right on that," Bunny said through another bite of truffle. Just then, the shop bell chimed and she turned to see Jerlene maneuvering her chair inside, guided by a portly man with thick glasses.

"Why, it's Bunny Sparks! Fancy finding you here!" Jerlene said. She gave her wheels a forceful thrust into the room. Teacups clattered as she bumped into a table. The man glowered as he followed her, righting a small vase that had toppled and setting a cup back in place.

Ivy flitted around the counter. "Don't worry about those," she said. "I'll reset it once I change the tablecloth."

The man gave a soft grunt in response.

"Ivy Tichner, this is my husband, Dave." Jerlene smiled up at him as he reached over her and offered a meaty hand. "And this is Bunny Sparks! She is Genie Sparks' granddaughter and lives in that big ol' house just over the hill from Gloryanne. You know where that is, don't you, Dave?"

Bunny wasn't sure if he was grimacing or simply didn't feel well. She waved a hand at him from her location near the counter. "It's a pleasure to meet you, Dave," she said.

He nodded in her direction.

Ivy unfolded a napkin from the table setting to mop up the spilled water from the vase. "You own the auto shop, right?" she asked Dave.

Dave nodded as he peered around the shop, frowning.

Jerlene wheeled herself over to the counter and surveyed the sweets on display. "We were just on the way to the pharmacy so Dave could pick up his medicine," she chirped.

Dave put his hands in his pockets and turned to look out the front window.

"He was out," Jerlene continued. "He's always losing his medicine lately."

"I didn't lose it," he grumbled under his breath, still staring out the window.

"You know you lost it, or we wouldn't have had to come get more," Jerlene clucked her tongue. "Unless you're saying someone stole it."

He walked over to the door. "I'll be in the van when you're done here," he said without looking back.

Jerlene snorted. "That man is a treasure."

Bunny and Ivy stood looking from the door to Jerlene for several moments before Ivy said, "So, Jerlene, can I tempt you into trying a delicious treat? I've just heard that the lemon truffles are to die for."

Bunny caught the little wink thrown her way. "Oh, yes. Truly scrumptious," Bunny said.

"To die for, eh?" Jerlene eyed the glass shelves, rapping on the glass with her knuckles. "I'll try some." She pushed her chair back from the case. "Speaking of 'to die for,'" she said with a grin, "did you hear the Sheriff thinks Victor was murdered?"

Ivy gasped.

Bunny took a step back and looked down at Jerlene. For a moment, she thought she should sit down to be at eye level with her, but couldn't bring herself to move.

"I *thought* there was something going on with Gloryanne. She never did have nothin' nice to say about Vic." Jerlene pushed and pulled the wheels of her chair, seeming to rock herself back and forth. "She must have said she was going to divorce him twenty times. 'I'll be divorced by Valentine's.' 'I'll be divorced by Easter.' 'I'll be divorced by Independence Day.' I swear, you could count on every holiday to be a new deadline. But she never filed, did she?"

Only the clock ticking filled the silence in the shop for a moment.

"You know," Jerlene added, "she actually said she was thinking of getting some herbs from you, Bunny, and doing him in."

Bunny's knees started to buckle and Ivy quickly pulled a chair from one of the tables and set it near the counter.

"Here, sit down," Ivy said, gently guiding Bunny into the seat.

Now at eye level, Bunny looked at Jerlene sternly. "Are you saying that Gloryanne was planning to murder Victor?"

"Or she was going to have you do it," Jerlene smiled. "She said you told her all about the digital."

Bunny looked up at Ivy and raised an eyebrow. Ivy raised one back.

"If you mean '*digitalis*,' Gloryanne and I have never really discussed it. In fact, she and I have never really discussed much of anything."

"Well, she told me it's growing all around your house, and all along the road, and you said it could kill. Or maybe your granny did... maybe she heard that from your granny, but she heard it from somewhere and she told me all about it. She was practically obsessed." Jerlene eyed the case of sweets, tapping her fingers against the glass.

Bunny tried not to stare at the cluster of oily fingerprint smudges left behind, but the desire to wipe them off was increasing uncomfortably. She looked down at her own fingers, still clutching the lacy napkin. She didn't know what to think. Was Jerlene actually accusing Gloryanne of murder? Or was this just the same gossipy child she remembered, now all grown up?

"She complained about his drinking, too. He was drunk all the time, you know? And with *his* heart issues, he shouldn't have been touching the stuff." She tapped the glass.

"What stuff?" Bunny asked.

"Alcohol, of course!" Jerlene hissed.

"Honestly, Jerlene, I don't know what you're talking about. Victor was sober. I never saw him drunk. I never saw him drinking. Not even once."

"Oh, so you lived with them, then? An awful lot goes on behind closed doors, you know."

"Did *you* live with them," Ivy asked, smiling.

Jerlene looked up at Ivy, who was now casually wiping the top of the desserts case with a tea towel.

"No. But I know things."

"Should we even be talking about this before the Sheriff has finished his investigation?" Ivy asked, just as casually as she moved the embroidered cloth.

"You're right," Jerlene said, sitting back in her chair. "I do that... talk too much. Bad, Jer. Bad." She tapped the back of one hand with the other.

The room was still, save the ticking of the antique clock. Bunny's eye caught the swinging of its silver spoon pendulum and the time on the clock face. It was after noon. She stood and balled the little napkin, looking for a trash receptacle, when the hanging beads parted. Fern stepped in behind the counter, her arms cradling a large stack of folded tablecloths and embroidered napkins.

"I'm back, Ivy! I just saw the most beautiful toad in the mint garden as I was coming in the back door, but that's not the most interesting thing. Remember that young man who always hangs out waiting for Misti from the library? What's his name?"

Ivy moved around the counter to join her and took the stack of linens. "Misti calls him Big Jake. I haven't seen him for a few days. Why?"

"The laundry said *they* haven't seen him in a few days, either. He's supposed to pick up deliveries for them, too, and they have stacks waiting. They called earlier this morning to ask if we wanted to wait for him or pick up our linens ourselves. I just went and got them."

Ivy set the linens on the counter. "I wondered where you were. It's hard to imagine he left town. He's so googly-eyed about Misti." She paused, fanning the napkins absentmindedly. "Oh!" she motioned to Bunny and Jerlene. "We have guests, dear."

Fern's eyes seemed to light up and she smiled broadly. "Oh, Bunny! You're here!"

Bunny nodded, returning her smile. "I thought I shouldn't wait to come in and see this amazing shop and meet your sister."

"I'm here, too," Jerlene said, raising a hand high in the air and waving. "I'm not invisible, am I?"

"Oh, no, certainly not," Fern said. She pushed her glasses up on her nose and looked over the counter. "It's just that..."

"Never mind," Ivy smiled. "We're happy everyone is here. Now who would like some tea?"

At that, the little bell above the front door jangled, announcing a new arrival. All four women looked toward the sound.

Jerlene lounged in her chair until she caught sight of Sheriff Greenwood. Then she brightened, twisting toward him with a smile that spread from ear to ear. "Why, Sheriff! What are you doing in here? Don't tell me you like tea and crumpets," she teased.

"Mrs. Bittle-Baer," he said, removing his hat. "Miss Tichner. Miss Booher. Miss Sparks."

Bunny pocketed the wad of napkin and moved to put the chair back, noting the seriousness of his expression.

Jerlene was still grinning broadly, waiting for her question to be answered. She was maneuvering her chair, in a somewhat stilted fashion, to better see him.

Ivy smiled in her inviting way and said, "It's nice to see you here this morning, Sheriff. Can I get you something? Hot or iced tea? A café au lait?"

Sheriff Greenwood nodded cordially, but didn't smile. "Thank you, Miss Tichner, but no thank you. I'm here on business."

Jerlene made a small "ooh" sound as she pushed her wheels forward and back, bumping the chair's rubber handgrips against the glass front of the display case with each backward motion.

Ivy reached back behind the counter and into the display, extracted a square of chocolate fudge atop gold foil, and presented it to Jerlene. "On the house," she said.

"Ooh!" Jerlene said, louder this time. Taking the little sugary gift in both hands, her chair came to rest.

Ivy winked at Bunny, then turned back to Sheriff Greenwood. "Well, you just let me know, Sheriff. Now, what can I do for you if not ply you with treats?"

"I'm making inquiries this morning, ma'am. Widow Stone from Dead Tree holler has reported that she hasn't seen her son in several days."

"Big Jake is missing." Jerlene offered. "Fern just said the laundry hasn't seen him in forever."

"Days," Fern corrected. "They said they haven't seen him in several days."

Sheriff Greenwood nodded. "I'm just making inquiries. If you happen to see him, let him know his mother is worried."

"You might want to check the library," Ivy suggested. "Jake comes in here regularly, but he's usually just waiting for Misti Meles to arrive in the morning or to take her lunch."

Jerlene snorted. "Big Jake and Misti? That's a laugh."

"Why do you say that?" Ivy asked. "He seems smitten and she's been meeting him here for tea in the morning at least three times a week."

"How long have they been meeting?" Sheriff Greenwood asked, pulling out a small notepad.

"Just a few weeks," Ivy said.

"Maybe only two," Fern added. "I mean, we've seen him almost every week since the shop opened, because we're on his regular delivery route. And we've seen Misti a couple of times a week, maybe. But in the last couple of weeks they seem to be meeting on purpose." She gasped. "You don't think they eloped, do you?"

Bunny shook her head. "If he did, he didn't take Misti with him. I just met her at the library this morning when I stopped in."

"Oh," Fern said. "Well, they sit over at that corner table in the back. It's kind of sweet the way they keep their heads down and whisper."

"You mean like Misti doesn't want to be seen with him." Jerlene snorted again. "Why else would they sit at the back so far away from the window?"

"Privacy?" Fern smiled. "People talk. Maybe they didn't want anyone to gossip about them."

"Like we are now," Ivy added.

Jerlene chortled. "Oh, sure. It's obvious that Misti wouldn't want people to see them together. She wants someone with money. Someone with polish. Big Jake doesn't have either. But, Big Jake? He'd want to shout from the rooftops that she was even talking to him. He hasn't ever even had a girlfriend."

"How do you know that?" Bunny asked. "Do you live with him?"

Jerlene grinned at Bunny. "I see what you did there. And, no. I don't live with him. Or his mother. But, people talk, remember?"

Bunny watched her pop the last of the chocolate fudge into her mouth and wipe her fingers on the hem of her shirt. Stifling any expression that might give away how she felt about what she'd just seen, she turned to Sheriff Greenwood. "Is there any news about Victor Tew?"

He pointed toward the front door with his hat. "Do you have a few minutes, Miss Sparks?"

"Of course, Sheriff," Bunny said. "I was just about to wrap up here." She looked at both Fern and Ivy. "Please, let's keep in touch."

"How could we not keep in touch with our new herbal goods distributor?" Ivy said.

Jerlene looked from Ivy to Bunny, to the Sheriff and back to Ivy. "What?" she squawked, making a face.

Bunny tried not to stare at the chocolate smeared around the grimace Jerlene was making and turned to Sheriff Greenwood. "Sheriff, do you need me to come into the office or...?"

"It's just a few questions, ma'am." He nodded at Jerlene, Ivy and Fern. "Ladies," he said, curtly. Pulling the front door open for Bunny, he put his hat on and waited for her to walk through, then added, "Miss Booher, we'll see you first thing tomorrow morning to get your ID and passwords updated."

"See you at eight, bright and early," Fern said, giving both a wave.

Jerlene called after him. "Don't you want to ask *me* anything, Sheriff? I know all sorts of secrets about that holler. I'm still available to fill in at the office, too. I'm free today, in fact. Earl don't need me at the pharmacy until tomorrow."

"Yes, ma'am." He turned to address her before pulling the door closed behind them.

Bunny squinted into the sun, now solidly above them, and waited for guidance about which direction the sheriff would lead. She watched him as he held a hand out in the direction he intended and quietly walked with him until they turned the corner at the intersection, heading north toward the station. "Do you have any leads, Sheriff?"

He stopped in the shade under a stately oak and pulled a bandanna from a back pocket. Removing his hat, he wiped at his brow. "It's going to be a hot one again today," he said.

Bunny shaded her eyes and looked up at the sky. "Clear, though," she said.

"Clear," he agreed. "There are some things that aren't clear, however, Miss Sparks."

Bunny waited silently for him to clarify his point. She wiped a hand across her forehead as she watched a bead of sweat make its way from his temple to the stubble on his jaw and noted the concern on his face. At least, she thought that's what it was.

He ran the bandanna across the back of his neck, scraped it across his chin, then stuffed it back into his pocket. "How much do you know about poisonous plants, Miss Sparks?"

Bunny studied his expression. "If you are asking whether I know about plants that kill people, I know a few. If you are asking if I've ever killed someone with a poisonous plant, the answer is absolutely not."

"I'm not asking if you've ever killed anyone." He looked up at the canopy of leaves. "I'm asking if you can identify poisonous plants. Like your granny could."

She watched his gaze move from the leaves above them to the mountain ridge west of the valley, to the ridge of a mountain to the south, then back to her.

"What do you know about foxglove?" he asked.

"I know that it is the plant from which digoxin is derived. It's a powerful stimulant to the heart. It's a powerful diuretic, too. And it really shouldn't be used for anything other than a beautiful cottage garden flower that feeds pollinators if you don't know what you're doing."

"Do *you* know what you're doing?"

Bunny breathed out a soft sigh. "I don't use foxglove as anything more than flowers to admire and to feed the bees."

The sheriff shifted his weight from one foot to the other, pulling his bandanna back out of his pocket. "Look, Miss Sparks, there are a lot of rumors that make their way around here at the best of times. I don't believe most of them and I want to give everyone the opportunity to own up to what's true or set straight anything that isn't."

"I've already been warned that people have been saying things about me, Sheriff. I like to keep to myself, and I guess that's cause for gossip. Maybe that's why Gigi had so many gatherings and gave so many talks. To keep people from making up stories about her. They did anyway, you know?"

He took off his hat and wiped his forehead. "Gigi?"

Bunny fanned herself with the stack of flyers.

The sheriff fanned his face with his hat.

They stood like this, each attempting to wave away the heat, until Bunny remembered only she and her sisters called their grandmother "Gigi." "Granny Gene," she said.

"Your granny was a fine woman, Miss Sparks. Most everyone in the holler loved and respected her. The only folks who made up stories about her were what you might call 'dissatisfied customers.'" He stopped waving his hat and held up a finger. "Don't misunderstand. I mean the kind of folks who want the impossible and then get a burr under their blanket when it's not delivered."

"Like when someone wants a love potion?"

"Yes. Like that. I know your granny would have helped everyone that came to see her if they could be helped, but there are a lot of folks who ask too much, and too often. And those folks get upset when their demands aren't met."

"I've dated 'folks' like that," Bunny mused.

Sheriff Greenwood chuckled. "We all have, I'd reckon."

They exchanged a brief smile at that.

"Your granny helped me solve a case once. Did you know that?"

"No, I don't think I did," Bunny said, flyers paused mid-wave.

"It's true," he nodded. "It was a case to do with poisoning, too. She called it the Tainted Tea case."

"Huh." Bunny smiled. "That's amazing. One day, I hope to find her diaries and learn all about her life. She really was something. "

"She really was. So, don't worry about gossip and rumors. I know how that goes in a small town. The holler is adrift with stories, and a lot of them are exaggerated or just plain false. Most of the time, it's not hard to tell the difference. You learn who you can trust and who you can't."

"I would guess you would have to in your line of work," Bunny said.

"You'd be right, there, Miss," he said, waving his hat a few more times. "I know you're knowledgeable about plants. I guess I just want to know who else has that knowledge."

"So, you're no closer to finding out what happened?" Bunny asked. "It sounds like you know Vic was poisoned, and that it was a plant?"

"We're still sorting things out," he said. "I'm just trying to collect as much data as I can so we can put together a good case. Jerlene and

Gloryanne have been doing a lot of talking. I'd like to hear a few other points of view."

"Well, as much as I'd love to help, Sheriff, I'm not sure how I can. I don't know who has that knowledge around here. I can tell you who doesn't, though."

"Who would that be?"

Bunny took a deep breath. "Don't get me wrong, Sheriff, I'm not trying to disparage anyone in the holler, but I don't think Gloryanne has that knowledge. I'm fairly sure I've seen her, like many people, get foxglove and fireweed confused."

"Do both grow around here?"

"Foxglove grows in the cottage gardens here and there. I have some in mine. Fireweed grows wild along the roadsides and in some of the fields. They look similar from a distance, and definitely to someone who doesn't know the difference between the two. But, then, some also get foxglove and mullein mixed up."

"I'm afraid I would be one of those who'd get plants mixed up," he said. "What about Jerlene? She said she and Gloryanne studied with your granny."

"Personally, Sheriff, I think they just annoyed my granny." Bunny sighed. "They hung around a bit when I was younger, and my granny did her best to be kind. She gave a lot of free talks, and I'll guess they attended some of them over the years. But, I'll bet it was more for the free lavender lemonade than to actually learn anything. They didn't listen much when they were little and I don't know that much has changed."

He let out a small chuckle at that, nodded, then asked, "Anyone else you can think of?"

"No." Bunny shook her head. "I honestly can't. And I guess that makes me a prime suspect?"

"Everyone and no one is a suspect at this point, Miss Sparks," he said. "I appreciate your cooperation. You have my number if you think of anything?"

Bunny nodded.

She stood there just a few moments longer in the shade and watched Sheriff Greenwood take long strides across the street, heading further west up the block. Before his cream-colored cowboy hat disappeared around the brick facade she presumed must be the Sheriff's Office, a small man stopped him. She couldn't make out everything he said, but his voice rose enough to hear snippets: "...progress on your investigation..." and "...do you know what my car is worth?..." and "why haven't we heard anything?"

She didn't mean to eavesdrop. She forced herself to shift focus and scanned the rest of the buildings on that same block. She stopped at the gold-leaf lettering stretched across a large plate-glass window: *Reiter's Antiques and Rare Treasures*.

It was only slightly uphill, but between the heat and the exertion, Bunny was panting by the time she reached the store front.

The interior was dark and a faded red and white "Closed" sign hung on the door.

Peering in through the window, Bunny cupped a hand over her eyes to better see inside. Her face was close enough to the glass that if the day were cooler her breath would surely have left a fog. It was difficult to make out much, but she did catch sight of a line of St. Joseph statues of varying heights. All in a row, they faced the display window. It looked as if another row lined the shelf behind an antique register near the door, but these were interspersed with what looked like a variety of other ceramic figurines. She squinted to make out their diverse and homely forms. There were green rabbits holding baskets, blue elephants with flowered hats, and pink-eyed horses wearing either sad or frightened expressions. It was difficult to tell which.

She stepped over to the door and tried the handle. Definitely locked.

When she looked back at the window, the blue sky reflected there was almost picture perfect.

Almost.

The line of white smoke cutting through the blue was distinct.

She turned to look in the direction mirrored in the glass. Definitely white smoke. Clutching her flyers, she hurried back to where the Keely was parked.

"Bunny! Yoohoo! Bunneeee!"

Bunny looked around in all directions as she put her flyers under a trowel in a gathering basket on the passenger seat and jumped in behind the wheel.

"Yoohooooo! Bunneeee!"

Chapter Seven

Bunny waved and started to back out of the parking spot as the bright magenta dress and clip-clopping of kitten heels on the cement rapidly approached.

"Wait, Bunny! Wait!" Gloryanne stuck her head in the open passenger window. "I'm glad I caught you! I need a ride, Bunny."

"Gloryanne, I'm in a hurry and I'm not sure I can take you where you need to go."

"Well, you're heading home, aren't you?" She held on to the Keely as if willing it to stay in place.

"I'm heading *toward* home. But, I'm not stopping there. I'm in a hurry, Gloryanne. Isn't there someone else you can get a ride with?"

"I've been trying all morning, Bunny," she whimpered. "My car is still in Dave's shop, being worked on and everything else. Vic took it in saying it was 'throwing codes again.' Something about the electronics. It seems like every time I turn around, he's telling me it needs something else. Dave said he was going to give me a ride, but now he can't."

Bunny leaned over and moved the basket from the passenger seat into the back. "Get in," she said, her voice flat with acceptance.

Navigating the winding back roads from town was usually enjoyable. Today, the steering wheel was too hot to grip fully. The air was thick. And then there was Gloryanne.

"So, I said to her, I said, 'You should just mind your own bees' wax.' I mean, I just lost my husband and everything else, you know? And she's accusing me of not caring because I said I would divorce him. Sure, I did. I said it lots of times. Especially after I started finding empty bottles of booze everywhere. But, did I?"

Bunny glanced over at her, then back to the road.

"What does she know, anyway? She said the reason all those bottles were outside was because he knew I would find them if he left them in the house. How dumb does she think I am? Are you really hiding something if you just leave it in a flower pot?" Gloryanne crossed her bare arms, with some effort, across her chest. "He didn't even care if I found out. She thinks she knows everything."

Without taking her eyes off the road, Bunny said, "Do you and Jerlene fight often? I thought you were friends."

"Friends?!" she huffed. "Why would I be friends with *her*? She was the one pointing out every single empty bottle. 'Did you see the one in *that* flower pot?' She'd yell stuff like that from Leo's porch sometimes. While I was on my way to work! How did she see it from all the way over there? She was probably snooping around. And she uses her limitations to get sympathy from the whole town. Have you seen her?"

Bunny shook her head, shifted into a lower gear to compensate for a steep incline, and kept her eyes straight ahead.

"Well, you should see her. She puts on this act like she's so feeble. If Sheriff Greenwood is in the office, all sudden like, she can't open a door or she's dropping things on the floor to see if he'll pick them up for her. He always does, because he's kind that way, but it's all an act. You should see her when no one's looking."

Bunny focused on the curves that wound their way deeper and further up into the holler.

"And you should see her with Dave. That's her husband. He can't even have a night out with the boys before she's calling all over to see where he is. And when she finds him, she demands that he come home for this reason or that reason. And you know what he told me?" She stuck her bottom lip out far enough that Bunny could see it in her peripheral vision. "He told me that Sheriff Greenwood and Doc Fisher are talking murder. That Vic was actually murdered. And he was most likely killed by someone he knew. And who knew him best? Me! That's what Jerlene is telling Dave. That she overheard that and now Dave shouldn't talk to me and everything else, because I'm a murder suspect. Can you believe that? Me! I mean, I couldn't stand him, but that doesn't mean I'd kill him."

She took in a quick breath. She hadn't meant to say the part about not being able to stand him, apparently.

Bunny kept driving, accelerating more than she might otherwise.

"Oooh! Isn't that the digital fox there?" Gloryanne pointed out the window at a cluster of flowers, their light magenta petals a bright spot in the shade just off the road.

"That's fireweed," Bunny said, taking a quick look.

"No. No. That's the fox plant." Gloryanne kept pointing.

"I heard you had a day of training to become a Master Herbalist," Bunny said. "Is that true?"

Gloryanne turned in her seat to better see the stand of flowers now well behind them. "I did," she smiled, repositioning herself in the seat. "I went into Morgan City and spent the whole day. I got a certificate and everything else. Do you have one? I can get you set up with the organization that gives the seminars, if you want. I know the coordinator and she said I can get $100 if I refer someone who signs up and takes the class."

Bunny smiled wanly. "Thank you, Gloryanne," she said. "I'm a little busy these days, but I'll let you know if I ever have the time to look into something like that."

"You just let me know if you have any questions about it." Gloryanne beamed.

Bunny squinted into the distance, checked her speedometer, squinted ahead again, then took a deep breath. "I do have a question, Gloryanne... and I guess there's no better time than now to ask it."

"You can ask me anything! I'm an open book, you know." She sat up taller in the seat and faced Bunny, smiling.

Bunny took another breath and focused on the road. Knitting her brows together, she tried to sound casual. "Friday night?"

"Yeah?"

"What were you doing?"

"What do you mean?" Gloryanne pulled at her hemline and shifted again in her seat.

"I mean, why were you running through my garden in the rain after midnight the night of the fire? What was going on?"

Gloryanne looked squarely in front of her at the road for the first time and pursed her lips together.

Bunny tried not to look directly at her, but she couldn't help but notice the mood change. "I get it if you don't want to talk about that night, Gloryanne, but I'd like to know why you were at my house at that hour."

Gloryanne kept her eyes fixed on the road for a minute, then looked down at her hands and the remaining fingers still tipped with brightly painted press-on nails. "I don't think I can tell you that, Bunny."

"Isn't that why you stopped by last night? To tell me? Now, you don't think I deserve to know? What would you have done if you got into the barn?"

Gloryanne stared straight ahead. "I can't talk about it right now, Bunny."

Bunny slowed the Keely as they rounded a corner and Hoodoo's store came into view. "Okay. I'll ask you again another time. But, I would like an answer and I think I deserve one." The parking area out front was empty, to Bunny's relief. She pulled in under the Cran General sign, the tires sliding on the gravel only briefly, and quickly shut off the engine. "I need to pick up a few things here. I'll only be a moment. Can you wait for me?" Bunny opened her door and hopped out without waiting for an answer.

Gloryanne furrowed her brow and leaned forward to look up through the windshield. "I should go in, too," she said. "It's hot and there's not a cloud in the sky. I'll just grab a few things myself."

Bunny looked up toward the sky. She wasn't looking for clouds, or the lack of them, as much as simply trying not to sigh. She'd been sighing a lot lately.

The heat followed them across the lot, clinging until Bunny pushed open the door. The interior seemed dark compared to the bright sunshine outside. Bunny took a moment for her eyes to adjust while she looked around. She had developed a sort of habit in the past few months of stopping in to see if Hoodoo had any packages for her or anything for G. Didi. The postal service delivered only letters to individual mail boxes. Larger items were left here.

She stood near the large wooden barrels that lined the front of the counter. They no longer contained bulk goods like flour or crackers, but they were such a fixture it was hard to imagine the store without them. Bunny only briefly let a memory flit through her mind of visiting Cran General when she was young. She and her sisters, walking hand-in-hand to deliver a note from Gigi, and Hoodoo always giving them each a piece of hard candy as a reward for making the trip.

She quickly scanned the store in hopes of finding him now and was suddenly propelled forward into a display when Gloryanne collided into her back.

"Oh, sorry, Bunny! I was looking at the summer clearance specials."

"Good afternoon! I'll be right with you," came a voice from the back.

Bunny stooped to collect the many silver spoons with their bowls hammered flat that were scattered on the floor from her collision. They were stamped with the names of various herbs: Basil, Rosemary, Thyme, Oregano, Parsley. She decided to save out several to purchase for herself and G.Didi.

Gloryanne sashayed past her and into the candy aisle, her kitten heels slowly click-clacking their way across the linoleum from chocolate bars to hard candies and back again.

"Bunny Sparks!" Hoodoo called out as he came around the corner from the back room. "Why, it's mighty nice to see you on this fine day!"

"It's nice to see you, too, Hoodoo," Bunny said, looking up at the tall gentleman.

He dabbed his face and the top of his balding head with a handkerchief while watching her place the many spoons on the counter.

"I dropped some of these, so I'd like to buy them." Bunny attempted to smile, but was sure her expression looked more like a grimace.

Gloryanne continued to click-clack back and forth in the candy aisle. "Don't you have taffy, yet, Hoodoo?" she called out. "I keep asking."

"Sorry, Mrs. Tew," he said, "Taffy is a New Jersey confection. Unless you mean the insincere flattery that gets floated around here sometimes."

Gloryanne puffed out a breath of disappointment. "Sometimes, Mr. Hoodoo, I question whether you are from the holler at all."

She resumed her click-clacking.

Hoodoo raised an eyebrow dramatically at Bunny and flashed a conspiratorial grin.

On any other day, Bunny would have felt privileged to be included on the inside joke, but the smile she returned today was strained.

"Oh," Hoodoo said, "I've got something for my dear friend, Miss Didima, Missy Sparks. Will you be seeing her soon?"

"I'm heading there now, as a matter of fact," Bunny nodded. "In a little bit of a hurry, actually, for that reason."

Hoodoo held up a finger to her as a signal to wait and slipped into the back room. When he reappeared, he was holding a beautiful blue jar filled with roots and twigs.

"Soapwort." Hoodoo held it out to her. "My niece in South Carolina grows it and Miss Didima just loves it. She, my niece, sends it to me every so often and I save it for Miss Didima. Would you mind making sure she gets it?"

He held the jar out to Bunny and she took it. "Of course, I will," she said.

"Do you want anything besides the markers? My niece made those, too. Aren't they something?"

"No," Bunny said. "I mean, yes, they are adorable. I'd like two of each so that I can gift G.Did... Miss Didima with some, too. But, no, I don't need anything else unless the mail...?"

She turned to look for Gloryanne, who was now in an aisle full of hair products and personal grooming items.

"Allow me," Hoodoo said, winking. "Mrs. Tew, my delivery man is scheduled for today. He usually gets here around one o'clock on Mondays. I'm sure he won't mind swinging up near your house, if you don't mind waiting. Can he give you a lift?"

"Oh!" Gloryanne cooed. "Do you mean Big Jake? Why, that handsome man can take me anywhere."

She click-clacked up to the counter and plopped down bags of fruit-flavored hard candies, chocolate covered cherries, and a box of peanut brittle.

"Thanks for the ride, Bunny," she said, smiling at Hoodoo. "I can wait for Big Jake to take me the rest of the way."

Bunny mouthed the words *thank you* as Hoodoo gave her an understanding smile, bagging her garden markers and the jar of soapwort.

"Oh! One more thing, Missy," Hoodoo said. "Something *did* come for you." He looked over at Gloryanne, then pointed toward the door.

Bunny turned, looked at the door, then back at Hoodoo as he gave Gloryanne a sign that she needed to wait a moment.

"I'll grab it for you and walk you out," he said, then stepped into the back room. When he returned, he carried a box wrapped in brown paper. It was big enough that he had to carry it with two hands.

When they were at the Keely, he placed it in the back for her. She looked it over. No return address. "When did that arrive?" she asked. "I wasn't expecting anything. I don't even see a return address."

"That came this morning. It was here on the porch when I opened shop." He looked down at her without smiling. "Be mighty careful, Missy. There's a current in the valley lately and it feels dangerous."

"A current?" Bunny looked up at him, studying the gray eyes set deeply into his heavily lined face. Stray hairs from long white eyebrows fluttered in the light breeze, as did the scant frills of silver above his ears.

"It's like electricity," he said, his eyes growing dark. "It's happened before. Just let Miss Didima know that I noticed."

"I will," Bunny agreed. "And if you see Jake, let him know that the Sheriff was asking around for him earlier today. He failed to pick up a delivery for the Tickety-Boo Tea Shoppe and his mother is looking for him."

Chapter Eight

By the time the old Keely lumbered over the hill, past the graveyard and onto the rocky path that led to Granny Didima's cottage, the smoke was dissipating and barely noticeable.

Bunny felt her heart jump a little upon seeing the sight that greeted her when she pulled closer to the porch. A group of women, quite a number of them, were gathered there.

She shut off the engine and tried to make out who they were, not seeing Granny Didima anywhere among them. Only when the group of women casually parted to let her through did she recognize a face. The other women, whose faces she did *not* recognize, chatted amongst themselves and occasionally nodded in her direction.

"G. Didi?" Bunny said, though her voice was less a statement than a query.

"Child, how good of you to drop by!"

Bunny began to point at the chimney, now devoid of smoke, when the sprite of a woman gently pinched her cheek and grinned. "I want to introduce you to a most venerated group of colleagues." She winked at Bunny and pointed at her winking eye. "Venerated."

Before Bunny could acknowledge a fine use of yet another "v" word, Granny Didima was twirling away and pulling Bunny up the porch steps with her.

"My fine friends," she announced, "allow me to introduce the granddaughter of Gene Sparks! This is Beatrice." She took a step back, as if presenting Bunny to a tribunal, although it felt to Bunny as if it might be a *friendly* tribunal, as each woman smiled a genuine smile.

One by one, they stepped forward and embraced Bunny warmly as Granny Didima named them. Bunny returned every hug, trying to remember names as they were offered, but they soon became a jumble.

By the time she reached the few remaining women, Bunny had almost entirely given up on the idea of keeping track.

"Parsy and Padda Peacock. They are our only true sisters on the Council and hail from Kentucky."

Bunny hugged them both at once and felt the rich velvet of their emerald green summer shawls cool her skin, much to her surprise. She would remember that, certainly. "True sisters?"

"We're actually related. By blood. Not just in the 'Sisterhood' of the Council, as it were. I'm Padda," said the taller sister. She squeezed Bunny's hand and stepped back, her jet-black hair undulating around a porcelain bare shoulder. "This is Parsy."

"Parsy Peacock," Parsy said, as she nodded, her own jet-black hair styled in a sharp bob, set off by a French beret in the same green velvet as her shawl. She plucked at the long peacock feather adorning the cap and grinned. "Too much?" she asked. "No one will tell me the truth."

Bunny shook her head. "No, it's beautiful. Really."

Parsy smiled. "I knew I'd like you."

Finally, the last introduction was made. "Madame Exene Zaayer, meet Beatrice Sparks. This is Gene Sparks' kin." Granny Didima assisted a wisp of a woman, other members of the council providing extra support, as needed.

The old woman's papery skin was so translucent, Bunny thought she might see through to her bones. "It's a pleasure to meet you, Madame Zaayer," Bunny said, gingerly accepting the woman's outstretched hand.

"I'm not breakable, chil'" she said, as she squeezed Bunny's hand. "But I know I'm scary lookin'. You don't have to pretend I ain't."

Bunny tried to appear unperturbed by the milky white eyes that met her own and wondered if the frail woman whose hand she cradled like a tiny bird was blind.

As Madame Zaayer was escorted to her seat, the rest of the women found places of their own to rest. Bunny looked about her at the colorful assortment of new acquaintances, vainly trying to recall their names. She felt awkward as she looked from one to the next. All were in their elder years, though some held an ethereal beauty and others struck Bunny as if they'd be quite happy under a toadstool.

Their good-natured greetings out of the way, Granny Didima motioned for Bunny to sit. "Thank you, one and all, for your presence and sagacity regarding the current situation. It isn't every day that we are privileged to have the Council meet with such attendance."

"It isn't every day we have an emergency meeting called," said Parsy, her green eyes solemn.

"Emergency? What emergency?" Bunny asked, looking squarely at Granny Didima.

"The energy in the holler has shifted," Parsy offered.

"There is something revved up and unnatural happening," Padda added.

Granny Didima nodded in agreement. "This has happened before. It feels familiar."

Bunny looked from face to face, noting the apprehension she saw. "I stopped at Hoodoo's on the way here," she said. "He told me to let you know that there was a 'current'... an electricity..."

"Your granny used to manage this on her own. She rarely called for help." Granny Didima's gaze drifted in a direction Bunny could only presume was the cemetery plot down the hill. "At that time, Gene was head of the Council. She put a great deal of energy into maintaining the energy here, protecting the land, and she generously assisted any Appalachian medicine woman who needed guidance."

Parsy and Padda were nodding enthusiastically. "She was our first teacher," Parsy said.

"She taught us how to keep our 'feelers' on," said Padda.

"Feelers?" Bunny asked.

"Heightened intuition, one might call it." Parsy smiled. "A type of energetic vigilance. You seem to have that innately." She leaned forward in her seat and tapped Bunny's shoulder lightly.

Bunny sensed Parsy's words were meant as a compliment, but the swirl of confusion clouded her mind, making it hard to accept the praise. "I'm not sure about that," Bunny said in an outrush of exasperated breath. "I have no earthly idea what's going on. I don't know why I was called here by the smoke signal. I don't know why you are all here, either. I don't know how I fit into all of this."

There seemed to be a sympathetic murmur that passed from woman to woman in the group.

"Just the same," Granny Didima continued, "there is a vexing energy in the holler that we have come together to address, and it feels only right to include you." She looked at Bunny and silently mouthed *vee word* and winked, but her expression became more serious the next instant.

"Can we get some details on what you've seen recently, Beatrice?" Parsy asked.

"You mean other than Victor dying in a fire? Which may or might not be murder with a side of arson to cover it up?"

"That," Parsy nodded. "And what else?"

Bunny pressed a finger to her temple and squeezed her eyes shut for a moment. "So many things have happened, it's hard to know where to begin or what to think."

Parsy nodded again, her jet black hair bobbing gently.

"Well, for one thing, Gloryanne was in my garden trampling a path to the barn in the middle of the night during a rainstorm. That was weird." Bunny tapped her temple lightly and frowned. "Then, she tried to get into the barn, which I found out later was because she wanted Gigi's Kee... the Jeepster." Bunny looked toward it, then back to the group. All were listening intently. "She was almost crazed, trying to pull the door open, and insisted that Gigi let her borrow it regularly... or maybe just occasionally, I can't remember."

"How about never?" Granny Didima offered.

"Yeah," Bunny conceded. "It sounded off to me, but I hadn't thought much about it until now."

Granny Didima motioned for her to continue.

"I insisted that she just let me drive her home, which is where I assumed she was going. She was all dressed up and trying to walk in heels."

"Dressed up?" Parsy raised an eyebrow. "As in?"

"As if she were coming back from being out on the town," Bunny said.

"Out on the town? What town?" Parsy asked. A titter fluttered around the porch and Parsy grinned. "I mean, really. Where's the nightlife that isn't feathered or furry?"

"Besides your last string of beaus, Pars?" Padda teased.

"Only one was feathered," Parsy said.

"And only after he was tarred first, as I recall," Padda added.

"Anyway." Parsy looked back to Bunny.

"Anyway," Bunny continued. "Gloryanne was there, out of nowhere and on foot. She can't have walked into town and back like that, even on a good night."

"I wouldn't," Parsy said.

"On top of it all, she seemed genuinely horrified about there being a fire, but later didn't seem even remotely sad about what happened. I didn't see her shed one tear."

"People handle grief differently, we know," Padda said, "But not seeming even a little upset?"

"Right?" Bunny said. "She didn't ask if Victor was okay. She didn't ask what happened. She wasn't even really upset that part of her house was charred."

Granny Didima said, "Her house is still standing, I hear. Didn't burn down. Hardly burned at all."

"The volunteers were already there when I finally got Gloryanne to accept a ride. It was out in no time, so it must not have been burning long. Jerlene was at Leo's so I can only guess that she called it in."

A murmur traveled between the women who had been, until that moment, mostly quiet.

Madam Zaayer clucked her tongue, her white eyes shining. "Jerlene," she harrumphed. "If she weren't Leo's kin..."

Bunny looked at the frail woman and waited for the end of the sentence. After a few moments, Bunny said, "Jerlene has been acting strange, as well. It's like no one wants to even admit this happened, and it *just* happened. It's not as if it's ancient history."

"Jerlene has always been a pill," Granny Didima said.

"We can all agree on *that*," Granny Zaayer concurred.

"If Jerlene is a pill, Gloryanne is the whole pharmacy," Padda added. Some chuckled at that. Most just nodded in agreement.

Granny Didima put a finger to her lips and motioned for Bunny to continue.

Bunny thought for a moment. She didn't personally know most of these women, though she wanted to and she knew if they were trusted by Granny Didima that they could be trusted. "Despite the perfectly timed zinger…" She nodded at Padda. "It actually sounds like he was murdered, and some suggestion he may have been poisoned before the fire."

"You think the fire was meant to hide something?" Parsy asked.

"I don't know." Bunny sighed.

Granny Didima stood up and stretched her legs. "Word around the holler is that Gloryanne has been setting a date for divorce by the calendar."

"I heard that from Jerlene, but thought she was just being Jerlene," Bunny said.

"Leo hears her declare she's filing papers by every holiday on the horizon. I think Labor Day was next as a deadline. Leo said she's been doing it for months. Drives him plum crazy."

Bunny wanted to add that *everything* was feeling a little crazy lately. Instead, she watched the antics of the goat kids on the hill as they danced around their grazing mother. When she looked back to the porch, the women were all starting to stand.

"We should get our official business underway," Madame Zaayer announced, her white eyes shining. "There's only so much time."

Bunny stood and held her arms open to give Granny Didima a quick hug. "I'm exhausted, so I won't take offense at being invited to leave early."

The old woman nodded and said, "I'm glad everyone got to meet you, Bunny. You head on home now and get some rest, if you can. I'll fill you in on what I'm able in a few days. Oh! Wait just one sec. I have a liniment for Leo's rheumatism, if you'll drop it by when you have time."

As she stepped inside to retrieve the remedy, each woman, in turn, embraced Bunny with such warmth she almost didn't want to leave.

Parsy was the last to step in. "Keep your eyes open, Buns," she said, in a low voice. "I can tell you want to keep to your own business, to keep your nose out of drama. If you close your eyes, though, you won't see a punch when it's coming."

In the afternoon sun, Bunny walked through the vegetable patch, trimming tomato suckers and gathering dark green cucumbers. She topped off her basket with plump radishes, Swiss chard, and crisp butter lettuce, then spotted a beautiful watermelon ready for picking.

A warm gust of air pulled at strands of hair, escaped from their place atop Bunny's head. As she pinned them back and adjusted the loose bun, Parsy's words replayed themselves in her mind. The thought of being punched in the nose and not seeing it coming. What had she been referring to exactly? She wondered if being called "Buns" was agreeable and smiled, knowing she would have bristled had it come from a less genuine person.

She surveyed the garden, lush and green, with bursts of color where ripening edibles caught the sunlight or riotous Zinnia blooms nodded in the breeze. The thought of lying down in the fragrant beds of thyme was tempting. Then she remembered the plant markers she forgot to give to G.Didi, the mysterious package she'd picked up at Hoodoo's, and the ointment she promised to deliver to Leo. After the recent summer storm, she expected he'd need it.

The bounty she harvested for dinner could wait. With the day pressing on, Bunny loaded the Keely and set off. Sheriff Greenwood's

114

patrol car was the first thing she saw, parked directly in front of Leo's, as she pulled up the drive. Leo rocked slowly in his chair on the porch.

Following his gaze, Bunny spotted Gloryanne and the sheriff standing near the Tew house across the way. Bright yellow police tape warning "Do Not Cross," strung between several lath stakes, prevented access to those who respected its boundary. She watched their backs as they faced the charred remains from the distance created by the illusory barrier. "Hi, Leo," she said somberly. "Granny Didima asked me to bring you this." She offered him the small, amber jar filled with earthy green relief.

He looked up and smiled. "Hello, missy. Thank you for taking the trouble."

"It was no trouble," Bunny assured him. Seeing his swollen knuckles prompted her to unscrew the lid before handing it over. "Would you like to use it now? I can work it into your hands and elbows, anyway."

He murmured a quiet thanks and went back to watching the sheriff and Gloryanne, still in conversation. Both were now looking toward Leo's porch. The aroma of crushed sage and lavender promised comfort as Bunny worked the shimmery balm over weathered skin.

"Your Granny Gene would be proud to know you're a healer, just like she was, young lady," Leo said, sounding almost sentimental to Bunny's ears.

"I'm not much for healing, Leo. Just helping."

Before she could ask where he wanted her to keep the jar, Sheriff Greenwood and Gloryanne were just reaching the porch. Gloryanne was first to speak. "It sure smells good over here. Whatcha been doing?"

Bunny placed the lid back onto the jar and stood up to acknowledge them. Leo began to rock his chair again, as slowly as before.

"Miss Sparks." The sheriff tilted his hat toward her. "I was just about to head over to talk to you after I finished here. Do you have time?"

Gloryanne gave him a sly smile. "Who wouldn't make time for *you*, Sheriff?"

He seemed to disregard her, though it was as polite a dismissal as Bunny could imagine.

"Of course, Sheriff," Bunny said. "I stopped by only to drop off this ointment for Leo. I'm available now." She waited for Gloryanne to teeter up the steps and plunk herself down into an empty rocking chair on Leo's porch before stepping down. "Is here okay?" she asked.

The sheriff gave a little shake of his head. "If we could..." He shifted his weight, his voice low and measured. "I'd rather it were a little less..."

Bunny thought he was intentionally trying not to look at Leo and Gloryanne. "Oh, of course," she said, "we can head over the hill. Is that okay?"

"Yes, that'll be fine." He placed his hat back in place atop his head, his expression unreadable. "Keep an eye out for Jake, will you both?" He looked from Leo to Gloryanne.

"Will do, Sheriff," Leo assured him.

"We certainly will, Sheriff," Gloryanne purred, her lashes fluttering.

Bunny parked at the barn and met the sheriff in the driveway. As he exited his cruiser, he said, "I don't want to keep you long, Miss Sparks."

"I appreciate that." Bunny tried to smile. She knew it probably came off as more strained and forced than she would have liked. "So, what you were saying at Leo's... still no sign of Jake?"

"That's right. Unless you've seen him."

"I haven't seen him, no." Bunny looked longingly at the covered porch. "Sheriff, can I get you some iced tea? I'd love some myself." She expected him to decline, so when he nodded and thanked her for the offer, she hesitated a moment.

The sheriff met her eyes and gave a small nod, stepping toward the porch. He waited there while Bunny put together a tray of cold lavender and honey tea, and when she reached the screen door, he was already opening it for her.

"You're not vegan, are you?" she asked.

"What?"

"Vegan? You're not, are you? I mean, I added honey. I'm sorry that I forgot to ask. I'm just so tired."

"No." He pushed the screen door, softly, until it latched. "I have a niece that's vegetarian. But, no."

She set the tray down and handed him a glass. He immediately put it to his forehead and held it there a moment or two. He looked like he could use a good night's sleep, too.

"Thank you, ma'am," he smiled. It was faint and overshadowed by his professional demeanor, but Bunny was happy she caught it, however brief.

"So, what did you want to ask me, Sheriff?"

"I need to know how involved you are or have been with the Tews," he said. He looked down the road before taking a long drink of the iced tea and putting the glass up to his forehead again.

"Not very. Growing up, my sisters and I spent our summers here. That's how I know Gloryanne. The Biggs, Biggs was her maiden name, lived in the house where she lives now."

"Yes, I've heard the story." He nodded. "So, you knew her because your grandparents were neighbors. How do you know Victor Tew?"

"I only met Vic when I moved back after Gigi died. Gloryanne brought him over and insisted he could help with repairs."

"Gigi?"

"Oh, that's what my sisters and I called Granny Gene, our grandmother."

"Right. And did he help you with repairs?"

"He did," Bunny said, pointing at the porch steps. "He worked for me for several weeks, replaced warped and rotting boards, built some shelves in the barn. He showed up when he said he would, charged a fair price, and did good work. Insisted he should do more."

"Was there any more to your relationship?"

Bunny's eyebrows shot up. "Meaning what?"

"Did you spend any time together beyond his doing handyman work for you?"

"None at all." Bunny considered the weeks when Victor Tew was a temporary fixture around the homestead. "He did his work, left when he was done. Neither of us were much for conversation, and I left him to it."

"He didn't talk to you about his relationship with Gloryanne?"

"Definitely not."

"Did you know that Gloryanne accused you of having your sights set on him?"

Bunny laughed. "You're not serious."

"Only about the accusation. It's fairly common knowledge that she has a habit of making either veiled or outright accusations about most women under a certain age in the holler coming on to her husband."

"I was taught not to speak ill of the dead, Sheriff, so I won't tell you what I think about *that* idea. Suffice it to say, if he *had* propositioned me, it would have been a hard 'no.'"

He gave a slight smile. "So, he never tried anything."

"No. He did the work we agreed on. That's all." She watched him for a moment before the thought occurred to her. "He *did* suggest too many times that I should have him come into the cottage to check things."

"Check things?"

"I'm not even sure what kinds of things he meant. Things that needed repair, I guess. He hinted several times that I should let him have a look around inside."

"And did you?"

"No, he only ever worked on the porch and parts of the barn. I thought he was just trying to be thorough, but I haven't even been in all the rooms myself yet."

The sheriff raised an eyebrow.

"I know." Bunny blushed. "It sounds silly."

He took a long sip from his glass, now dripping with condensation, and set it down. "How well do you know Jake Stone?"

"Big Jake?" Bunny paused, registering the shift. "I know he's the delivery driver for various businesses in the valley. I met him for the first time at Hoodoo's when I first moved back. That's pretty much all I know, beyond the fact that he's missed some deliveries. But does that mean he's missing? Maybe he's ill. Maybe he had an accident. Has anyone checked the hospital in Morgan City?"

"His mother has." He glanced away, as if weighing a decision. "I'm going to tell you something, Miss Sparks. I probably shouldn't, but I think you need to know. The state, maybe even the feds, are getting involved now." He rubbed the back of his neck, clearly uncomfortable.

Bunny watched him. He sat with his elbows resting on his knees, his forehead glistening with sweat despite the shade of the porch. The heat of the afternoon still clung to everything, even the occasional faint breeze. She said nothing.

He shifted in his seat and wiped his forehead with the sleeve of his shirt, avoiding her gaze. "They're already looking at you, Miss Sparks. I can't see that you did anything... even anything at all suspicious, but... I don't know. After a small handful of locals, you're gonna be the first person they look at. And I couldn't... I couldn't sit here and not tell you. You deserve to know."

Her porch, usually a place of comfort, suddenly felt stifling. When he finally looked directly at her, his concern was clear, but it was edged with something heavier.

"Why are you telling me this, Sheriff?" Bunny asked softly. "Isn't everyone a suspect? That's what they always say on television crime shows."

He smiled wanly. "I was supposed to handle this. It's my job. But now... now, others are sticking their noses in... as if I can't. Handle this, I mean. And from the sounds of it, they're looking in all the wrong places." He let out a low sigh, again rubbing the back of his neck and what Bunny could only assume was the tension knotting there. The clench of his jaw belied more than frustration.

"So, you don't think I killed him?" It wasn't really a question.

The look in his eyes was both weary and fervent, at once. He shook his head and whispered, "No."

"How do you know, though?"

"After more than thirty years of doing this job, you develop a nose for the truth."

"And your nose tells you I'm innocent?" Bunny asked.

"What I think isn't going to matter much. If they send down the man I think they're going to, any years of experience or common sense aren't going to matter much either."

Bunny noticed his knee start to bounce and wondered if it was fatigue or irritation. He picked up his glass and put it back down. "That bonehead has been itching to—" He cut himself short and looked at her. "I don't need to bore you with someone else's ancient personal drama. I'll just say I know who'll be first in line from Morgan City as volunteer to whip us all into shape and wrap up the case, tying a neat little bow on the quickest resolution possible. Right or wrong." He stood up and walked to the edge of the porch. Facing away from her, he said, "They are sending someone to take over the investigation. My office will be their office for now. Unless Blagg gets his way and finds a way to push me out."

Bunny said nothing.

Sheriff Greenwood turned to face her. "Do you understand what I'm saying?"

Bunny nodded. "I think so."

"You don't seem to have much to say."

She leaned back in her chair. "What do you *want* me to say? You're telling me that someone may come push you out of your position as sheriff for some reason, a reason that you don't want to get into, apparently, and that I'm likely going to be pegged as the prime suspect in a murder I didn't commit." She stood and picked up their glasses. "I need time to process run-of-the-mill surprises... I'm not sure how long it's going to take me to process *this*. I don't even know what questions I should be asking. I've never been in a situation like this before."

He shook his head. "You're right. I'm not sure how I would react either. I suppose it would make me angry."

"I haven't had time to be angry, Sheriff. You *just* laid this on my doorstep, and I'm so tired I'm on the verge of feeling numb. But I am confused about why anyone would suspect me. Because he did work for me?"

"I think it has something to do with the plant material at the scene."

"I'll admit that was odd... but I still don't see how that implicates me."

He turned and looked at her. "If Victor Tew was murdered by poison, and the poison came from a specific plant, and that specific plant grows in your garden, and you know the toxicity of that plant and how to harvest it... Should I go on?"

There was a moment when the two of them just stood there, looking at each other. Bunny wanted to ask if the look she saw in his eyes was his pleading with her to understand what he was saying or if he was just exasperated that she was confused about the implication.

She shook her head. "Sheriff, I'm quite certain the plants left all over the ground were common fireweed. It grows everywhere along the road. I don't grow any in my garden."

"And if you're wrong?"

"We'll have to cross that bridge when we find out."

He nodded grimly. "Jerlene Bittle-Baer said they are undeniably foxglove. She said Gloryanne Tew confirmed this."

Bunny laughed. "Undeniably?"

"That's what she said."

"Sheriff, honestly. I have a hard time believing that either of them could identify two dissimilar plants, much less two plants that are sometimes confused with each other."

She caught a faint twitch at the corner of his mouth, as if he were fighting a smile. Like her, he seemed to find the situation unexpectedly funny.

Just as quickly, his jaw tightened and his expression hardened. "I could probably get into trouble for discussing this with you at all, but I thought you should know."

"You know, Sheriff, that's the second time in as many days that someone has offered a sort of protective caution."

"Your Granny Gene was well-loved in the holler, Miss Sparks."

"I'm aware that Gigi had a sort of standing. She was active in the community and helped a lot of people here. As much as I'd love to live up to her expectations of me, I'll never fill her shoes." She felt tears welling up and decidedly pushed them down. "I was hoping just to settle into a quiet life here… grow beautiful gardens, like she did, maybe teach a little about plants if anyone in the holler was interested in learning. Otherwise, I just want to mind my own business."

She took a steadying breath as the thought caught up with her. "Now I might be pulled into a mess for my troubles?"

Her eyes were already beginning to puff. She focused on keeping her voice even. "What makes you think anyone is going to suspect me, anyway? Growing a poisonous plant doesn't make me responsible for its misuse." She tried not to sound as if she were demanding an answer. "You said you don't consider me a suspect, even if not in those exact words."

"Don't ask me how I know. Just… just keep your head down, alright? They'll have their own way of handling things."

"You mean the 'bonehead' who wants to take over the investigation?"

"Possibly," he said.

She pulled the door open and stepped inside. "Thank you for your concern, Sheriff. I mean it. And, I don't want to appear rude, but unless you need anything else… or want to tell me anything more… I'm going to wash up, grab a little something to eat, and go to bed. I'll come up with a way to feel about it tomorrow."

He nodded and stepped off the porch. She watched him as he walked slowly toward the cruiser, carrying his hat in one hand, before he turned to see her still standing in the doorway. "I'm just saying, Miss Sparks, things might be about to move faster than you're expecting. Faster than any of us are."

Chapter Nine

The small bell above the door chimed as Bunny stepped into Cran General store and called out for Hoodoo. She knew he'd be here, despite the early hour of the morning. She was met with the heady scent of pipe tobacco and old leather. She stood admiring a fresh display of strawberry jams, sweet clover honey, and peach preserves when he emerged from the back room, wiping his hands on a dish towel.

"Well, if it isn't Bunny Sparks," he said with a warm smile. "Come on in, sunshine. What brings you out so early?"

Bunny returned his smile, though she knew he could see the tension on her face. She had hoped to come in with a light heart, but the weight of the past few days was pressing on her. "Good morning, Hoodoo," she said, walking toward the counter. She hesitated a moment, then leaned in a little closer. "I mean, good rising. I forgot about the morning and mourning thing."

"The importance of words, yes. Your Granny Gene reminded me often." He smiled, the lines on his face softening as he remembered. "What can I do for you this fine morn... day?"

"I really just wanted to talk to you."

He smiled. "What a gift! I *have* been curious. Who sent the package?"

"Package?"

"You know, the box that came for you... no return address?"

"Oh, *that* package. I forgot all about it. I haven't even opened it yet. It's still on my porch." She bit her lip and lowered her voice. "I wanted to ask you something, actually. It's important... and confidential, really."

The old man raised an eyebrow, setting the dish towel aside on the counter. "I regard you as a favorite granddaughter, once-removed. You know you can count on my discretion. What's on your mind, child?"

Bunny took a deep breath. "I had a conversation yesterday with Sheriff Greenwood. Essentially, he gave me a warning. Someone from the state or federal police are looking into things... looking at *me* in connection with Vic Tew's death. They think I'm involved. And I need to know that you know I'm not involved."

For a moment, the elderly man studied her face. He nodded slowly, his expression serious. "I don't have any doubt, missy. Don't you go worrying about that. Is that all?"

Bunny felt the weight on her chest lift slightly. She hadn't expected to need his reassurance, but she was relieved to have it. "I was also hoping for your insight about someone from town. She also gave me a warning."

"Okay, shoot. Who?"

"Fern Booher, Ivy Tichner's sister. Ivy owns the Tickety-Boo Tea Shoppe. Do you know her?"

"Hon, just about everyone in the holler has to come to this ol' place at some time or another. I'm the closest thing to a Piggly-Wiggly this side of Morgan City, even if I'm up the hill and out of town a ways."

Bunny resisted the urge to glance around Hoodoo's store, where memories clung to every corner. She knew it too well—the soft hum of the chest freezer in the back stocked with ice cream bars and popsicles, the round table by the window where daily checkers games were played, and the poker nights that filled Fridays with laughter and clinking coins.

Hoodoo picked up the dish towel and slowly polished the counter between them. "So you want to know if Fern Booher is trustworthy?"

"She dropped by unannounced, and uninvited, mind you, to warn me about town gossip." Bunny thought back to the conversation. "Oh, and she said she was hoping to get a business arrangement going between me and Tickety-Boo, which sounded promising, but I don't know now." She picked up one of the jars and traced the raised lettering of its label with her thumb. "The gossip was about me, of course. She seemed genuine, but I don't know if I should trust her."

Hoodoo's gaze softened even more, and he gave a slow, affectionate nod. "Fern has been here just a bit longer than you've been back in the holler. If I had to bet, I'd say she's a good soul. She's tough, a little blunt at times, but her heart's in the right place. I would trust her."

"You would?"

"I would," he said.

She let out a breath. "I wish that was all it took to make me feel better."

"Are you planning to have a talk with her?"

"Just as soon as I talked to you." Bunny nodded. "If I didn't get a good sign, I figured I'd have to use Plan B."

"What was your Plan B?"

She put the jar back in place and put both elbows on the counter, resting her forehead in her palms. "Truth be told, I didn't have a Plan B."

Hoodoo set the towel aside. "There will be a lot of gossip about a lot of folks, hon. The fact that Fern Booher came to you before she believed any of what she heard speaks volumes, as they say."

"True." Bunny looked up and attempted a smile. "I'm not trusting my instincts like I should. Have you heard any of that gossip?"

"No." He shook his head, his expression shadowed with concern. "But I have heard other goosefat, as Mrs. Kettel likes to call it."

"About me?" Her stomach tightened.

"No, not about you, child, about Big Jake," he said solemnly. "No one's heard from him since the night of the fire. Some folks are saying he might have had a hand in it."

"Big Jake? Really?"

He sighed, rubbing the white stubble on his chin. "He's a good boy, just... caught up in things. I think he might've been misled by someone around here... maybe by someone who knows him better than they should. But until we get some answers, he's as much a suspect as anyone."

Bunny absently picked up the jar again. "You don't think he has anything do with Vic, do you?"

Hoodoo met her gaze. "I do. And I think he's in trouble. More trouble than anyone realizes. But right now, we've got to focus on finding out the truth. Not just about him, but about everyone involved."

She nodded, absorbing the weight of his words.

Hoodoo pressed his lips together and looked out the window, his gaze distant. "Missy, this holler has secrets, but you know that already." He looked from the window back to her, his face softening once again, then gently took the jar from her and placed it in a paper bag. He folded the top, giving it a crisp edge. "Give this to Fern for me when you see her? And be careful, child."

She leaned across the counter and gave him a quick hug. "Thanks, Hoodoo."

He gave her shoulder a squeeze and handed the bag to her. She slipped it under one arm and stepped out into the bright morning light. It was still early, and the bird song was as crisp and clear as the blue sky. She had a loose plan coming together. Carefully setting the bag in backseat, she got behind the wheel and pulled out of the lot before she could second-guess herself.

The winding road that led deeper into the valley toward town was empty and smooth as she picked up speed, the cool morning air blowing through her hair. The soothing rhythm of the road beneath her tires was a stark contrast to the turmoil churning in her mind. When she reached Tickety-Boo, her stomach started growling. She was certain it was more to do with nerves than with hunger and tried to ignore it as she parked and walked the short distance to the door.

Standing outside the tea shop door as the faint scent of bergamot, lavender and chocolate drifted out with the morning breeze, her mouth watered, nonetheless. She could almost feel the weight of Sheriff Greenwood's warning still lingering. It held an eerie echo of Fern's warning about town gossip, a strange combination of concern and caution. She hesitated, her hand on the door handle. The valley was a tight-knit place and she saw herself as something of an outsider, despite the many summers she spent in the holler as a child. Who could she really trust here?

Glancing down the quiet street offered little comfort. She wasn't sure just why she felt so compelled to give this woman the benefit of the doubt. Maybe because, like her, she was also still finding her way in this strange little valley. Or maybe, deep down, Bunny needed at least one other person to believe she wasn't guilty of whatever was being whispered about her.

When Bunny finally pulled the door open, the welcoming aromas wrapped around her and pulled her gently inside. At the display cabinet, Misti Meles stood casually with the fingers of one hand tapping gently on the side of a to-go cup. "Hi, Misti," Bunny said brightly, as she reached the counter. "You're here early."

Misti jerked toward her quickly, so quickly that droplets of liquid splashed out and onto the pristine edge of her pink cashmere sweater. "Oh no!" she gasped. She set the cup atop the display cabinet and frantically gathered a handful of paper napkins, dabbing the fabric.

Bunny spotted another pile of paper napkins further down the counter. She retrieved several and offered them to her. "I'm sorry. I didn't mean to startle you. Are you okay?"

Misti looked up at her, pulling her lips into a strained smile. "Startled," she said, through clenched teeth, "it's just... a special sweater."

Bunny looked down at the expensive fabric, soft and luxurious, and wondered if it had been a gift. Her eyes then caught sight of a shimmering string of pearls that draped gracefully over Misti's collarbone. These were not the kind of plastic costume pearls that might be found in a discount store. Matching teardrop earrings dangling from each earlobe. She watched as Misti's collarbone, along with her cheeks, went from pale cream in color to a vivid pink, deeper in hue than her exquisite sweater.

Ivy called out from the kitchen, "I'll be right there. Just taking the gateau out of the oven now."

Misti called back, "I'm in sort of a hurry, Miss Tichner." She balled up the many napkins in her hand, furrowed her brow, and focused her attention on finding a place to dispose of them.

Ivy stepped through the beaded curtain, wiping her hands on an immaculate apron, and smiled at them both. "They just need to cool a little before I can add the toppings," she said. "Morning, Bunny. What can I get for you?"

"I just stopped by to see if I could chat with Fern." Bunny smiled. "But I'd love a chai latte, if you have time."

Ivy smiled. "You got it," she said. "Would you like to try one of the new chocolate gateaus? I'll be icing them in just a moment. Then, a sprinkle of crushed walnut and they'll be almost heaven."

Misti placed the clump of napkins on the counter and stepped away from them both, still focused on her sweater.

"Is that what you're having, Misti?" Bunny asked.

Without looking up, Misti murmured, "Mm-hmm."

Ivy measured out a fragrant spoon of chai into a shiny copper French press. "I promised Misti's meemaw she could have first dibs on the new dessert I'm testing," she said, over her shoulder. "Today's the day. Fern shouldn't be too much longer. She had to make another run to Morgan City, early, so we'd have what we need for the week. We were really hoping for Big Jake to be back, but..."

Bunny watched Misti turn a deeper shade of pink.

Ivy carried a tray around the counter and set it on a nearby table. "Have you heard from him, hon?"

Misti looked at Ivy, then Bunny, then back again. She shook her head and bent down to closely examine something on the glass of the display case.

Bunny decided that all this tiptoeing around and not asking direct questions might be polite, but it wasn't very efficient. "So, were you two dating?" she asked.

The question hung in the air like dust in a sunbeam.

Misti, determined to concentrate on the extraordinarily interesting but invisible thing on the glass in front of her, pressed her lips together and shook her head. "Hm-nn."

Ivy cleared her throat and made her way back to the kitchen, presumably to ice the chocolate gateau and anoint it with nuts.

"I only ask because you were seen with him quite a bit, and everyone is wondering where he is." Bunny sat down at the table and slowly depressed the plunger of her chai. "Do you know where he went? Did he tell you anything?"

Misti pulled herself upright and smoothed the cuffs of her delicate sweater. "No. I don't know where he is, and I don't mean to be rude, but if I *did* know where he is then I'm not sure how it's any of your business, Miss Beatrice Sparks."

Bunny couldn't fight the urge to smile at this, with less humor than amusement. "You must tell your memaw that I'll stop by and see her soon and bring her some fresh veggies." She slowly poured the hot, milky liquid from the French press into a charming porcelain cup. Steeling herself, she watched the graceful steam and breathed in the savory aroma rising from it. "Your memaw is well-loved… well-respected… I can only imagine that she impressed upon you that calling someone by their given name is intimidating." She stirred the contents of the cup without looking up. "Tell her I'll be sure to include some fresh corn on the cob. I know how much she loves sweet corn."

At this, just as Ivy returned carrying the decadent round of chocolate in both hands, Misti turned on her heel and stormed out.

"What in the world?" Ivy set the dessert on the counter and watched as Misti walked briskly past the plate-glass window, one hand clutching her sweater closed, the other over her pearls.

Fern called out from the back, "Can you come help me, Sis?"

Ivy looked up from icing another chocolate gateau, spatula raised artfully. "I'm in the middle of something, Fern!" she called.

Bunny stood and peered back through the beaded curtain separating the kitchen from the tearoom. "I'll help," she said, placing her empty cup onto the serving tray she'd seen used to bus the tables.

Ivy visibly relaxed. "Thanks, Bunny." She pointed toward the storeroom with the spatula. "She's probably got boxes full of supplies."

Fern's eyebrows shot up in surprise when she saw Bunny and not her sister.

"Ivy's icing," Bunny said, extending her arms. She took the carton filled with lemons and fresh flowers.

Once the boxes, bags and cartons were all safe inside the storeroom, Ivy offered to make a special brew of iced jasmine and fresh lemon tea as a thank you. She carried it out on a tray for the three of them to enjoy under the corkscrew willow that shaded the bistro set in the back courtyard. "I've got the chime receiver, in case anyone comes in while we're out here," she said, placing the black box on the table between them. "How were the markets?"

Fern slumped in her chair. "Tiring," she huffed. "When is Big Jake going to be back?"

Ivy looked at Bunny and lifted her glass. "Bunny was doing a little interrogating about that this morning and Misti chewed her out and left."

"Misti chewed you out?" Fern looked incredulously at Bunny. "Really? I thought she was such a prim."

Bunny chuckled. "She didn't chew me out exactly. She told me it was none of my business, though."

Fern gasped. "She told you where Jake might be is none of your business?"

"No." Bunny shook her head. "She told me what *she* knows about it is none of my business, which now makes me wonder what she *does* know."

Ivy leaned back in her chair and looked up into the willow. "She didn't even wait for the special gateau she ordered."

Fern blinked slowly, deliberately emphasizing her disbelief. "I'll walk it over to Mrs. Kettel after I've finished." She took a long sip from her glass. "So, she snapped at you?"

Ivy nodded keenly.

"Yes, I suppose she did." Bunny chuckled. "She seemed to be angry that I asked."

"She even called Bunny 'Beatrice,' as if she were scolding a child." Ivy grinned.

Fern theatrically covered her mouth in mock horror. "No!" she cried. "How dare she?!"

"I know." Bunny smirked. "It was terrible."

The three women shared a short moment of laughter, until Bunny quietly set her glass on the table. "The truth is," she said, "I think she knows something."

"Does she though?" asked Ivy. "Fern and I lightly, and I do mean lightly, teased her a few times about Jake being her boyfriend and she bristled like a polecat poked with a broom."

Fern nodded. "Practically hissed."

Bunny leaned back in her chair and squinted into her iced tea. "So, if she wasn't dating him…"

"Why were they together every week for the past month?" Ivy finished the thought. "Exactly."

Fern chimed in, "Not only that, they always sat at the only table nobody ever wants."

Bunny raised an eyebrow. "The one in the corner?"

Fern nodded. "It's tucked behind the tea cabinet. Half the time I forget it's even there. You have to really *want* to be out of sight to pick that table."

The three women sat in silence until the little black box on the table let out a soft ding-ding sound like a silver spoon tapping the side of a teacup. Ivy set her glass down and stood. "Be right back," she said, straightening her apron.

Bunny leaned in. "I'm glad we have a moment," she said, "I wanted to thank you for coming out to talk to me. About the gossip, especially."

Fern's expression softened. "I wasn't sure I should." She looked into her glass and laughed. "And, I must say, you looked like you'd rather have hidden behind a potted plant or something."

Bunny gave a little laugh, too. "I'm sure I did. But, it meant a lot, actually. Not many people would have bothered."

Fern shrugged. "Well, small towns, big talk, huh? Anyway, I wanted to be sure you knew you were welcome here. Ivy and I were excited to have the best herbal blends and remedies this side of the Rockies when your granny agreed to be a local supplier." She looked up, offering Bunny a pained smile. "Everyone loved her."

"I know," Bunny whispered. "I miss her." She took a deep breath, then cleared her throat. "I'll never fill her shoes, but I'm determined to pick up where she left off, if I can. And I think it might just start with making friends. As a start, I brought a gift. It's from Hoodoo, actually, but.." She set the jar of jam on the table between them.

Fern leaned across the table and squeezed Bunny's hand. Just as quickly, she sat back in her chair, eyes wide, as the screen door creaked open.

Bunny watched Fern's attempt to hide surprise as Misti approached the table. For a moment, no one said a word.

"Forgot my memaw's dessert," Misti said quietly, holding up the Tickety-Boo bakery box. "She about had a conniption." She blushed, then added, "Sorry about this morning, Bunny."

And just like that, she turned and quickly walked away, clutching the box as if it might explode.

Ivy returned to the table and picked up the pitcher. "Fern, can you watch the counter for a minute? I just saw Jerlene up on a ladder in the pharmacy, so Earl must be out. You *know* I've been trying to catch her."

Fern groaned. "Again?"

"I keep missing her," Ivy said, pulling off her apron and folding it neatly. "We all know she doesn't need that wheelchair."

Bunny blinked. "Really? But she told me she has M.S."

Fern nodded slowly. "She *says* that, but Doc Fisher wrote in her file that she doesn't. He said it's psychosomatic."

Bunny couldn't hide her surprise. "How do you know *that*?"

"The tea shop isn't always busy. When the students are gone for the summer, the town slows down a lot. You'll notice how busy it gets in

September if you come into town more often." She smiled. "Hopefully, you will. Anyway, I had to find something to supplement working for my sister, so I've worked in his office off and on since I moved here, trading hours with Misti Meles. Whenever he needs someone to fill in at the receptionist desk or do any extra filing. I do the same for the Sheriff's Office."

Bunny stared at her, hoping the look on her face was neutral. It must not have been.

Fern took a sip of what was left of her iced tea. Looking over the rim of her glass, she said, "I know, I know. What about HIPAA and all that?" She leaned in, a little smirk on her lips. "I don't think it applies if you're a mean old biddy."

Bunny let out a startled laugh, then immediately looked around to be sure they were still alone in the little courtyard. "You're terrible," Bunny said, trying to sound disapproving.

Fern shrugged. "I just think if you're going to fake a medical condition, you should at least be nice about it."

"But how can you be sure she's actually faking?" Bunny asked. "Even if it's psychosomatic, she at least believes she's sick, even if she isn't."

"True. But, if you ask me, she *knows* she's not. She just likes the attention. And the free handicap parking. Ivy and I have literally watched her get up out of her chair, pull the rolling ladder, and climb up without a problem."

Bunny shook her head. "No... really? How in the world?"

"She works part-time in the pharmacy just down the street, kitty-corner from the library." Fern pointed in that direction. "From the counter in the shop, if the light is just right, we can see right into the back area of the pharmacy through their window. It's only in the mornings, when the sun is just right." She grinned, looking up at the sky.

"Like now, I'm guessing," Bunny said. "Do you think Ivy will catch her this time?"

Fern shook her head, looking back across the table. "Only if Jerlene doesn't see her first. That woman has the instincts of a feral cat."

Chapter Ten

Bunny swirled the last of her melted ice in her glass, then set it down with a soft clink. "Can I tell you something else?" she asked, keeping her voice low even though they were alone.

Fern leaned in automatically. "Of course. What is it?"

"Yesterday, I had a conversation with Sheriff Greenwood." Bunny hesitated and focused intently on a loose thread at the seam of the long linen apron she wore over her sundress, realizing that she'd forgotten to remove it before leaving that morning. "He didn't come right out and say it," she said, "but he hinted —strongly— that there might be some... outside interest in Victor Tew's death, and that they might even look in my direction as a suspect."

Fern sat back a little, her mouth pressed in a tight line. "I know. At least about the 'outside interest' part. There is definitely tension in his office about it, for sure," she said. "When I was there yesterday morning covering for Gloryanne, a call came in from someone at the state's investigative division — definitely not just checking in. They used a tone."

"A *tone*?"

Fern nodded sagely. "You know. The kind that says, 'This isn't just a courtesy call, sweetie, we're about to roll in like we own the place.'"

Bunny's stomach dipped. "Ugh... that can't be good."

"Nope," Fern said, drawing out the *p*. "And if Cal Greenwood is unnerved, that's saying something. He doesn't rattle easily."

"He also seemed especially sour about a guy that might be part of the outside investigation, if it happens. Called him a 'bonehead with a grudge.' Something like that. He said 'bonehead,' anyway."

Fern perked up at that. "Did he now?"

"You know who it might be?"

"I might," Fern said slowly, eyes sparkling. "There's a name that's come up before. Rufus Blagg. A big goon with the state office. He went to high school with Sheriff Greenwood, if it's the one I'm thinking of. Sheriff can't stand him."

"Why?"

"Okay, this is just hearsay, you understand?" Fern leaned forward, putting her elbows on the table. "But, I have it on good authority that the guy stole his high school sweetheart. Ended up marrying her, too. Word is, she's actually a nightmare. Deputy Rawlings teases the Sheriff about it from time to time. 'You dodged a doozy of a bullet there, Cal, my pal,' he'll say. Sheriff usually just nods, but you can see relief all over his face."

Bunny squinted in the sun. "So, this state guy... he's got a professional incentive *and* a personal grudge?"

"Bingo." Fern leaned in again, lowering her voice conspiratorially. "If he cracks a high-profile case and nails it, he could be looking at a promotion. Something his wife is always insisting on, I hear. He might even make a play for the position of Sheriff here in the holler."

Bunny exhaled slowly, an unpleasant tension building in the pit of her stomach.

Fern casually flicked a crumb off the table. "And you didn't hear this from me," meaning, Bunny was absolutely about to hear it from her, "but that call that came in yesterday? It was about something going on with Baer's Garage."

Bunny narrowed her eyes. "Dave Baer? Jerlene's husband?"

Fern nodded.

"Why would they be interested in Dave's place?"

"Well," Fern said, drawing the word out like honey, "I don't know *everything*, but I know Deputy Rawlings made a face when he hung up. And then he muttered something about 'that place finally catching up with itself.'" She let that hang in the air, looking for more crumbs to flick off the table.

Bunny sat up straighter. "Wait, are they trying to connect what happened with Vic to *Dave* then?"

Fern gave a little shrug. "Maybe. Or maybe to Gloryanne, who is... was... married to Vic, and she sure hangs around Dave's place a lot. Can there really be so much wrong with one car?"

Bunny stared at her. "Maybe she bought a clunker."

"And then there's Jake," Fern continued. "He was always in and out of there at *the* oddest hours. How many deliveries can one small-town garage get in a week, every week, month after month? And Gloryanne used to gush over him. Have you ever seen that?"

Bunny felt a chill crawl down her back. "No, I don't think I have." She gave a little shudder. "Or maybe a little. When Hoodoo said she could probably catch a ride with him, since he was scheduled to be there soon at Hoodoo's store. But, he wasn't there at the time. Sheesh... Who knew so much was going on around here?"

"Small towns, eh?" Fern mused. "Funny, though, that the sheriff thought he should warn *you*, when there seems to be so much to look into that has nothing to do with you." Her expression grew dark. "Warning you. That alone is interesting. I wonder..." she tapped a finger on the table.

"What?" Bunny asked.

"I'm just thinking," Fern said slowly. "The night Vic died... didn't you think the fire was, well, theatrical? Like it was meant to draw attention?"

"I don't know," Bunny said quietly. "It didn't destroy much, but that might just be because of all the rain that night."

Fern nodded. "And those plants."

Bunny glanced up. "You heard about the plants?"

"Of course. They're still waiting for the toxicology report in the office. They found foxglove all around the scene, right? Which is mighty convenient, given your garden."

Bunny's jaw tightened. "Except they *weren't* foxglove."

"I know that," Fern said gently. "Sheriff said he believes you. But we still have to wait for the report to be sure. And, either way, everyone in town hears there was a poisonous plant at the scene and your name follows in the same breath."

Bunny exhaled slowly, the tension in her shoulders refusing to leave. "Do you think someone's trying to frame me or just make things more confusing?"

Fern sat staring into her glass. "Let's just say, if someone wanted to point a finger your way, they did a decent job of planting the idea. No pun intended."

Bunny looked out toward the trees beyond the courtyard, her mind spinning. "So the fire hides the evidence, and the plants direct suspicion at me. It's a little too clever, don't you think?"

Fern sipped the last little bit of watered-down tea, eyes sharp over the rim. "Exactly. That's what's bothering me."

"What do you mean?"

"I mean, it's messy. It *looks* like someone wanted to burn everything to the ground, but it didn't work. And those plants? They weren't scattered, they were placed. Arranged. Like someone wanted them *noticed*. I saw the crime scene photos."

There was a moment of silence.

"And who knows that you grow foxglove?" Fern asked.

Bunny stared at her. "Everyone knows. Everyone who knew my granny knows. It's not like I'm hiding it. It's all around the mailbox."

"Still. It narrows the field," Fern said. "Not everyone would know foxglove is poisonous, or what it looks like, or where to find it. But someone did. Or thought they did." Her eyebrows shot up as she spotted something in the undergrowth surrounding the patio. "Oh, look! There's a little toad! I wonder where he came from." Fern was still watching the tiny toad, her head tilted, when the door creaked open behind them.

Ivy stepped out, wiping her hands on a clean dish towel.

"Well?" Fern asked, looking up.

"No dice," Ivy announced, exasperated. "Jerlene must have shimmied down that ladder like a possum before I could get to the door."

Fern snorted. "Unreal."

"It's only a matter of time," Ivy muttered, reaching for their empty glasses. "Alright, ladies, fun's over for me. I've got three more chocolate gateaus to frost and get ready for the lunch rush, fingers crossed."

Bunny smiled. "Thanks for the tea, Ivy."

"Anytime, sugar." Ivy gave a warm smile in return, then swept back into the shop, white linen skirts billowing like sails, hand towel slung over her shoulder. The screen door clattered shut behind her.

Fern looked over at Bunny. "You've got a look."

"What look?"

"It's a familiar look. I see it on my own face when I've decided to do something I probably shouldn't but have already made up my mind."

Bunny hesitated only a moment. "I want to get into Dave Baer's garage. Just... take a look. See what's what."

Fern raised an eyebrow. "Uh huh. And by 'see what's what,' you mean break and enter?"

"Maybe," Bunny said cautiously.

Fern leaned forward, putting both elbows on the table. "Okay, I'm in. When do we go?"

"Oh, no." Bunny shook her head. "I'm not involving you in this."

Fern crossed her arms and leaned back. "Well, you're not going alone. I'm coming with you."

"I can't see that as a good idea, Fern," Bunny said, still emphatically shaking her head.

"Oh, but *I* do." Fern sat forward again. "You might have a green thumb and know plant magic, Bunny Sparks, but how are your sneaking skills? Mine are stellar, just ask Ivy. And I'm sure you could use a look-out, at least. What if someone shows up to find you poking around?"

Bunny opened her mouth to protest, then closed it again. "You do know we could get into serious trouble. I've already been warned to keep my head down."

"So, we'll walk doubled over." Fern grinned.

Bunny smiled back at her, but the tension lingered in the air, quiet and unspoken. "I've never done anything like this, you know?" Bunny confessed.

Fern nodded, knowingly. "Well, I might have... a time or two.

The streets of Cranberry Creek were mostly quiet this time of night, filled only with the soft hum of a few sparse streetlights, the occasional dog bark echoing down an alley, and the faint chirr of crickets holding court somewhere in the holler. Bunny wrapped her long braid up into a bandanna, per Fern's instructions. They'd met behind Tickety-Boo, as agreed. The walk to Baer's Garage was short, but the night air was still and hot, so it felt much longer. Bunny rolled up her sleeves as they walked.

"By the way," Fern whispered, "I love those overalls."

Bunny looked over at her, but kept up her pace. "Break-in approved?"

"Definitely break-in approved." Fern agreed. "Dark green though? You don't own any black?"

Bunny shushed her. "I don't have any hoodies, either," she teased, flipping the hood hanging limply behind Fern's collar.

"This is my gardening hoodie," Fern grinned. "It's got pockets and questionable stains. Nothing says *innocent bystander* like potting soil on your elbows, right?"

When they reached the Baer's Garage sign, its bulbs flickering in slow, stuttering blinks, Fern whispered, "This way." She led Bunny behind the building until they were crouching beneath a grime-streaked window. She gave it a slight tug, and it creaked open with surprising ease.

Bunny stared. "How did you—?"

Fern grinned in the dim light. "After you left, I made a little detour."

Bunny looked at her, incredulous. "A detour?" she whispered.

"I walked over and told Dave the Tickety-Boo bathroom was out of order and I *really* had to go," Fern said, putting extra-heavy emphasis on *really*. "He didn't even ask why I didn't just use the pharmacy or library or literally anywhere else between here and there. He just grunted, pointed toward the grease pit of a bathroom, and went back to cursing at a carburetor."

Bunny shook her head in disbelief. "And you unlocked the window while you were in there?"

"With a paper towel, of course. I didn't even want to *breathe* in that room, let alone touch anything."

"That is disturbingly impressive."

"Why, thank you," Fern whispered as she gave a mock curtsy.

She climbed through first, landing with a soft thud on the oil-stained concrete floor inside. Bunny followed, wincing as her shoe made a quiet squelch on something unidentifiable. "Ughhh," she whispered.

"Don't touch anything if you can help it," Fern said.

"I wouldn't dream of it," Bunny coughed.

"Also, no fingerprints. Here." Fern pulled several disposable serving gloves out of her pocket. "Oh, and I brought flashlights." She fished two small, black, metal cylinders out of her other pocket and handed one to Bunny.

They moved slowly, the twin beams of their flashlights sweeping across the cluttered garage filled with racks of tools, mismatched car parts, and an abandoned mug with something fossilized in the bottom. A thick, musty scent hung in the air, tinged with grease, mildew, and the unmistakable sharpness of engine fluids.

"I'm not sure where to even begin," Bunny said in a low voice. "Everything is cluttered and dirty."

"Check that side over there," Fern suggested, jerking her chin toward a workbench stacked with novelty license plates.

Bunny took her suggestion, and after a moment of quiet rummaging, stopped and pointed her flashlight in Fern's direction. "Why are you really helping me?"

Fern looked up, the flashlight beam catching the curve of her cheekbone inside the black hoodie. "You mean, besides the thrill of committing a misdemeanor on a Tuesday night?"

Bunny gave her a look.

Fern shrugged. "Honestly? I guess... I felt like you needed a friend." She turned back to the desk, pretending to study grease-smeared paper on a cracked clipboard. "And, to be honest some more, life in the holler's kind of boring. I mean, most weeks, the biggest drama is whether someone saw Jerlene up on a ladder."

"Boring? Someone was murdered. Someone else is missing. Some criminal activity is going on right under everyone's nose in this garage... possibly." Bunny was quiet a moment. "Are you saying that you need a friend?"

Fern looked at her again, more seriously this time. "I'd love to have a good friend."

The silence that followed was comfortable enough.

Fern turned back to the desk and muttered, "Although, if I disappear after this, tell my sister I died stupidly."

"Deal. So what exactly are we looking for?"

"Wait," Fern said, just a little too loud, "wasn't it your idea to break in here?"

"It may have been," Bunny said. "But, you're the one with the experience, remember?"

"You've never broken in to anything before? Ever?"

"No. Why would I?" Bunny shined her light in Fern's direction.

"Not even when you were little, like into your parent's closet to get a peek at Christmas gifts?"

Bunny moved her flashlight beam back to the floor in front of her. "My mom was the only parent I had, and she struggled."

"Oh," Fern said softly. "Well, I'm not sure I have anything in my past that matches *this*, but let's look for anything that seems less like a typical mechanic's shop and any hint of something shady."

"Like that?" Bunny aimed her beam at a workbench in the back, where several boxes were stacked neatly and labeled with shipping tags. She stepped closer and squinted. "These all read 'Jake.'"

Fern came to stand beside her. "As in, for delivery pick up?"

Bunny shook her head. "I don't know. He's been MIA since Vic's death, right?"

"Only so far as we know." Fern leaned closer to the boxes, her eyes narrowing, then pulled a little purple UV light out of another pocket. She switched it on and held it close to one of the labels.

"You brought a blacklight?" Bunny whispered, impressed and mildly alarmed.

"What? You don't have one in your EDC?"

"What the heck is that?" Bunny asked.

"Every Day Carry." Fern shined the light up at her own face and rolled her eyes. "Clearly, you're not a prepper."

"Clearly," Bunny agreed, looking back at the boxes.

Under the UV glow, faint stamps appeared on a few boxes that were virtually invisible under normal light. Letters and numbers, in seemingly random patterns. Fern squinted at each one. "This is interesting. If I didn't know better... I've seen stamps like these before."

"Really?" Bunny gaped. "Hidden stamps that can only be seen with a blacklight? What would be the purpose?"

"It was months ago. I was filing old cases and Deputy Rawlings was helping me decide what went where," Fern said. "One of the case files was huge, so I opened it and asked if he knew what it was about. He said everyone with a television would remember because it made national news. A few hollers over, there was a black-market auto-parts ring and massive smuggling operation. They used inventory marks like these and their shipments went all over the world."

Bunny leaned in. "These haven't moved in a while. Look at the dust. They're just... waiting?"

Fern nodded. "Maybe because Jake's not around to move them. And, if these are meant to be shipped, someone somewhere is waiting for them."

"We shouldn't open these, should we, to see what they are?" Bunny wondered out loud.

"I'm sure we shouldn't, but why come all this way if we aren't going to see what's in there?" Fern asked.

They stood in silence, staring at the choice before them, until the soft *click-hiss* of a two-way radio broke the quiet. Then a faint crackle of static and a garbled voice, low and far off. Fern glanced around. "Dave must've left the shop radio on or something," she whispered.

The thought that this might be an important clue that could shed light on what had happened felt heavy. Bunny rubbed the back of her neck, contemplating how they might open a box without leaving any signs they'd been there.

Cradling her flashlight in her elbow, Fern bent to look closer. "What's that on the floor?"

Bunny squatted down, shining the beam on the ground. "Is that a sobriety pin?" She reached out to pick it up, then—*clank.*

They both froze.

Something had shifted deeper in the garage. A soft metallic thud, followed by stillness.

Fern mouthed, *Mouse?*

Bunny shook her head, mouthing back, *Bigger.*

Fern's eyes widened. *Worse?*

Bunny motioned toward the window. *Let's go.*

As they crept back toward the side window, trying not to breathe too loud, Bunny's heel caught on something behind her. A dull knock, followed by a sharper *clack*, and the trunk of a car sprang open a few inches before settling, the latch giving way with a soft metallic cough.

Fern slowly lifted her flashlight again, just enough to angle the beam downward. The light skimmed the trunk's interior, stacked with black boxes and tangled cords. "That's a lot of GPS units," she said. "And look at all the dash cams."

Bunny felt a tightening behind her ribs. "Isn't this Gloryanne's car?"

Before Fern could answer, another sound echoed. Bunny couldn't tell if it came from the garage, the lot outside, or somewhere else. She tugged at Fern's sleeve and they eased backward the way they'd come, careful not to bump anything else, their breaths shallow, flashlights dark.

They didn't look back.

After dropping quietly out of the bathroom window into the parking area, they crept around the side of the garage, keeping low. Bunny's mind was reeling. Whatever they'd found, it felt like a big deal. As they rounded the back corner of the building, everything exploded.

Two state police cruisers were angled in the lot, bright spotlights blazing, pointed directly at them.

"Freeze! Hands where we can see 'em!"

For one wild second, Bunny thought she could still run. Her legs tensed, ready to spring. But Fern was faster. She grabbed Bunny by the wrist and yanked her sideways, hard, toward a line of scraggly shrubs that had overgrown the edge of the parking lot. "Get down and don't move," Fern hissed, pushing her into the thicket of leaves.

Bunny dropped, thudding onto her side just behind the hedge, her pulse thundering in her ears. She watched, incredulous, as Fern sprinted away toward the alley beyond the parking lot. The spotlight beams immediately shifted direction, slicing through the dark after her.

"Suspect on foot! West side!"

Bunny curled tighter behind the hedge, the brambles biting into her arms as two officers took off running, chasing Fern. She barely had time to breathe before another flashlight snapped directly onto her. This one didn't waver.

"You, on the ground! Hands over your head! Now!"

Bunny didn't speak. She just slowly uncurled from the hedge, raising her hands. Her knees hit the gravel, rough and sharp. She barely registered the cuffs locking in place as the metal bit into her wrists. Her gaze stayed locked on the alley.

No sign of Fern.

The officer that pulled her to her feet said, "Looks like your friend gave us the slip."

Bunny didn't respond. She couldn't. Her mouth was dry, her heart still pounding, apparently unaware that the chase was over.

The two officers who'd chased Fern jogged back across the lot toward them, one shaking his head, the other looking ticked off and winded. "Lost him behind the tackle shop," one of them said. "Gone like a ghost."

The officer holding Bunny gave a humorless snort. "Figures."

Bunny stared at the ground, jaw tight. She hadn't moved because Fern told her not to. Was this some kind of set up? The pit of her stomach was threatening to turn itself inside out.

Chapter Eleven

Bunny sat on the bench in the holding cell, elbows on her knees, palms pressed against her eyes. Her adrenaline had long since drained away in the hours since her arrest. Now she was just sore, damp, and more than a little angry—at herself for doing something so stupid as to break the law to snoop around, and even angrier at Fern, who encouraged her and then bolted, leaving her to take the fall.

A soft *thunk* broke the silence. Metal springs creaked. A yawn followed, then a small sniffle. Whoever was in the next cell must have been sleeping when Bunny was brought in. Then came the faint scrape of bare feet on the cement floor.

And then, "Dang you, Victor Alan Tew."

Bunny froze. She said nothing. She had her own problems.

But the voice came again, louder this time, half a mutter, half a grumble. "Look what you did to me and everything else."

She thought so. "Gloryanne?"

"Bunny? Is that you? What the heck are you doing in here?"

"I could ask you the same thing," Bunny shot back. "But I'm not sure I'd like the answer. In fact, it's probably best you don't tell me. Unless, of course, I need to use it in my own defense." Bunny glared at the wall separating their cells.

Gloryanne's voice tightened. "What's that supposed to mean?"

"It means," Bunny said, her voice dropping in tone, "if you killed your husband, started a fire to cover it up, and then planted evidence to frame *me* in the process..."

"I did *no such thing*, Bunny Sparks!" Gloryanne sputtered. "I wasn't even home!"

Bunny stood and walked to the bars of her cell. "Right... where were you then? I hope you have witnesses. Besides me, that is, because I only saw you after you killed Vic and set the fire."

"I did not set fire to my own house," she huffed. "And, unless he forgot to take his heart medication, Vic isn't even dead."

The silence that followed was thick enough to chew.

Bunny blinked. "Can you run that by me again?"

Gloryanne huffed. "Well. He told me he'd make it *look* like he was, that's all."

"Go on."

Gloryanne sighed.

Bunny could hear more than a little regret at her having already said this much, but she'd never known Gloryanne to hold a secret longer than one-Mississippi.

"He said we needed money. And he was right. We always need money. So he said he had a plan. Not easy, but easy enough. He said, 'Don't worry, Glory. I won't *actually* be dead. Just pretend. You file for the insurance, we collect, and then I'll meet you somewhere.' Said we'd be set for life and everything else."

"You didn't think that might be, oh, I don't know — *insane*?" Bunny asked, stunned. "No one ever gets away with stunts like that."

"I thought it was *risky*, not insane. And I didn't agree right away. I just... we needed the money."

"So... where *is* Vic?"

"I don't know," Gloryanne said, her voice quieter now. "He said he'd be in touch. Told me to just act normal until then."

Bunny leaned her head against the cool concrete wall. "'Act normal'? Like a grieving widow who's not really grieving and is fine with her house being charred?"

"I didn't start that fire," Gloryanne said quickly. "I wasn't even there."

"I know. You were trying to break into my barn."

The pause that followed was long. Bunny could hear muffled voices coming from the other side of the door that separated the holding cells from the booking area. She listened, hoping to hear someone familiar. She couldn't. She walked back to the metal bed bolted to the wall and sat on the edge.

"I was out..." Gloryanne said, finally. "With Dave, if you must know."

Bunny's eyebrows shot up. "Dave Baer?"

"Don't you start with me, Bunny Sparks. I got enough flak from your Granny Gene about it. And for your information, Big Jake never did come get me when you left me at Hoodoo's, so he was my only ride."

Bunny ignored that. "And then you went out with him? Dave Baer? What were you doing out with *him*?"

"Not that it's any of your business, but we used to go out. You know, back in high school and everything else."

Bunny shook her head. "You're not in high school anymore, though. Dave is married. Remember? And you are married. Remember?"

"I know how it sounds," Gloryanne said. "But Vic isn't exactly warm and fuzzy. And Jerlene... well, Dave's not exactly living the dream, either. And if your granny had just given me the potion I wanted, everything coulda been different."

Bunny let the silence speak for her.

"Turns out," Gloryanne went on, "I didn't need a potion after all. We went out, and that's that."

"I know I'll hate myself for asking..." Bunny looked up at the ceiling and the bright fluorescent buzzing above her. "...but what did you do?"

"We went on a date. A real one. He took me to dinner and treated me like I was his wife."

Bunny couldn't see Gloryanne smile, but she might as well have by the syrupy sound in the answer. "Treated you like his wife? You mean, he left you at home alone and spent time and money on another woman?"

Gloryanne blew out a haughty breath.

"And why didn't he drop you off at home then? Walk you to the door, even? What were you doing at my barn after midnight in the rain?" Bunny asked.

"He got uptight all the sudden and said he had to go home," Gloryanne whined. "In the middle of our date, and everything else. He didn't want Vic to see him, neither..."

"So, he dropped you off over a mile from your house, in the pouring rain, after midnight?" Bunny said. "Is that how a man treating you like his wife acts?"

"None of this even matters," she puffed. "Vic isn't dead."

"Someone is," Bunny said flatly. "Someone was in that fire."

Gloryanne hesitated. "It wasn't Vic. Maybe it was just... a mannequin or something."

Bunny's voice dropped. "They took a *body* out, Gloryanne. A real one. Doc Fisher came. They're probably waiting on dental records, and I'll bet they're doing an autopsy. I don't think you can autopsy a mannequin."

Another long silence.

"But... that wasn't part of the plan," Gloryanne said faintly.

When the main door to the cells creaked open, Bunny startled. She was surprised she had any adrenaline left.

"Come on, Miss Sparks," Deputy Rawlings said, jangling his keys as he opened the door to the holding cell and stepped back. "You've got someone who wants a word."

Bunny sat up straighter, her neck stiff. She could only ask, "Sheriff Greenwood?"

Rawlings' face was tight, his eyes focused on the floor. "No. Let's go."

She slid off the bench and followed him. As they passed the sheriff's office, Bunny caught a glimpse of Greenwood sitting at his desk, arms folded, jaw clenched. He didn't look up. She made a soft *ahem* sound and he glanced toward the door, just for a second. When their eyes met, she tried to read his expression. Frustration? Regret? She couldn't tell, and he didn't say a word. Rawlings led her around a corner to a reinforced door at the end of the hall. He focused on opening the door, motioned for her to step into the small, windowless room, and shut the door. She turned to see a cold metal table bolted to the floor and a single chair on either side. And she wasn't alone. Already seated in one of those chairs, leaning back, arms folded, was Officer Rufus Blagg.

"Miss Sparks," he said coolly.

Bunny hesitated. "Um, who are you?"

"Name's Blagg. And, before you ask, Sheriff Greenwood's been sidelined." He gestured to the empty chair. "This is a state-level investigation now."

"Since when?" Bunny folded her arms, still standing. "This isn't about me trespassing?"

"It's a little bigger than that," Blagg said, smiling like a man who'd been waiting all day to be smug. "Orders from above."

"Above who? The sheriff?"

He leaned forward. "Above all of us."

Reluctantly, Bunny sat. The metal chair was cold and unforgiving. So was the stare Blagg gave her as he opened a manila folder, clearly for show.

"Ms. Sparks," he drawled, "mind telling me why you were skulking around a closed garage after midnight?"

"I wasn't skulking," Bunny replied flatly. It was all she could think to say.

He smirked. "That your official statement?"

"Do I get a phone call?" she asked.

Blagg started to tap the folder on the table with his oversized index finger when a knock on the door interrupted. The door opened and Deputy Rawlings poked his head inside. "Agent Blagg, there's a phone call for you."

"I'm in the middle of an interrogation here, Deputy," Blagg blustered. "I don't know how you do things around here in the backwoods, but where I come from..."

Deputy Rawlings didn't wait for him to finish. "It's your superior. He said he wants to talk to you now."

Blagg's face seemed to turn a shade of red Bunny was sure she'd never seen before. He turned to look at her, eyes hard, lips clamped so tightly together they were white at the edges. Through the open door, she could hear a different kind of commotion. A woman's voice echoed down the hall. "That woman grows heirloom tomatoes and gives away lemon balm for free. What's the charge? Fermenting too many vegetables? I demand she be released right now!" She heard Sheriff Greenwood then. "If you don't pipe down, you can get *yourself* in a lot of trouble." She could hear another woman. "Just tell me how much it costs to bail her out, Sheriff. I'll mortgage my tea shop, if I have to. She's innocent and you know it."

Bunny recognized the voices now, and as Blagg stood and hiked up his utility belt, she heard, "These are for Bunny. If I find out she's in there without food, water, or basic human decency, someone's getting a cinnamon roll to the face."

Blagg swiped the file folder from the table with irritation and stomped out.

Deputy Rawlings still held the door open. "It shouldn't be long now," he said, then rolled his eyes. "'Where I come from...'" He pulled the door closed and Bunny was left alone in the room.

Bunny sat still, hands folded in her lap, the cold metal chair doing nothing to soothe the dull aches she was sure would be purple at some point in the day. The silence in the room stretched on, broken only by the faint hum of the fluorescent light in the ceiling and a murmur of voices beyond the door. Eventually, the door creaked open again, and Deputy Rawlings stepped in. He held a clipboard and a sheepish look on his face.

"You're free to go, Miss Sparks," he said. "At least, for now."

Bunny arched a brow. "Really? Just like that? No mug shot? No orange jumpsuit?"

"Let's not push our luck."

He held the door open, and she followed him down the hallway, past the holding cells, and into a narrow corridor that led to the front of the station. The hum of conversation grew louder. She could smell stale coffee, old leather, and definitely cinnamon. They rounded the last corner, and Bunny stepped into what looked like a reception area. A half-empty tray of cinnamon rolls sat on the front counter. Ivy and Fern, both seated in a sort of waiting area, immediately stood.

"There she is!" Fern beamed. "Alive, upright, and we brought cinnamon buns in case your blood sugar is low."

Bunny wasn't sure what she felt about this... part relief, part gratitude, a little embarrassment, some anger. She was still confused. "What are you two doing here?"

Fern held up a second container. "We brought something for you to eat, after they check for metal files."

Ivy held up her checkbook. "We thought we might be able to help."

As Bunny looked at the release form Deputy Rawlings handed her to sign, Blagg's voice boom from an office down the hall. "This is *my* investigation. You can't just order the release of suspects without hearing from me first."

Rawlings focused intently on the form, a little too intently, in fact. Bunny thought she saw that same sheepish grin on his face as he waited, then he nodded. "You're free to go," he said.

Fern and Ivy flanked Bunny the moment she stepped away from the counter, like two protective bodyguards.

"I've got a special blend for the nervous system waiting at the shop, Bunny." Ivy gave her a small smile and a look that said they had some catching up to do.

Fern linked her arm through Bunny's. "Come on. Let us feed you. I'm sure we need to catch up."

She turned to Fern. "You didn't ditch me, then?"

For half a second, Fern's smile faltered. She cleared her throat, squeezed Bunny's arm, and lowered her voice. "Not on your life," she said. "We have a lot to talk about."

Ivy added, in a hushed tone, "And Sheriff Greenwood said he's going to come by later. For now, let's get you out of here."

Bunny didn't argue. She just nodded and let herself be guided toward the door.

Chapter Twelve

Ivy steered Bunny toward the back of Tickety-Boo and up the stairs to the small apartment above the shop. A fresh, lush towel and soft robe were already laid out near the clawfoot tub in the bathroom. "Go on, hop in. We'll have tea and treats waiting," she said gently. Bunny hadn't realized how gritty she'd actually felt until the beauty of the little shop wrapped around her. The aromas of lavender, cinnamon, and fennel floated in the air in a way both soothing and surprising. For the second time in a day, Bunny didn't argue. The cool water and oatmeal soap made quick work of the grime and tension clinging to her. It wasn't a miracle, but when she emerged twenty minutes later, wrapped in Ivy's robe and feeling human again, the world seemed a little less off kilter.

Out back in the courtyard, the small bistro table was set. A silver teapot was nestled among delicate china cups and a three-tiered tray of scrumptious slices of cake, sugary cookies, and scones stood in the center. "Sit, sit," Fern said, pulling out a chair with a flourish. "You're officially under house care now. Or rather, Tickety-Boo care. Ivy made the blend based on your Granny Gene's recipe—skullcap, oatstraw, and lemon balm. Calms the nerves and soothes the soul."

Bunny sank into the chair. The cup handed to her was warm, slightly lemony, and instantly grounding. She took a sip, then closed her eyes, listening to the wind chimes tinkling gently in the background. When she opened her eyes again, she stared flatly at Fern. "You pushed me into a hedge and ran."

"I'm sorry," Fern said, setting her cup down. "But, technically, it was meant to save you. That was the plan anyway. I run. You wait until I make a big scene and draw them away, then you run. Except, you didn't run and I didn't realize there were more than two of them."

Bunny nodded. "I thought you were leaving me to take the fall." She stared at her cup and blinked back tears. She was still too tired.

"Never," Fern said firmly. "Wanna hear something funny, though?"

Bunny looked up at her.

"They thought I was a guy." Fern laughed. "I heard one of them yell 'Get him!' to the other one."

"Seriously?" Bunny asked. "Did you run track in high school?"

"High school is a long way in the rearview." Fern smirked. "But you'd be surprised at what a little crosstraining and a whole lot of adrenaline will do." She slid a plate of scones across the table. "I told Ivy you'd be half feral by the time we got you out of there."

Bunny picked one with cherries and dark chocolate and took a bite. She chewed slowly, closing her eyes and lifting her face to the morning sun.

Fern helped herself to a lemon-poppyseed bar. "I called the sheriff right away and told him the truth about the garage… about the boxes, about what we saw. I didn't mention you by name, at first. I just said 'we,' but he already knew."

Ivy, from her seat across the table, gave a proud little hum. "He called *me* right after. Said State had already shown up. He was not happy."

Bunny tilted her head. "You two weren't together when you talked to the sheriff?"

Fern shook her head emphatically. "No way," she said. "I ran them around in circles until I lost them, and by then I was behind the library. I saw the lights on, so I peeked in the window and Mrs. Kettel was there." Fern licked a little glaze off her fingers. "I don't know what she was doing. I guess she never sleeps. When I knocked on the window and asked if I could use her phone, she was complaining about neighborhood watch."

Ivy gave another little hum. "When the sheriff called me, he told me where Fern was and to go pick her up. Then he told me, and I quote, 'I need a distraction with excellent snacks and terrible timing.'" She smiled broadly, adjusting her voluminous skirts. "I told him I'd be honored." She lifted her teacup with a small bow of her head.

"So... that was staged? He knew you were coming?"

Fern laughed. "When I started ranting about heirloom tomatoes and fermenting with intent to distribute, he was smirking. He asked for a distraction and I wanted to give him one."

Ivy added, "And while Fern was raising the volume, the sheriff was calling Blagg's supervisor."

"What in the world could he have told him?" Bunny asked.

"We might just find out now." Fern nodded toward the door.

A shadow fell across the courtyard as Sheriff Greenwood stepped through the back gate, still in uniform, hat in hand. His eyes landed on Bunny first, then drifted to Fern and Ivy, whose teacups paused midair.

"Ladies," he greeted them, nodding politely.

"Sheriff," Ivy said, her voice smooth. She stood and offered him a seat with a practiced elegance. "Would you care for a scone? We have cherry-chocolate and a lemon drizzle that will forgive even a small felony."

Greenwood ignored the plate and looked at Bunny, while Ivy excused herself quietly and slipped into the tea shop. Fern put both elbows on the table and leaned forward, waiting.

"So, I told you to keep your head down, I think," he said.

"You did," Bunny agreed.

"It doesn't look like you listened."

Fern pulled her chair closer to Bunny's and said, "Bunny didn't do this alone, Sheriff. I encouraged her to do it, and we're in this together."

He placed his hat on the table and pulled out the empty chair. As he sat down, he let out a long protracted breath. "It's fortunate that Dave Baer heard what happened. Or saw, more like."

"Why is that fortunate?" Bunny asked. "It was his garage we broke into. And how would he see it?"

"Security cameras. He recently had some installed."

While Fern shrunk back further in her seat, Bunny fought the urge to look at her. "Okay, Sheriff, I'm still not following," she said. "He installed cameras. He may have seen Fern and I snooping through his garage... Maybe even in real time..."

"Someone reported you, but it wasn't him." He looked over the many dessert offerings on the table, nodding when Fern nudged them a few inches closer to him.

"Do we know who did?" Bunny asked.

"No, the call went to Blagg's team. I don't know why yet, but I will," he said, gingerly picking up a mini lemon tart. "When Baer got wind of it, he called in and talked to my deputy."

"Rawlings?" Fern asked.

He nodded, then popped the tart in his mouth and looked around for a napkin. Fern handed one across the table to him.

"I don't want to look a gift horse in the mouth, Sheriff, but I'm still confused," Bunny admitted.

"According to Rawlings, Baer told him to pass along a message. Not to me, but to Blagg. 'Dave Baer will refuse to cooperate if Bunny Sparks is charged.'"

Bunny blinked in confusion. "He refused to press charges?"

"He refused." The sheriff wiped his mouth and sat back. "I'd like to know what you know, Miss Sparks."

"I only know there's something going on in that garage," she said, looking at Fern. Fern nodded enthusiastically at him. "We found boxes of what we can only assume to be contraband of some sort."

"Contraband," he repeated.

"We were considering looking further to see what it actually was, but we got spooked," she said.

Fern nodded in agreement.

"So, you completely disregarded my warning and went so far as to firmly land yourself in a possible illegal smuggling ring," he said.

Bunny looked at Fern, then pointed at her.

Fern shrugged. "Are there any *legal* smuggling rings?"

"Well, your timing couldn't have been better." He leaned toward the sweets once more. Once more, Fern nudged them just the tiniest bit closer to him. "Blagg already had plans to roll in this week. Now he's fit to be tied and wants somebody's head on a stake." He sat back in his chair, picked up his hat and twirled it casually between his knees. "Blagg's from the same place I am... but now he's with the State Bureau, so we're too dumb or too slow around here to know what's going on."

Bunny shuddered. "He looked like he wanted to skin me and make a pair of boots."

"That's why we were called in," Ivy said, as she brought a tray of fresh iced tea. "Please, don't refer to us as the 'cinnamon huns with the cinnamon buns,' though. Deputy Rawlings needs to have a talking to about that."

"We brought a dozen," Fern added, nodding solemnly.

"Only two were weaponized." Ivy smiled as she set down the pitcher.

Bunny couldn't help but laugh when she saw Sheriff Greenwood trying not to. She covered her face with both hands and just breathed for a minute. "I thought I was going to be charged with federal crimes."

"I have a feeling the state boys are more interested in whoever those boxes were meant for," Greenwood assured her. "For my part, I've been charged with finding Jake Stone. If he's got something to do with the murder... or a smuggling ring... or if something's happened to him... it's way more complicated than a little B&E."

Bunny nodded slowly, her eyes distant. "You ever get the feeling something's a lot worse than it seems... and it already seems bad?"

Greenwood gave a dry huff. "Every gal-darned day lately."

A dry wind stirred the chimes, low and eerie, and Ivy moved quietly around them, collecting items from the table as unobtrusively as possible. Bunny didn't look up. Her voice was quiet, and almost to herself, she said, "This feels really bad, doesn't it?"

Sheriff Greenwood exhaled slowly, his face hardening with a subtle grimace. "Yes, it does."

The wind picked up again, the chimes ringing out a melancholic tune as Ivy continued to move quietly around the courtyard. Bunny felt a knot form in her chest. They had barely scratched the surface of whatever was really going on. The strange feeling she'd had from the moment she set foot in that garage, the unease that now crawled under her skin, was only growing.

"This may be bigger than anyone imagined," Greenwood continued, his gaze never leaving her. "I'd like you to do what I suggested. Keep your head down." He looked at Fern. "You, too. There's a lot at play here."

Bunny let his words sink in. "I'm beginning to see that," she whispered.

"What I don't understand," Fern said, "is how all this is connected? The fire, a possible murder, maybe a smuggling ring in the valley... Big Jake did all of this?" Her voice trailed off.

Bunny watched her stringing the relevant pieces together. "What about Gloryanne?" she added. "Why is she in custody? Is she being held as a suspect in Vic's murder?"

Greenwood shook his head, more in disbelief than disagreement.

Fern also shook her head. "She tried to move cash out of a life insurance policy. The insurance company flagged it and alerted law enforcement. She's being held for questioning around falsifying documentation."

The sheriff looked at Bunny, then at Fern, and back again. "Looks like you have a pipeline to all our secrets," he said. The somber expression on his face darkened. "There are too many people involved in this. And the stakes are too high for you both to be playing detective."

Bunny's gaze met his, a silent understanding passing between them. For a brief moment, the scent of lemon and cinnamon drifting on the warm afternoon breeze, Bunny almost felt a sense of togetherness for the first time in a long time.

Sheriff Greenwood stood slowly, putting his hat back on. "I'll be in touch," he said, his voice low and measured. He offered a nod to Fern. "I'll see you tomorrow morning, if I decide to stop in to my hijacked office before heading out." He turned to Bunny. "Keep your head down this time. I mean it. Don't do anything reckless."

Bunny gave him a nod of her own. She didn't want to be reckless. But it seemed like the more she knew, the more impossible it was to stay out of the storm. As their eyes locked, she knew he was serious. There was no smile in his expression, no small-town charm, just quiet intensity.

He held her gaze until Fern cleared her throat, gently but deliberately. "I'll keep her out of trouble," she said, injecting lightness into her voice, but her hand found Bunny's shoulder and gave it a squeeze.

The sheriff smiled, but it didn't reach his eyes. "Or get her into it," he muttered. "See that you don't." Then he nodded to them both and took the long way out, slipping through the back gate without another word.

Chapter Thirteen

When they were alone, Fern let out a low whistle. "That was interesting," she said.

"How so?" Bunny was still watching the back gate and feeling unsettled.

"Well, for starters, he's stretched tighter than a banjo string. I'd chalk that up to Blagg, mostly." She stood up and stretched. "I've never seen him linger like that. And he shared a lot of information. I have to wonder why."

Bunny turned to look at her. "What are you suggesting?"

"I'm not sure. I'm just saying that it's interesting."

The warm breeze rustled through the willow again. Bunny looked down at her hands. "Maybe he's hoping I won't make things worse."

There was a long pause between them. Finally, Fern asked, "What are you thinking?"

"I'm thinking that I forgot to tell him about Gloryanne insisting Victor's not dead."

"She may well believe that. Reality and Gloryanne have always had a flexible relationship. What else are you thinking?"

Bunny took a deep breath. "I'm wondering why so many people seem to be involved in crime around here. And I don't want to be one of them, but here I am."

Fern smiled. "You don't mean the break-in, do you? We were just looking around. No harm, no foul. Besides, Dave is letting you off the hook there."

"Yeah," Bunny mused. "What's up with that? Sheriff Greenwood may want me to keep my head down, but I need to know what's going on. And I think I know where to start."

Fern straightened. "Please don't say the garage again. It smells in there."

Bunny shook her head. "No, not the garage. I need to talk to someone first."

Fern narrowed her eyes. "Who?"

Bunny stood and brushed any lingering crumbs from her lap. "Mrs. Kettel. She's been watching everything from that window for more than fifty years, and I'd bet my best tincture formula she's seen more than she lets on."

Fern tilted her head. "Mrs. Kettel? The original Neighborhood Watch? I heard she once called the volunteer fire brigade because the Cran Pharmacy sign was 'smoking in a suggestive manner.'"

Bunny laughed. "Yes, her. She's been in the holler her entire life. She's observant. And completely underestimated."

Fern grabbed her bag. "I'll come with. If she's in gossip mode, she won't even notice me poking around. I've been meaning to check out what's going on with the community board anyway. Half the flyers look like they've been chewed by squirrels."

Bunny smirked. "You mean you want to see into the Cran Pharmacy window from the library to catch Jerlene."

Fern gave her a mock innocent look. "Can't a girl multitask?"

They walked the three blocks in companionable silence, the streets unusually quiet for late afternoon. The town kept its pleasant rhythm, though Bunny was no longer fooled by it. The fact that nothing about the day seemed unusual was what unsettled her most.

Mrs. Kettel's quaint, pale green bungalow was tucked in on the other side of the library and had a tiny front porch overrun with aggressively flowering begonias. The curtains twitched before they even reached the library and the door to the bungalow swung open wide. "Why, Bunny Sparks," Mrs. Kettel called, clutching a tea towel and squinting. "And Miss Fern. Well, isn't this a treat. I was just finishing my supper. Do you need the library?"

Bunny waved. "Just thought I'd check in, Mrs. Kettel."

Mrs. Kettel stepped outside and waved them over to her porch. "Are we talking fresh goosefat, then?"

Bunny watched Fern wrinkle her forehead in confusion and decided she'd either catch on during their conversation or find out later.

"Come on in." Mrs. Kettel stepped aside and motioned with her tea towel. "I hope you brought some more of that chocolate cake my granddaughter picked up this morning."

Fern smiled wide at her. "I didn't, but I know where I can get some."

Inside, the little house smelled of lemon polish and ginger snaps. Bunny eased into one of the floral wingback chairs, while Fern wandered over to the front window and peered through the curtain. Mrs. Kettel eased herself into the wingback across from Bunny. "Let's hear it, then."

Bunny smiled. "Hear what?" she asked.

"The goosefat, chil'," she said. "Or were you hoping I had some to spill?"

"Well..." Bunny elongated the word.

Fern, still peering through the curtain, said, "Oh, you've got a great view of the alley behind Dave Baer's garage from here, don't you?"

"I do." Mrs. Kettel pressed her lips together in a little smile.

Bunny rested her elbow on the armrest, hoping to seem casual. "We were wondering... have you noticed anything unusual over there recently?"

Mrs. Kettel narrowed her eyes. "You looking for something in particular, or just stirring the pot?"

"I'm really just hoping to find out what's been going on," Bunny said gently. "Because we think something *is* going on."

There was a pause. Then Mrs. Kettel leaned back, clicking her tongue. "Well, you're not wrong. I've seen a few things over there that don't sit right. Lots of late nights with too many folks comin' and goin'. Someone even broke in there last night."

Fern made an innocent face. "Did you see who it was?"

"I didn't get a good look, no." Mrs. Kettel tugged her glasses from her small face and used the tea towel to polish the lenses one by one. "I'd say they was young teens, though. Maybe the Haywood boys. They're always getting into trouble."

Bunny nodded absently.

Fern stepped away from the window. "We were wondering if you saw anything with boxes."

"Boxes?" Mrs. Kettel put her glasses back in place and peered at Fern intently.

Fern nodded. "You know, deliveries that seem to be coming or going after hours?"

Mrs. Kettel nodded. "I keep a little log," she said, lifting a small notebook from the side table.

Bunny caught her breath. "Can I see it?"

Mrs. Kettel hesitated, then held it out. "I don't much show that to anyone, mind. Even Misti don't know I keep it. But, I 'spect it won't do no harm to show you, Bunny."

Bunny flipped through the pages, her finger stopping on a scrawl:

Aug. 05 — 10:42PM — Baer's Garage.
  White van, no plates. Unloaded boxes.
  Left before midnight.

Aug. 08 — 12:18AM — Baer's Garage.
  Jake Stone's delivery truck in alley.
  Loaded boxes.
  Victor Tew yelling at Jake.
  Dave yells at Victor.
  Jake leaves before 1:10AM.
  Victor leaves 1:15AM.
  Lights off 1:16AM.
  Dave leaves.
Aug. 10 — 12:30AM — Baer's Garage.
  Flashlights inside.
  No trucks. No sign of Dave Baer.
  One suspect apprehended.

Bunny looked up. "Wow."

Mrs. Kettel lifted her chin, just the tiniest bit, with an air of humble satisfaction.

"Are you sure this was Victor Tew and Jake Stone, Mrs. Kettel? It couldn't have been anyone else?"

Mrs. Kettel folded her tea towel, primly. "I may be old, but I'm not blind. Both of 'em move like they's made of the same sized bricks, but Jake slouches like he's always lookin' for dropped pennies and Victor can't stop pullin' that pencil from behind his ear and puttin' it back."

Bunny nodded slowly. Now that Mrs. Kettel said it out loud, she could see it clearly.

Fern walked back over to the window and peered out. She turned to Bunny, eyes wide. "Um… I think you're going to want to see this." When Bunny seemed not to move fast enough for her, she reached out and snagged Bunny's sleeve. "Okay, *now* you really want to see this," she said in a low hiss.

Bunny rose to join her and followed her gaze. Through the wide plate-glass window that ran along the front of the Cran Pharmacy, kitty-corner across the street, the lights were on, despite a CLOSED sign hanging on the door.

Inside, Dave Baer stood near the counter, shoulders hunched, arms slack at his sides, and Jerlene was standing—on her own two legs.

Bunny opened her mouth, but no sound came out.

"See?" Fern whispered.

"I see," Bunny whispered back.

Chapter Fourteen

Bunny and Fern stood at Mrs. Kettel's living room window and watched as Jerlene leaned forward, gesturing sharply at Dave. Even from across the street, they could see her face was flushed an angry shade of red. Dave stood slumped in front of her, staring at the Cran Pharmacy floor, when another figure appeared from the back. In an instant, Jerlene dropped like a stone into her wheelchair, her arms limp in her lap, as if she'd been unplugged. She even lolled her head slightly to one side.

"Earl," Fern whispered. "He owns the place. Do you know him?"

Bunny shook her head as they watched Dave nod at Earl, take a small prescription bag from the counter, and walk out the front door of the pharmacy with his head still low. They continued watching as he shuffled away from the pharmacy, across the parking lot, and into the alley that led to his garage.

Mrs. Kettel, who'd been quietly folding and refolding her tea towel, spoke up. "She does that sometimes. Thinks no one sees."

Bunny turned. "You've seen her?"

"Of course," Mrs. Kettel said. "Usually when the place is supposed to be closed, but she messes up sometimes and does it right in the middle of the day, right in front of the plate glass."

Bunny turned from the window and looked at her. "Why do you think she pretends?"

"Attention, most likely," Mrs. Kettel said. "She and Dave were fightin' like hell cats until she got sick. Then he was all flowers, and 'sweetie,' and home in the evenings."

Fern nodded. "I wasn't here then, but I heard about it. Doctor Fisher said it was quite a transformation in Dave."

"That must not have lasted. Dave goes out now, I hear, including out of town," Bunny said. The night of the fire flashed through her mind, Jerlene casually explaining the overnight stay at her uncle's as if it were almost routine that Dave would be away on business. "And she really wasn't sick?"

"Well, not according to Doc," Fern said. "At least, the tests in her chart don't show anything abnormal."

"Misti told me the same thing," Bunny said. "But why would Jerlene keep up the act when it's not working anymore?"

"I suspect Jerlene discovered somethin' unexpected in all the fuss." Mrs. Kettel stood and tossed her tea towel onto the back of the chair. "Dave wasn't the only one payin' attention, and she liked bein' noticed. Don't seem to matter much who's doin' the noticin'. Now, I need you girls to help *me* with somethin'."

"Of course," Bunny agreed. "What is it?"

Fern gave Bunny a gentle elbow to her side and exaggerated an expression of surprise. "Wait, I thought *we* were the ones pokin' around."

"Oh, don't think I haven't noticed." Mrs. Kettel turned to Bunny, eyes sharp. "But I got a few questions of my own."

Bunny sat back down. "What is it?" she asked.

Mrs. Kettel huffed. "It's my granddaughter." She waved a hand. "That girl's been sneakin' around like a fox with a feather in its teeth. Goin' out late, coming back later. Dressin' in clothes she ain't got no money for. New earrings, pearls. Wears 'em like a skunk tiptoein' through the perfume aisle at the Five & Dime. She must be thinkin' nobody'll notice, but I do. I always do."

"A boyfriend?" Fern and Bunny blurted, together.

Mrs. Kettel nodded. "Jake Stone. She won't admit it, but I've seen him waitin' for her when she tells me she's 'goin' on a break,' whatever that means."

Fern muttered, "Sounds like my last relationship. But, he went 'on a break' with the woman who cut his hair."

Bunny just looked at her.

Fern shrugged. "Who gets a trim every week and still looks like a mop in a pinstripe?"

Bunny turned back to Mrs. Kettel. "We're actually trying to find Jake. No one has seen him for several days. Do you think Misti has been meeting with him? Have you seen him at all?"

Mrs. Kettel looked up at the ceiling. "Come to think of it, I haven't. And Misti has been moody as a girl left watchin' her fella dance with someone else all night."

"Interesting image," Fern said, tilting her head. "That mop in the pinstripe comes to mind again, only now it's doing the tango with a flirty broom."

Bunny gave her a sharp look, willing Fern to save her stand-up for later. "Have you ever seen her go into Dave Baer's garage?"

Mrs. Kettel shook her head slowly. "No. She don't own a car."

"But you've seen Jake there, quite a lot." Bunny lightly tapped her temple with one finger.

"Not lately, though," Mrs. Kettel reminded her.

"Right..." Bunny kept tapping.

The door creaked open just as Mrs. Kettel seemed to remember something.

"Hey, Memaw!" a bright voice called from the hallway.

Fern's eyebrows shot up.

Misti stepped around the corner into the little sitting room and froze. "Oh!" she said. "Didn't realize you had company."

Fern stood smoothly. "We were just on our way out, actually."

Bunny followed suit. "Just stopping in to say 'hello' to your memaw."

Mrs. Kettel didn't stand. She didn't smile, either. Her eyes flicked from her granddaughter to Bunny, then back again.

"You girls get home safe now," she said, a distinct edge to her voice. "And don't forget about my request."

Fern nodded quickly. "We'll look into that missing mechanic's manual. Promise. No library should be without one."

Misti walked over and patted her grandmother's arm, then turned to look at Bunny. "I really am sorry about earlier, Bunny," she said. "I don't know what's got into me lately. And look..." She lifted the corner of her sweater, holding it out for Bunny to see. "No stains."

Bunny smiled at her. "I'm glad, Misti. You two have a lovely evening."

After saying their good-byes, Fern and Bunny walked in silence toward the tea shop, the afternoon sun casting its last long shadows of the day before dipping behind the ridge.

Fern finally let out a low breath. "Okay. That was a vibe."

Bunny didn't answer. Her mind was still spinning from what they'd seen and what they hadn't had time to find out.

Fern went on, "And who is wearing a cashmere sweater in this heat?"

Bunny continued to walk in silence.

When Fern spoke again, her voice was quieter. "What if Misti really was seeing Jake? And what if Jake killed Victor?" She stopped walking. "And what if Jake left town and now Misti is heartbroken?"

Bunny stopped and turned to look at her. "Why?" she asked. "What would Jake gain by killing Victor?"

Fern kicked a pebble with the toe of her shoe. "Maybe he and Gloryanne have something going on. I mean, Jake looks an awful lot like Victor, wouldn't you say? Same size, same build. Sort of the same look. But Jake is disarming, everyone thinks he's innocent, right? And Victor... well, he was nice enough, but had a sort of 'I've seen the dark side and I liked it' thing about him."

Bunny stared at her.

"See? Gloryanne didn't like Victor. She said so herself *all the time*. To *everyone*," Fern continued, undeterred by Bunny's lack of response. "And if Gloryanne thought she could have a better life with someone charming but manipulatable... plus a little insurance money to get their new life started?"

Bunny resumed walking. "Gloryanne's in jail. So Jake just... left her?"

Fern picked up her pace. "Maybe they're planning to rendezvous when the heat is off, but she jumped the gun and tried to cash in too soon. Maybe he's waiting for her somewhere. Maybe Misti was a distraction this whole time to keep us from catching on to the real affair."

"That's a lot of maybes, don't you think?" Bunny said, frowning.

"Sure," Fern agreed. "But you saw Misti's face. That wasn't just moody. That was *wrecked*."

Bunny looked ahead, eyes narrowing as the tea shop came into view. "If Jake really is gone," she said, "can we even figure out where he went? That's not keeping our heads down, is it?"

Fern glanced sideways. "Only one person was told to keep her head down."

A breeze stirred the hem of Bunny's dress. As she instinctively reached down to keep it from lifting, a dark sedan with tinted windows rolled past. They watched until it turned the corner. "Who do you think *that* was?" she asked rhetorically, making note of the license plate:

New York GT2GO

This wasn't about infidelity or missing persons anymore. This was organized. Intentional. Dangerous.

And it had already cost someone their life.

Chapter Fifteen

D riving home, Bunny rolled the window all the way down, letting the night air rush in. The moon hung low over the hills, casting a pale sheen in patches across the winding two-lane road. Her headlights caught the soft flash of night moths and the occasional glint of an old reflector nailed to a tree.

Fern had tried and failed to convince Bunny to stay with her and Ivy for the night, but she preferred the comfort of her own bed, and she needed the quiet. Her thoughts were loud enough on their own.

She kept one hand on the wheel and the other resting lightly on the door frame.

So much had happened in so little time.

She'd been arrested. That was a tad too scary. She sent a wish up to the nearest star that nothing more came of it.

Dave Baer had insisted on her release. Why? He could've pressed charges. Instead, he made sure she walked out the door. Was it guilt? Or something else?

And then there was Misti—bright-eyed and sugar-coated, but wilting around the edges now. The earrings, the sweater, a secret in her voice. Had Jake given her those things and then just vanished? Was it a breakup? A setup? Was it really a broken heart she was nursing? Or was it about losing a gravy train studded in pearls and lined with cashmere?

She eased into a curve, tires humming softly, as the shadows between the trees grew deeper, blurred slightly by her headlights. A raccoon darted across the road ahead and she braked gently, watching it vanish into the brush. Or was that a badger?

Was Jake buying Misti's affection with smuggling money?

And then there was Gloryanne, still in a holding cell. Bunny was sure that even there her lipstick would be painted on a little too thick. Had she really said Victor wasn't dead? Does she actually believe that or is she simply in the denial stage of grief?

The Keely reached the top of a rise where the trees thinned, and for a moment, the sky opened up, stars sprinkled overhead. The world quieted. It felt sacred. Still. Peaceful.

Then, Bunny's eyes landed on something not quite right.

Just ahead on the shoulder was a broken line of saplings, pale and jagged where they'd snapped. Something dark glistened in the dirt, snaking toward the edge. She hadn't noticed them before. Maybe it was the way the moonlight filtered through the trees just now, low and silver, catching the shadows just right. But, it was suddenly obvious.

Bunny was sure this was about where the gravel pit would be, but the road that dropped down into it was farther along, just past the curve. She pulled off the road, half in the weeds, cut the lights and got out. As she stepped closer to the edge, her stomach tightened. The woods were thick here. The smell of pine, damp moss, and something faintly smoky yet metallic hung in the air. She had to step carefully or end up at the bottom of the pit herself.

Then she saw it.

Down below, half-hidden in the shadows of jagged piles of granite, chalky in the moonlight, sat the husk of a vehicle. A box truck. The cab was blackened, the metal frame warped and sagging in the middle like it had folded in on itself. The edges still glinted faintly. She strained to see without leaning too far over the edge. The windshield was gone. The side panel was scorched. No logo. No lettering. There was no mistaking it, though.

Jake's delivery truck.

Her breath caught in her chest. She couldn't tell if someone was inside. It was too dark. She was too far away. She stepped back, her heart pounding. She had to get to a phone. For the first time since she'd been in the valley, she regretted that cell phones were useless here, but who would she call? If she called the Sheriff's office, it would be Blagg. That was a hard no.

She hurried back to the Keely and slid behind the wheel. Hoodoo's was on the way. She would stop there. She only hoped he would be there.

When Bunny turned off the road and crunched over the familiar gravel lot in front of Cran General, the storefront was dark, shuttered for the night. But a soft amber light glowed from the back windows. She cut the engine, and for a moment sat in the quiet, her hands still gripping the steering wheel. A small flutter of anxiety was making her nauseous. It was late and dropping in like this was not something she ever wanted to do. Hoodoo was one of the kindest people and getting on in years. He deserved his rest.

Still. She had seen what she'd seen.

She got out and walked around to the back. The window where the light shone was a bit fogged at the corners, but she could see him standing over the stove, stirring something in a small pan. His profile was calm, domestic. Safe. She rapped gently on the glass. He turned, instinctively glancing toward the sound. The second his eyes met hers, Bunny saw the shift in his expression. Concern. Readiness. He understood this wasn't a casual visit.

He set the spoon down and moved out of view. A moment later, the side door latch clicked open.

"What is it, Bunny?" he asked, pulling the door wide. His voice was low but sharp with worry.

She stepped inside, trying to catch her breath. She hadn't been running, but her body didn't seem to know that. "There's a truck," she said, "down in the gravel pit. It looks burned out. I didn't see it until the moon hit it just right, and then…" She shook her head. "It's Jake's. I'm sure of it."

He led her inside without another word, closing the door gently behind them.

"I need to call someone, but I'm not sure who," she said. "The Sheriff's Office has been commandeered by a State guy, Rufus Blagg. I don't trust him as far as I can throw a watermelon uphill."

Hoodoo nodded once. "You don't have to explain. Sit down."

She hesitated, still jittery.

"Sit," he said again, firmer this time. "I'll call the sheriff myself. I've got his direct line and his home number."

Bunny sank into the nearest chair, finally letting her shoulders drop, while Hoodoo made the phone call. By the time he'd hung up, Bunny had wandered to the window. She stood quietly, arms crossed, eyes on the dark treetops rippling silver beneath the rising moonlight.

"He's on his way," Hoodoo said. "Said he'd call Rawlings first, get him moving."

Bunny glanced over her shoulder. "I met Rawlings. Seems like a decent guy."

Hoodoo nodded as he stepped back to the stove and stirred the contents of the pan before turning off the flame. "Sheriff wouldn't let just anyone wear that badge. He's old-fashioned about that. He comes from a line of lawmen, did you know? His daddy was a sheriff. His grandpappy, too. He has an idea about a man's character… it's either polished or tarnished daily."

Bunny smiled faintly and turned back to the window. "Wish that kind of standard caught on elsewhere."

"Well," Hoodoo said, setting the spoon aside. "Now all we can do is wait."

She nodded and sat back down while he filled two bowls and brought them to the table, setting one before her.

"Hungry?" he asked.

She shook her head. "Stomach's in knots, really. A lot has happened."

He waited. So she told him everything. Gloryanne's strange behavior. The plants found at the scene of the fire. The accusations. The things they saw in Dave's garage. Misti's pearls and cashmere. The arrest. Blagg. Her unexpected release. Jerlene. And somewhere in the middle of it all, her voice faltered.

Hoodoo listened with the kind of patience born of long winters and slow cookers. When she finished, he leaned back and rubbed his jaw. "I remember seeing those plants scattered around the fire site. They were everywhere, like someone'd dumped out a bushel in a hurry. Some of us thought that was odd, but there was no cause to question it." He looked toward the window himself now, voice lower. "We're lucky the storm came when it did. Sky opened up like a kicked bucket. Kept the fire from spreading." He gave a soft, dry chuckle. "Old folks used to say when fire meets rain under a hunter's moon, truth's not far behind."

Bunny raised an eyebrow. "Is that real mountain wisdom or something you just made up to sound impressive?"

"I plead the fifth." Hoodoo grinned at her, but not with a full face.

"A Hunter's moon is in October," she said, attempting to sound lighthearted.

"At any rate, it *was* poker night. The volunteer crew was already here, playing cards and complainin' about how quiet things were. Fastest response this holler's ever seen."

Bunny's brows drew together. "But who called it in? Leo was here that night, too, wasn't he?"

"Jerlene," he said, his face growing more serious. "She said she was up at her uncle's. No clue why. But if she hadn't been there, she wouldn't have seen the flames." He hesitated, then looked her in the eye. "She *thinks* she saw Jake. Or someone like him. Big man, ball cap. Heading off on foot, away from the smoke."

Bunny couldn't hide the shock of hearing that.

Hoodoo held up a hand. "Don't go telling that around. It's not common knowledge and the Sheriff wants to be careful with it. Could spook whoever might be involved."

Bunny nodded slowly. Her mind was already turning over new threads, new possibilities.

"Whatever this is," Hoodoo said quietly, "it's crawling up outta the shadows now."

Outside, the moon inched higher, and they waited. It was just after ten when the sound of engines echoed up the hill. Bunny and Hoodoo stepped out into the open air, the moon hanging high and full over the store. The first vehicle that eased into the gravel was Rawlings', in a department-issued SUV, his headlights washing briefly over them before he parked under the store sign. He left his vehicle running. A moment later, the sheriff followed in a dusty old Ford, the kind that some would say didn't look like much but was reliable, and likely still had enough torque to drag a stuck cow out of a creek.

They parked side by side. Both men stepped out at once, boots hitting gravel in unison. Rawlings gave a short nod in greeting. "Evening," he said, though his tone suggested he'd rather skip the pleasantries and get moving.

The sheriff didn't smile. He looked tired, like maybe he'd been up since before sunrise, and this night was testing what was left of his patience. But his gaze was steady, assessing Bunny in one glance, and then turning to Hoodoo.

"Sheriff." Hoodoo offered his hand, and the sheriff clasped it in a firm, no-nonsense shake. Bunny observed the quiet respect of men who'd weathered more than one storm on the same side.

"We went to the site on the shoulder," the sheriff said, without preamble. "Just like you described. We didn't go down yet."

"Too dark," Rawlings added. "Too steep, too. Gotta do it right."

Bunny folded her arms. "Did you see the truck in the bottom of the pit? I can take you there. I know exactly where I saw it."

The sheriff shook his head. "No need. We've got it mapped. We'll go in slow. Cautious." He turned back to Hoodoo as if Bunny hadn't spoken at all. "Appreciate the call. And the quiet. Didn't want this on the radio."

Hoodoo gave a single nod. "Didn't seem wise to stir up noise until you'd had a look."

The sheriff's jaw tightened, but he gave a small grunt of agreement. Rawlings, meanwhile, had already taken a few steps toward his vehicle, shifting from one foot to the other like a dog waiting to be let off-leash. The sheriff turned to Bunny. "Best you head home, Miss Sparks. You've done your part."

"But—"

"I understand," he said, interrupting gently. "You saw it. You alerted us. That's good work. Now go home and try to get some rest." It was polite. It was firm. It wasn't a request.

Bunny felt that wave of nausea return. "I'm already involved, Sheriff," she said. "Whether either of us want me to be or not."

Hoodoo stepped closer, voice quiet. "He's just trying to protect you, Bunny. Doesn't mean he doesn't respect what you've done."

She looked between them, reading something in Hoodoo's tone. Maybe Greenwood wasn't being dismissive. Maybe he had enough on his hands. She didn't *want* to be involved in any of this.

"You'll be kept updated," the sheriff added, glancing at Hoodoo as though entrusting him with the responsibility. "Through Hoodoo," he added and tipped his hat slightly toward Hoodoo before heading back to his truck. Rawlings was already pulling out onto the road.

"Go on home, Bunny," Hoodoo said gently. "Nothing else you can do out here tonight but lose sleep."

She looked once more into the darkness, where the trees swallowed the edge of the world. Then she turned back toward the Keely and opened the door. As she slid behind the wheel, she met her own eyes in the rearview mirror, the moonlight catching the worry lines on her face. Whatever was down in that gravel pit, it wasn't just ashes and wreckage. It was a piece of a very convoluted puzzle, and she wanted to know where it fit.

Chapter Sixteen

T he cottage windows glowed softly with their flickering lights as Bunny pulled into the drive, headlights sweeping the familiar shapes of foxglove and roses. Before she cut the engine, she noted the mysterious package was still there on the porch, unopened, in its plain brown wrapper. She stepped out and thought again about bringing it in, but the night had stretched too long already. She left it where it was and let herself inside.

The cottage was just as she'd left it. She was embraced by the faint scent of amber, which lingered from somewhere in time. The rich beams overhead, hand-hewn and old as the holler itself, stretched across the low ceiling like the arms of ancient ancestors. Their dark grain caught the lamplight in soft gold streaks, and she could almost hear her granny's voice reminding her that beams like these weren't just for holding houses together, they held families together. She closed the door behind her and leaned against it just long enough to soak in the comfort of being home. The tension didn't leave her all at once, but it began to soften at the edges.

In the kitchen, she made herself something simple and cooling. Cucumber slices, a sprig of mint, a splash of lemon, and a few ice cubes in a tall glass of fresh spring water. It wasn't much, but it calmed her. Just the act of preparing it, slowly, brought her back to earth. She carried the glass upstairs, the familiar creak of wood underfoot and the soft whoosh of the attic fan lulled her further. She settled into bed. The linen sheets were soft on her skin, the open windows waiting for a breeze to carry in the scent of night-blooming jasmine, the kind of sweetness that didn't ask anything of her.

The sheriff was right. She should let go of all this and let the people trained for it do the work they are expected to do. She'd been reckless, letting Fern's enthusiasm fan a small idea into something far bigger than she'd intended, something that ended with her arrest. Only now was she thinking about the cost of that mistake, in a town where she was still being sized up and judged. Breaking into a local business was not going to endear her to anyone, least of all those who already thought she was living off her granny's reputation. What had she been thinking?

The image of the little pin came back to her, the one she'd seen on the floor in Dave's garage. She wished she'd taken it with her. It was a sobriety pin, she was sure of it. Victor had one like it and wore it like a badge. But, it could have easily been Dave's. Or anyone else's, really.

Her eyes fluttered closed. Let it go, she told herself. Let it go and let it be someone else's burden. She was just drifting, that soft weightless feeling before sleep, when the sound reached her ears.

Chirp.

The chirp of a car locking with a key fob. It was short, sharp, and unmistakable. Her eyes snapped open. No one in the valley locked their cars with those things. Most didn't bother locking their cars at all. And no one around here, certainly no one she knew, would make *that* kind of noise this late. She sat up, heart thudding, held her breath and listened.

There it was, the crunch of gravel underfoot. It was faint, but it was there. Footsteps.

She rolled slowly out of bed and stepped across the room to the window. There it was. A dark sedan, parked just beyond her drive. It was sleek, low to the ground, and too polished for this road. She could almost read the license plate. She wouldn't have seen it at all, but it was rimmed in a garish blue light. "No one around here would drive that," she murmured.

Well, maybe Gloryanne. But even she wouldn't tint the windows so dark.

Bunny backed away from the window, pulse pounding in her ears. She didn't know what this was, but she knew it wasn't nothing, and she *wasn't* going to wait to find out. She crept down the stairs, careful not to let the old boards groan beneath her feet. The kitchen was dark now, save for the moonlight spilling in through the windows. She didn't turn on a lamp. No need to announce herself. She moved quietly out the back door and stayed in the shadows.

She knew the land by heart, the winding paths between the flower beds, the way the creeping thyme grew in fragrant tufts along the stone wall, and where the stepping stones were. Keeping low and moving in silence, Bunny stayed alert, though the man ahead of her sounded unlikely to hear anything short of metal boots on stone. The road was only forty yards ahead, and she could see him clearly in the moonlight, his hard soles crunching over the gravel as he muttered a steady stream of curses. She slipped into the line of pines that flanked the ditch, where the elderberry grew. The breeze was coming off the ridge behind her, rustling softly through the higher branches. Good. She was downwind.

She would have known that without a wind, the stench of too much cologne biting her nostrils. It was a cologne that cost too much, all musk and ambition, thick enough to be offensive. Beneath that scent, the chemical undertones. She held her breath and crouched low behind the wide bole of an old spruce, and watched. There was just one man. *Wearing enough cologne for a dozen.* His dark hair was gelled back with precision, but a single practiced curl dipped over his forehead, the kind of detail that came from vanity, not accident. She shook her head, pinched her nose, and tried to stay focused, watching as he paced back and forth near the dark sedan, clearly agitated.

He checked his phone again and again, holding it up, frustrated. No signal. He cursed some more and shoved it back in his pocket.

The sedan's headlights flooded the roadside and highlighted his shiny accoutrements. His shoes were definitely not meant for backwoods travel. She guessed they were Italian. Fancy. His belt matched. His watch, his belt buckle, and a thick chain inside the collar of his shirt, all caught the light like polished brass. Gold, or at least plated. Expensive-looking. Loud.

The New York plate framed in that gaudy blue neon was the same. *The same car*. This must have been the guy they saw earlier. But what was he doing here?

Then, click. The headlights finally went dark.

Time-delay headlamps, Bunny remembered. They stayed on for a bit after shutting the car off. A nice feature for a nice car, in a place that didn't need either.

The man let out a louder curse this time. He popped back into the car and opened something. A paper? A map. Bunny could just make out the flutter of the page as he unfolded it, reading by the interior light. She watched him slam his hand on the steering wheel and mutter something she couldn't hear. But she caught the map. He was looking for something.

For someone.

He restarted the engine, eased the sedan forward, and turned the car until he was facing toward the fork in the road that led over the hill to the Tew's place. And Leo's. Bunny watched the red taillights disappear around the bend.

He wasn't here for her and she was flooded with relief, though her mind raced. If he was heading to Victor's, then the sheriff had more on his hands than just a burnt-out truck. If he went to the wrong house, it could mean trouble for Leo.

Bunny exhaled, slowly. She had a choice. She could go inside and pretend none of this happened. Let law enforcement do their job. Or she could grab her keys and follow. She hesitated only a moment before slipping back inside for her keys. She didn't bother with looking for shoes. She stepped into her garden clogs by the door and grabbed the garden trug, in case someone caught her. She could say she was doing some night harvesting. She wasn't sure what else she was doing. She just knew she couldn't let Leo deal with this alone.

If some slick-haired flashy thug, or worse—a *wannabe* gangster—showed up at Leo's in the middle of the night, she was at least going to create a scene. She slid behind the wheel, engine barely above a hum as she backed down the drive. She didn't switch on the headlights. The moon was high, and she knew these roads the way she knew her own gardens. Every bend, every dip, every place where a deer might dart out or gravel might slide was known to her. Far ahead, cresting the hill, she caught the red glint of taillights. He was driving slower than molasses. Must not want to ding the chassis. She slowed to keep a safe distance, heart tight in her chest.

When she reached the turnoff, she didn't follow. Not all the way. She pulled off the road instead, easing in behind a thick stand of sugar maples, and killed the engine.

Up ahead, the road split. One path led to Leo's cottage. The other looped past it and to the left, to the house where Victor and Gloryanne had lived. She stayed to the right, toward Leo's, moving along the edge of the woods where the shadows were thickest. The grass was tall enough to brush against her calves, and, somewhere above her, an Eastern Screech Owl belted out a tremolo that almost dropped her to the ground with fright.

When the Tew house came into view, she felt a flicker of relief. The sedan had rolled all the way up the drive, lights still on, aimed directly at the warped siding of the house. The charred remains of what was once their side door was now boarded up. Leo's handiwork, probably. He wouldn't have left the place open to rain or raccoons.

She crouched beside Leo's porch, keeping low, heart pounding in her ears. When Oscar Wildecat let out a little mew, Bunny looked up to see him on the porch, right beside Jerlene. She clamped her hand over her own mouth to stop herself from yelling out. When she caught her breath, she whispered, "Jerlene! What are you doing out here?"

Jerlene didn't look over. Her voice was low and calm. "Making sure that man doesn't bring trouble to my uncle's. He's asleep inside."

Bunny glanced back toward the Tew house. The man was outside now, pacing in short, angry strides, shining a phone flashlight into the windows. He didn't knock. He just walked the perimeter like he had every right to be there.

Jerlene nodded toward him, her jaw tight. "Dave told me he was probably heading out this way. Said he was looking for Victor."

Bunny paused, considering. "Why would Dave know that?"

Jerlene exhaled, slow and heavy. "Because he knows these guys are looking for Vic. Dirty crooks. Dave never shoulda fallen for Victor's scheme in the first place. But he did. Stupid man."

"What scheme?" Bunny asked. She had an idea, having seen what she'd seen in the garage, but wanted confirmation.

"Stealing car parts from rich tourists. Junk from their cars. If they weren't bright enough to take their valuables out, they stole other stuff. Money. Jewelry. Have you seen Misti's new pearl earrings?"

Bunny swallowed hard. "Those came from Dave?"

"No." Jerlene scoffed. "Those came from Victor. Along with a bunch of other trinkets to get her to do his bidding."

"Wait," Bunny said, remembering the man demanding answers from Sheriff Greenwood. She couldn't really hear, he was too far away, but she could tell he wasn't from the valley and he was upset about something not being done about his car. "Victor and Dave were stealing from tourists and Victor was giving stolen jewelry to Misti?"

"Jewelry... and other things. And Dave said nothing when he found out," Jerlene continued. "Dave's not a clever man. He's a big talker when I'm not around. But, he didn't know they'd be stealing anything. Victor sweet-talked him with promises of easy money and said he just needed a little mechanical help and to use his garage. Then he said he had connections in New York. That he knew how to keep things under the radar. Dave fell for it."

The man outside stepped in something. He let out a hiss of disgust and scraped his shoe on a rock, muttering big city curses that carried on the night air.

"Jake must have fallen for it, too?" Bunny whispered.

"Yep. Vic roped him in, too. That's what Misti was being bought off for, I think. To get Jake in on the scheme. But Dave didn't cover his tracks," Jerlene said. "Never could. I saw the signs. I made him come clean and when it looked like bigger fish were onto them, I made him come clean to them, too."

"'Bigger fish'? So, the sheriff?" Bunny asked.

"No. No, not the sheriff." Jerlene raised her voice, then dropped it when she saw Bunny's eyes widen. "I wasn't about to have our name dragged through the mud in front of the whole holler. And certainly not in front of the sheriff. I've worked in that office. I know those people." She adjusted in her chair. "I mean the State. Maybe higher."

"So, you made him cooperate?"

"I didn't make him. I just made it clear what would happen if he didn't." Jerlene's mouth pressed into a line. "That man out there? He was at the garage already. Picked up whatever Vic had waiting for him. But Victor's dead, and they still want the money they're owed. Maybe he don't believe Vic's dead. Now he's sniffing around, and when he doesn't get answers, he'll look for someone to squeeze."

Bunny watched the man shine his light into the boarded-up window, then pace back to his car.

"Where do you think he'll go next?" Bunny asked.

Jerlene shook her head. "No idea."

There was a pause. Then Bunny said quietly, "While we're sitting here, there's something I have to ask."

Jerlene continued watching the man.

"Why do you use that chair when you can walk just fine?"

The silence that followed was sharp.

Bunny also kept her eyes on the man, who was cursing again as he kicked mud off his polished shoes. "I saw you," she said. "Through the pharmacy window. I was visiting with Mrs. Kettel and her front window has a pretty direct view. You were chewing Dave out and you were standing as you did it. Clear as day. At least, until Earl walked in."

Jerlene was quiet for a moment. "I was chewing him out because he said he lost his heart medication. I told him a hundred times before that our insurance don't cover replacements. Lose your meds, you pay out of pocket 'til the refill."

"I've heard that," Bunny said gently. "But that's not the bit I'm asking about."

Jerlene sighed, deep and gravelly. "It wasn't always like this, Bunny. I was hurt once. Bad. I had to be in a wheelchair for a while. Things changed because of it. I got a little more of his time. Dave, I mean." She adjusted in her seat. "I also found out people don't treat you the same when you're in a chair. Some people are a lot nicer. Some just don't pay you no mind, and so you hear stuff you wouldn't otherwise."

Across the road, the man finally gave up. He got back into the sedan and slammed the door so hard the echo bounced off the trees. Then he started down the gravel, faster this time, until the undercarriage scraped hard over a dip. He cursed again, louder, smacked the steering wheel, then slowed the car with exaggerated care and rolled back toward the main road.

When the taillights disappeared, Bunny exhaled slowly. She turned to Jerlene. "We need to tell the sheriff what's going on."

Jerlene didn't argue. She adjusted in her chair, eyes still fixed on the bend where the sedan disappeared. "I've got Blagg's number," she said finally. "He's the State contact Dave's been working with." She turned to Bunny. "We're past small-town secrets now."

Chapter Seventeen

The sun had barely cleared the ridge and Bunny was already on the porch, draped in a light sundress, both hands cradling a mug of chicory root, chaga and lion's mane. The steam curled gently into the morning air as she watched the early light stretch long and golden across the garden, softening everything it touched—Gigi's roses, now near the drive, the dew drying on the hollyhock, even the brown paper of the package still sitting on the porch. It seemed somehow less ominous than it had, but she still wasn't ready to open it. She sipped her concoction and mulled over the events of the last several days. She knew what she *should* do. She should tell the sheriff what she'd seen. Maybe not what she'd done, necessarily. Following that man had been dangerous, she conceded that much to herself. The thought of telling him, though, made her stomach knot. He'd already warned her to stay out of it. Twice. Or was it three times, now? She could already imagine the look on his face when he found out she'd gone creeping around again. No matter how good her intentions.

She was glad she'd told Jerlene flat out: *"I'm not dealing with Blagg. Keep me out of that one."* But that left them in an awkward little triangle of secrecy. Jerlene didn't want the sheriff to know anything. Bunny didn't want to deal with Blagg.

Victor might be dead, but everything he'd stirred up wasn't gone. Neither was the man with too much cologne and too-shiny shoes. If he had a gun, Bunny knew it would be too shiny, too. She needed to talk to someone who would listen and not berate her. She thought about driving up to chat with Granny Didima and glanced up the ridge in that direction. No smoke. Bunny wondered how deep she'd be in it by the time she'd make it back that way for a visit, and what kind of light G.Didi would cast on it all. What a mess of secrets. Then she remembered the delightful group of women that were there at the meeting she'd stumbled into. Parsy and Padda, and so many bright, sharp women with deep roots. She hadn't stopped thinking about them since. At least, in the quiet moments. Admittedly, there had been too few of those recently. She hoped she'd see them again. Not just because they were fascinating, and friendly, and stylish in an enchanted way, but to feel again how it feels to be with women who know exactly who they are. No apologies.

Bunny exhaled, then almost laughed. Fern! She would tell Fern. Fern would listen and not berate her. She'd also probably come up with three plans, all of them wild. But she'd listen. Bunny took one last sip, set her mug down, and stood. She left the package where it was, grabbed her keys, and was already easing the Keely down the drive before the sun climbed any higher.

Passing Hoodoo's on the way into town, her window cracked just enough to let in the fresh scent of juniper and cedar, she slowed and was tempted to pull in. Instead, she gave a little wave toward the low building and told herself she'd stop on the way home, both to thank him and to ask whether he'd heard anything more about Jake's truck. It could wait a little longer. She wanted to tell Fern everything that had happened and she didn't like talking on the phone.

When she stepped into Tickety-Boo, the clatter of cups and saucers greeted her, followed by a melange of scent that filled the air—cinnamon, cardamom, and vanilla.

Ivy looked up from behind the counter, smiling brightly. "Good morning, Bunny," Ivy said. "Tea? Coffee? A muffin?"

"Goodness," Bunny said, looking around her. "I've never seen the place so busy."

"Thursday mornings seem to be the busiest. Something about the research schedule. I've never figured it out. It'll change in September when the new students are settled in," she said. "You're just in time for the last of the honey biscuits. Sit. I'll bring you one with a strong blend. Looks like you could use it."

Bunny looked around for an open seat and discovered only the table that she'd come to think of as Jake and Misti's was available.

"Fern's not here just yet," Ivy said, returning with a small tray. "She's working a shift at the sheriff's office. Helps out some Thursdays, mostly morning filing, while Gloryanne's still out... well, you know where." She said it in a hushed tone, lightly glancing around. "She shouldn't be too long, I wouldn't think." She set a French press filled with a dark steaming liquid on the table. It smelled heavenly to Bunny. "Fern just keeps them caught up on things. She likes the order of it."

"I like order," Bunny said, moving her cup and napkin to make a straighter presentation. "I sure haven't seen much of it lately, though."

"I think it's good for her," Ivy said, taking a quick look around before pulling out the other chair and sitting. "When she first showed up here, she was all shadows. No spark in her. Broken hearts and all that, eh?"

Bunny nodded slowly. "Ah," she said, with a knowing smile. "The mop."

Ivy tilted her head. "The what now?"

"Oh, just something Fern said."

Ivy laughed, her eyes kind. "Well, whatever happened, and she still won't really talk about it, she seems better now. Cheerier. This town can be a hard place to land when you don't have roots. Even for folks with a backbone, like Fern. It can get lonely here." She shifted in her seat, adjusted the many bangles adorning her wrists, and looked around to be sure she wasn't needed immediately.

"It does," Bunny said, feeling the truth of it. "It really does."

They fell into easy conversation. Ivy asked about the garden and herbs. Bunny asked about baking and recipes. They chatted comfortably, Ivy getting up occasionally to grab another cinnamon bun or refill a cup of tea for someone. When she returned to the table once more, Bunny looked at the fanciful clock on the wall. "What time did you say Fern would be back?" It had been almost an hour and a half and she could feel herself start to grow restless.

Ivy wasn't concerned. "She should stroll in any moment, I would expect." She happily picked up empty cups and cleared away the tables as customers finished and went on their way.

"I wanted to tell you both, at the same time, about what happened last night," Bunny said, standing slowly. "I'm beginning to wonder if that's why Fern is later than usual. Maybe there is a lot more going on in the office."

"What happened?" Ivy asked, sitting back down. "You alright?"

Bunny offered a smile that wasn't quite as breezy as she meant it to be. "I'll definitely share. Later. I'm just going to pop over to the library and have a word with Misti."

"Will you stop back by after that?" Ivy asked. "I'm making a killer quiche for lunch."

"Sounds amazing." She already knew it would be.

The door to the library closed softly as Bunny stepped inside. The front counter was empty. Glancing around, the entire place seemed empty. It was unusually quiet, even for a library. Not peaceful or studious, but eerie. She walked slowly to the front desk. "Hello?" she called.

A faint noise answered. It wasn't a voice, but a soft sound, like a book shifting. Or maybe someone sniffing quietly.

Bunny turned and ventured into the area with reading tables and old computer monitors. No one. She walked through the A-F section of shelves. Empty. Then G-O, where she found Mrs. Kettel standing behind one of the book carts, a paperback clutched in one hand. Her cardigan was buttoned one button too high, and her usually immaculate bun had started to list sideways. "Mrs. Kettel?"

The older woman turned. Her face, so often a blend of pragmatism and no-nonsense, looked stricken, held together only by will. "Oh," she said faintly. "Bunny. It's just you."

Bunny nodded. "Just me. Are you alright?"

Mrs. Kettel swayed slightly and looked down at the book in her hand as if she'd only just realized it was there. "Misti didn't come home last night."

Bunny waited to see if she would say more.

"She always comes home," Mrs. Kettel continued, her voice tight. "Even if she's upset. Even if she's stayed out too late or stormed off about something I said. She always... comes home."

Bunny stepped closer. "She didn't call?"

Mrs. Kettel shook her head and stared at the book in her hand, which was shaking slightly. "I told myself not to worry. She'd be home. But, she ain't."

Bunny's mind turned quickly now, the image of the too-shiny man at the Tew house jumped into her thoughts. "Is there anywhere she might be?"

"If I knew where she *might* be," Mrs. Kettel snapped, and then immediately softened. "Forgive me, missy. I just... I'm not used to worrying like this." She lowered herself onto the edge of a window seat, both hands clasped together around the book she held. Her knuckles had gone pale.

Bunny sat down beside her. "What did she say the last time you saw her? How was she dressed?"

Mrs. Kettel thought for a moment, then finally set the book down, its cover severely warped. "She had on her new pink cardigan, the really soft one. Pearls. A pretty dress. She was dolled up, that's for sure. She looked like she was heading out for a night on the town."

Bunny nodded, encouraging her to go on.

"You don't go out on the town in the middle of the week, though, do you? Around this ol' holler? That'd be a weekend in Morgan City, as far as I remember." Mrs. Kettel's eyes were glistening.

"She didn't tell you who she was meeting? *If* she was meeting someone?"

Mrs. Kettel simply shook her head, one tear threading its way down and over the many lines of her cheek.

"We'll find her. I'll help." She touched Mrs. Kettel's hand and stood again, heart pounding a little too hard.

When she left the library, the sun was higher but feeling oddly cold on her skin. Her thoughts were reeling. She should go straight to the sheriff. *That* would be the obvious next step. But if Blagg were there...

The thought stopped her on the sidewalk. She'd told Jerlene she didn't want to deal with him, and she meant it. The man more than grated on her. The way he oozed entitlement in taking over an investigation. The way he seemed to thrill in being in on a secret no one else knew. The pleasure he seemed to take in looking down his crooked nose at her. Still, she had no idea who *was* at the office right now. Sheriff Greenwood may or may not be there. Fern might still be filing. Or not. Bunny didn't know, and it made her nerves jangle in the worst way.

She considered calling, just going back into the library and picking up the phone. She could leave a message for him and say her piece. But she didn't want to leave that message with just anyone, and she didn't have his number. Not his *real* one, anyway.

Hoodoo, though. *Hoodoo* would have the number. She almost turned to walk back into the library then and there. But the idea of going through a third party, even one as dear as Hoodoo, just to pull him into a wild goose chase... It felt like sending up a flare from the bottom of a well.

She glanced up the street, the Tickety-Boo sign was clearly visible from where she stood. *Maybe Fern was back by now.* She started walking, her stride quickening. As she passed the pharmacy, she caught sight of a familiar figure through the wide front window. Jerlene. She was sitting, squarely, in her wheelchair, arm extended upward toward a shelf that was clearly too high. Her hand opened and closed around empty air. Earl must be somewhere in the building. Bunny hesitated, then sighed. *Jerlene knows things.* She changed course and crossed the street.

When she pushed open the door, the buzz-snap sound and acrid smell of pine-scented floor cleaner hit her squarely in the nose. She stepped inside, scanning the aisles for Earl. Whatever they ended up discussing, she didn't think he needed to hear it.

Jerlene's arm dropped when she saw it was Bunny. She pushed her chair away from the shelves and folded her hands neatly in her lap. Neatly for Jerlene, anyway. "Hmph," she grunted. "Didn't expect you."

Bunny ignored the tone. "I didn't expect to come in," she said flatly. "I think we need to talk, though."

Jerlene looked her over, taking her time. "About?"

"An awful lot has gone wrong around the holler lately. I think you know things, Jerlene. I know you don't think much of me." Bunny took a deep breath. "Frankly, I don't know that you think much of anyone."

Something flickered across Jerlene's face, not surprise exactly, but something. When she didn't respond, Bunny continued, "Did you know that Misti is missing?"

"Nope," Jerlene said, her voice even. "So?"

Bunny shook her head. "Mrs. Kettel is beside herself, and that woman's not easy to rattle. I just want to know if you've seen anything... if you know anything."

Jerlene gave a small hum, pressing her lips into a line.

"Look, I have the feeling you expect me to run around town telling everyone I know your secret," Bunny whispered. "Don't worry. That's not what I'm here to do. But, I know you know more about what's going on than you let on, and I'd like you to tell me what you know."

"You're walking awful close to things that ain't your business," Jerlene said in a low hiss. "You really want to step in it?"

"What are you talking about? I'm in the middle of—whatever *this* is—whether I like it or not," Bunny snapped. "Victor's dead. Gloryanne's in jail. Jake's gone. Misti's missing. And your husband, lest I need remind you, owns the business at the center of all this. I'm not in the mood to play games with someone who lies every day." Bunny tapped the wheel of Jerlene's chair with the tip of her shoe.

Jerlene didn't flinch. Her jaw set hard.

Bunny bent down and looked her in the eye. "I don't want to be involved, but I *am*. So if you know something, now's the time." The air between them felt stale.

Finally, Jerlene exhaled through her nose in a sort of snort. "Dave got pulled in too deep. He didn't know at first. I believe that. But once you know, you're in it, and Vic made sure of that. He tied folks up in small ways. Ways that felt like favors at first."

"And the man from New York?"

"Victor promised him deliveries. Regular ones. He started with car parts, then moved to jewelry, maybe other things. Dave thought it was small-time. A fence-and-forget kind of thing."

"And Jake?"

"Was useful," Jerlene said dismissively. "He moved things. Didn't talk."

"And Misti?"

"Pretty girl. Big dreams. Not too bright. She was getting gifts for her part."

"And what *was* her part?"

"That part, I'm not sure about," Jerlene said, looking around for Earl. "I know what Dave knows. Dave doesn't know everything."

"Misti didn't come home last night," Bunny repeated. "If this man from New York came looking for... missing deliveries? Money owed to him or his bosses. Answers. Wouldn't Dave know?"

Jerlene was silent for several moments. "He's not supposed to talk. Even to me. Blagg gave him an ultimatum."

"He gets no immunity if the investigation is compromised by..." Bunny mused.

"By his big mouth," Jerlene finished for her. "Fine by me. I don't want anyone to know what a fool he's been. Especially the sheriff."

"So, you don't know where Jake is. You don't know where Misti is. You have no ideas about either one."

"No, but I know both of them were acting weird before I left my shift here on that Friday. I saw Jake leave the Tew house the night of the fire. At least, it looked like him. And I know there was another fire that night. I passed it around the same time I saw Misti off the road with armfuls of flowers like she was taking up arranging." She stared at Bunny.

"Where did you pass the other fire? And Misti gathering... flowers?"

"I passed both on the way to Uncle Leo's when Dave said I should find something to do because he had business in Morgan City."

Bunny's heart stuttered. "Where would you say the other fire was?"

"Smelled like someone making a bonfire in the old gravel pit," Jerlene said. "You know, the kind macho men who don't know how to start a fire make, with lots of kerosene or gasoline or..." She didn't finish.

"Like it would smell if you set a delivery truck on fire?" Bunny looked around at the aisle they occupied, as if searching for a sign. "Maybe someone should look there," she said, more to herself than anyone.

Jerlene looked up at her, eyes sharp now. "You know something I don't?"

"I honestly can't say." Bunny turned and walked toward the door.

"You can't? Or you won't?" Jerlene called after her. "I've told you all I know, Bunny Sparks. Now, what are you going to do with it?"

"Whatever I have to."

Chapter Eighteen

When Bunny returned to Tickety-Boo for the second time that day, the space had quieted significantly. The sunlight was now casting long shadows outside. Only one customer remained, a man seated near the window, reading a paperback. Fern stood behind the counter, wiping down the display cases. When she looked up and saw Bunny, a smile broke across her face. Until she really saw her. Then her brows knit together.

"Where have you been?" she asked, coming around the counter.

"I'll tell you. But not here." Bunny glanced at the man still nursing his tea.

From behind the beaded curtain, Ivy called out, "Is that Bunny? I saved you a slice of quiche, Bunny! Missed you at lunch."

"That was kind of you," Bunny called back, managing a smile. "I appreciate it. But I'm too jumpy to eat just now."

Fern motioned toward the kitchen. "Let's go help Ivy. She was just starting cleanup. We'll talk in the back."

Bunny nodded, following Fern through the beads and into the cozy chaos of the kitchen. Ivy was already stacking plates, humming under her breath. "Oh good," Ivy said brightly, not turning. "More hands."

"We've got more than hands," Fern said. "We've got news."

That got Ivy's attention. She turned fully, hands on hips, and looked at Bunny. "Is this about Misti? Mrs. Kettel called and asked if we'd seen her. She sounded afraid."

"It's not entirely about Misti," Bunny said, picking up a stack of dessert plates. "But she's definitely involved. Listen..."

As they moved about the kitchen, clearing counters and washing dishes, Bunny filled them in. How she'd spotted the burned-out wreck of Jake's truck from the road above the gravel pit. How she hadn't gone all the way down to look—too steep, too dangerous—but she knew it was his delivery truck all the same.

"How long has it been down there?" Ivy asked.

"I don't know. Long enough to no longer smolder, I guess. I stopped at Hoodoo's and he got in touch with the sheriff."

"I heard!" Fern said.

"The sheriff was in this morning, then?" Bunny asked.

"Oh, yes, he was in and all sorts of news was whipping around the office. Blagg was red-faced and huffing like the Big Bad Wolf, and the sheriff stayed cool as could be. Though I know he can't stand the guy." Fern grinned. "But, tell me what happened to *you*."

"The sheriff and Deputy Rawlings showed up and told me to go home." She put the last of the dishes in the sink. "I was dismissed. So, I went home."

Fern raised an eyebrow. "That's not where this ends, I assume."

"No. After I was in bed, looking forward to a good night's sleep, I heard that beep cars make now when they lock or unlock. That car was the same car we saw from New York."

"It showed up at your house?" Ivy was incredulous.

"It was parked on the side of the road nearby. The man driving it wasn't looking for my house, though, he was looking for the Tew's house.

He had a map and was teed off about not having a signal on his cell phone."

"Yeah, everyone is upset about that, at first," Ivy nodded. "I was. Until I embraced the quiet and not being tethered to everyone all the time."

Fern nodded in agreement, then looked back to Bunny. "How did you know it was the same car?"

"That plate," Bunny said. "It was the same one."

"You remembered that?" Fern and Ivy asked, in unison.

"It was a vanity plate. Hard to forget," Bunny said, "New York GT2GO."

Ivy mused. "Get to go? Like a take-out place?"

Fern looked up at the ceiling. "No. No. Got to go. Like, a cry for help between rest stops. The driver has incontinence."

Bunny laughed, despite herself. "I've no idea what it means, but it was the same car, that's certain."

Fern got serious. "Then what happened?"

"When he left, I followed him. He headed toward the Tew house. Leo's place is just across the drive, and I thought... well, I couldn't let it go. Not if Leo might be in trouble."

"So you tailed him," Ivy said flatly, not surprised.

"I followed him," Bunny confirmed. "And when I got there, the man was prowling around outside the Tew house. He didn't see me, but he was checking the doors, peering in the windows. Cursing a lot because his very shiny shoes were getting dirty."

"And Leo?" Fern asked.

"I didn't see him. But I saw someone else. Jerlene."

"What was *she* doing?"

"She was sitting on Leo's porch, just watching. Like she'd been there a while. I didn't even know she was there at first."

Fern and Ivy both wiped counters, both waiting for the next part of the story. "Then what?" Ivy demanded.

"We watched him, the guy from New York, and we talked. She knows a *lot* of things, Fern. A lot of things about what's been going on in Dave's garage, a smuggling ring that she said Victor got them all tangled up in, and she said that guy from New York is here to collect."

"So, what was in the boxes?" Fern asked. "Drugs? Guns?"

"According to Jerlene, car parts, mostly. Jerlene wasn't sure about everything they were smuggling. What she *was* sure about is that man from New York. She said he already cleaned out Dave's garage. Took what his bosses wanted. Now he wants Victor."

"But Victor's dead," Fern said quietly.

"Maybe," Bunny said. "Remember what Gloryanne said? She said he isn't."

"Gloryanne is grief-stricken," Fern said.

"Possibly. I don't know," Bunny said, peering back out into the shop to see if the last remaining customer was still there. He was sitting quietly, peering into his cup.

When Ivy peered out, too, she wiped her hands and headed out to see if he needed anything else. She gave both of them a look that said, 'I don't want to miss anything.'

Fern waved at Bunny. "I'll fill her in later. Go on."

"Not much more happened. He left. But today I wanted to ask Misti what she knew and Mrs. Kettel said she didn't come home last night. I've never seen her so upset."

"That's not good," Fern said. "I suspect she'll turn up though. She's probably mad that we were grilling her grandma. Anyway, I have news, too. Wanna hear?"

Bunny nodded, though her stomach wasn't so sure.

"So..." Fern began, "I was in the Sheriff's Office this morning, doing my filing. Blagg was storming around the office like a bull because the sheriff got some reports back and wouldn't let him see 'em. He said they were all to do with Jake's disappearance and that was *his* part of the investigation. Rawlings couldn't help but snicker every time Blagg turned his back."

Bunny didn't want to hear about Blagg. "What did the reports say?"

Fern peeked into the front. Ivy was collecting things from the now-empty table. "Well, first, the toxicology report came back," she said. "The plants weren't poisonous. But they did find digoxin and a lot of alcohol."

"So, he *was* poisoned," Bunny gasped.

"There's more," Fern said. "There was an accelerant used on Jake's truck, and it *was* Jake's truck, by the way. And the same accelerant was used on Gloryanne's house the night of the fire."

Ivy quickly returned and put the cup and saucer she'd collected on the counter. "What'd I miss?"

"You've already heard this part," Fern told her, turning back to Bunny. "Digoxin." Fern said. "Heart medicine. That's digitalis... from foxglove. Right?"

Bunny nodded. "Right."

"That means someone knew what they were doing," Ivy said grimly.

They stood silent for a moment, the tic-tic of the clock in the other room the only sound.

"Did you know that Dave Baer takes heart medication?" Bunny looked from Ivy to Fern and back again.

Both looked at her, eyes wide. She tapped her temple, quick and light. "This is a lot. Misti's missing. That's what we need to focus on, I think. Where is she?" It was a question, but she didn't seem to be asking anyone in particular. "The man from New York may or may not be a problem.

Jake's missing and his truck is destroyed. And now we know someone poisoned Victor and then tried to make it look like I had something to do with it but they chose the wrong plant."

"Oh, there's one more thing," Fern added. "Gloryanne is starting to sing like a canary." She grinned. "A very plump canary with brassy hennaed feathers."

"Wait. Gloryanne's talking to *Blagg*?"

Fern slid the last stack of clean plates onto the shelf. "Oh, she's practically putting on a floor show down at the station."

"She did call the insurance company looking for money," Ivy said, drying her hands on a dish towel and nodding solemnly.

"Which is how Blagg got to drag her in. Insurance fraud, conspiracy, 'premeditated filing,' whatever charge fits best in his fat binder." Fern tossed her dish towel on a hook, peeled off her apron, and swiped her forehead with the back of her hand. "Anyone want something cold? We're all done here, right, Ivy?"

Ivy nodded and began to untie her own apron, then changed her mind. "You and Bunny head out to the courtyard," she said. "I've heard this part. I'll bring out the refreshments."

On the patio behind the tea shop, Fern scanned the clouds. "Looks like rain is on the way."

Bunny looked beyond the courtyard gates at the trees. "It's possible," she said.

Fern continued. "Anyway, Blagg doesn't care about charges for Gloryanne unless it leads directly to nabbing the ring leader of the smuggling operation."

"And that would be... Victor, right?" Bunny asked.

"Yep," Fern said, punctuating the 'p.' "Gloryanne is insisting he isn't dead."

"The sheriff is just letting Blagg lean on her?"

"Oh, he's letting it happen alright. Gloryanne loves the sound of her own voice and being center stage. I think the sheriff would like that... shall we say, 'quality,' put to good use for once." Fern grinned. "Rawlings can't get enough of it. He sees the look on Blagg's face after he's spent more than five minutes with her and has to excuse himself before he busts a gut."

"I don't know if that's genius or just plain mean."

"Could be a little of both," Fern said.

They both looked up when Ivy brought a tray out to them, setting it on the table and looking at Fern. "What'd I miss?"

"Bunny thinks the sheriff is a sadistic genius," Fern said.

Ivy gave her a look. "What?"

"For what he's doing to both Blagg and Gloryanne... and all at the same time," she explained.

Ivy nodded. "You think she knows what happened to Misti?"

"If she does, she hasn't said anything that's gotten around the office," Fern said.

Bunny took an icy glass of fragrant tea from the tray and took a long sip. "I can't shake the feeling that the man from New York got her. She's involved. She must be scared to death. If she's not..."

There was a long pause.

"Dead?" Fern said, finally.

Both Ivy and Bunny gaped at her.

"What? Don't act as if we weren't all thinking it," Fern admonished.

"You don't think Jake killed her, do you?" Ivy held her glass to her forehead. "I mean, if he killed Victor Tew, why not her?"

"Why would he kill her, though?" Bunny asked. "He had a thing for her, didn't he?"

"Yes, it was more than obvious," Ivy agreed. "The way he looked at her. The way he asked about her when he was waiting. She always kept him waiting, by the way. He'd show up, eager as ever, and ask if she was here. A jumble of nerves until she showed up. She didn't feel the same. You could tell."

"Maybe that's why he killed her," Fern said.

Ivy shook her head. "I think Jake was sweet."

Fern nodded. "Maybe he was tired of being strung along. I also think he was tired of being broke, tired of making deliveries for peanuts."

Bunny chewed her lip. "So, he burned his own truck, killed Victor, then killed Misti? Why?"

Fern picked up her glass and looked through it at the clouds rolling in. "Maybe he was also tired of being played."

Bunny looked down, her voice low. "Jerlene did say she thought she saw him leaving the Tew place the night of the fire. But..."

"But, Jerlene is blind as a bat."

Bunny gave her a look. "Bats aren't blind, you know."

Fern stared at her. "You get the point. Jerlene's spectacles are thick as Crown glass. She could've seen Bigfoot on a bicycle."

"Everyone seems to be lying," Ivy said quietly.

They looked at each other in heavy silence, the shadows deepening across the patio. Finally, Fern spoke, her voice grim and steady. "So, Misti's missing. Victor might be alive. Jake might be anywhere. Gloryanne's the star of her own soap opera. And somewhere out there is a man with shiny shoes from New York who wants something. What?"

Bunny felt the truth settle in her gut like a cold stone. "He wants something, that's certain. And I don't think he plans to leave empty-handed."

Fern turned and faced Bunny, her face serious. "What should we do?"

Bunny steeled her resolve. "I don't know exactly... but I think I know where we need to start."

Chapter Nineteen

The road curved like a lazy ribbon through the woods, the trees casting long shadows as the sun slipped lower. It would be behind the ridge soon. Bunny eased her foot off the pedal, squinting toward the embankment.

Fern leaned forward, elbows on the dash. "Is this it?"

"Yes," Bunny confirmed. "Jerlene said it was right around here, a mile or two before the gravel pit."

Fern looked hard, shaking her head. "Didn't she also claim a bobcat stole her uncle's canoe?"

Bunny glanced at her, steering carefully along the gravel shoulder. "Maybe, but *this* story came without moonshine." On the slope to their left, a burst of purple-pink blossoms, tall and luminous, swayed gently in clusters. "I think this is it," Bunny announced. "We'll walk from here."

The air smelled warm and earthy, the way a forest does before rain. Bunny bent, brushing her hand along slender stalks of flowers and tall grass. Fern squatted down next to her. "How will we know she was here? What are we looking for?" she asked.

"I'm not sure."

Fern stood and moved a few feet ahead, looking around her. "What'd you say these are called again?"

"Fireweed," Bunny said. "Some people confuse it with foxglove, but it's not poisonous. In fact, the flowers are edible. The grannies used to make a beautiful pink jelly with the blossoms. No part of foxglove is edible."

"Does it have medicinal properties?"

"Not many, as far as I know," Bunny considered.

Fern stood and surveyed the area. The fireweed grew throughout the clearing, with a few patches near the line of trees that led deeper into the forest. "Oh, look. These look cut clean. A whole bunch of them, cut right near the base." She pointed toward a cluster of jagged stems, the flowering tops nowhere in sight.

"Well, Jerlene was at least right about someone cutting flowers here," Bunny said. "But was she right about it being Misti? And was Misti the reason they were left all around the Tew house when it was set on fire?"

"And, did she do it on her own, or did someone tell her to do it?" Fern offered.

"And did that someone mean for it to be foxglove, but they didn't know the difference?"

Fern looked at her sideways. "You mean... like trying to make it look like you had something to do with the murder or the fire, or both?"

Bunny didn't answer. She brushed her hands off on her apron. Yet again, she'd forgotten to take it off before she left that morning.

"What next?" Fern asked.

Bunny tracked the sun to see how much time they might have. Not much. "Let's go to the gravel pit. See if Jake's truck is still there."

They walked back to the Keely in silence and drove the rest of the way without speaking. The road dipped and curved, framed in alder and pine. As they neared the place where Jake's truck went over, the young trees splintered in two were obvious now that that Bunny knew where they were. The grass was still flat where the sheriff and Rawlings parked to inspect the area. Bunny slowed and pulled onto the shoulder near the caution tape flapping in the breeze, half torn from the lathe where it was tied.

"So, he just drove over the edge?" Fern said, pointing to the tire gouges.

Bunny nodded absently, scanning the ground. She took a step, then stopped. Something caught her eye. Half-buried in the gravel was a long, flat carpenter's pencil. She bent down and held it up.

Fern peered at it. "Weird place for one of those."

Bunny turned it in her hand. "Did you ever meet Victor Tew?" she asked.

Fern thought. "More than once. He walked over and got coffees whenever he was at Baer's Garage, which lately was a lot." She thought a moment more. "He always had one of those pencils, come to think of it. Behind his ear."

Bunny slipped the pencil into the pocket of her apron and they followed an overgrown path down the embankment to the gravel pit below. The air changed as they descended, growing cooler. The truck was still sat at the bottom, crumpled and charred. The air still smelled of burnt oil. Fern circled the wreck, careful not to touch anything. "Wow," she said. "Just wow."

Bunny peered into the cab. "You'd think if someone wanted to disappear, they'd do a better job hiding their tracks."

They poked around for a few minutes, looking around the shell of the truck. Fern picked up a stick and opened the rear door of the trailer a little wider. The sound of rusted hinges creaking echoed around them. She pulled out a flashlight and shone it inside the cargo box.

"You thought to bring a flashlight?"

Fern smirked at her. "You didn't? Now that it's officially dark, we're lucky *one* of us thought ahead."

Bunny shook her head in disbelief. "You're amazing."

"Hey, look," Fern said. "Is that a hidden compartment?"

Bunny looked intently where the beam of light indicated. "I don't know. Maybe."

Fern continued to look. "Think I should crawl up in there and check?"

"Definitely not." Bunny was emphatic. "The sheriff will already be mad at me for just snooping around. If we mess up evidence, he'll kill me."

Then Fern froze. "Did you hear that?"

Bunny straightened. "What?"

Crunch.

A footstep, slow and deliberate, on the gravel behind them. Then a beam of light cut through the dusk, *blinding*. A voice followed, low, brusque and far too amused. "Now, what would two lovely ladies be doing poking around a burned-out truck in the dark... all alone?"

Bunny's blood ran cold. Fern stepped slightly in front of her, squinting into the beam. "Victor?"

The beam of the flashlight dipped slightly, just enough to reveal the glint of Victor Tew's smile. "Well, well," he said. "You're quicker than you look."

Fern bristled, a flash of irritation crossing her face. Bunny took a slow breath, keeping her posture relaxed, but her insides were blasting a silent alarm that said 'we are in serious danger.' She stepped out from behind Fern. "Victor, what in the world are you doing here? Everyone thinks you died. Horribly, in fact."

Victor chuckled and stepped closer, the flashlight swinging casually at his side. "I didn't expect you two. I figured Blagg's goons would be sniffing around first."

"They are," Fern said. "Everywhere, in fact. We just beat them to Jake's truck. Maybe we're smarter than they are."

He smirked. "That's not saying much." He swept the light past them, landing briefly on the wreckage, then back to Bunny's face. "You want to know how I did it, don't you? That's why you're here."

Bunny didn't blink. "Not really. We've already figured most of it out."

Victor tilted his head. "Oh yeah?"

"Apparently, you faked your own death. Set fire to your house." She paused while her mind raced, the pieces falling into place like a dark puzzle. She couldn't risk revealing too much. Forcing her voice to steady, feigning curiosity, she asked, "Where's Jake? Did he help you?"

He laughed. "You've got it all figured out, huh?"

"What have you done with Misti?" Bunny pressed on. "How in the world did you get her to go along with this stupid scheme?"

Victor gave another short laugh. "You think she needed convincing? Please. Misti jumped at the chance to feel important. All I had to do was string her along with a few shiny things."

"She trusted you." Bunny's voice softened, just slightly. "So did I."

Victor snorted. "She's naive. Small town girl gets a promise of big city lights? A pearl here, a diamond there. She was easy."

Fern shifted beside Bunny, tensing. Bunny kept her tone even. "And Jake?"

"Jake was a useful tool for awhile, but when you don't need a tool anymore, then they're just dead weight," Victor said bluntly.

"Was?" Bunny felt something inside her sink.

Victor swung the flashlight around in a circle, the beam arcing over them. "He was a lovesick puppy with no sense of reality. Misti had him wrapped around her little finger faster than a bluegill on a spinner."

"So you used her to *kill* Jake?" Bunny felt her stomach lurch. She reached out and grabbed Fern to steady herself.

"Like I said, she was easy. I told her I needed him for just one more delivery, that's all. She didn't even ask why. She didn't want to know.

She never did, really." He smirked. "And it didn't take much to convince him."

Bunny released Fern, who was holding on tightly, and looked around them. The sun was below the mountain now, and it would soon be pitch black. She felt anger mixed with the fear in the pit of her stomach. Jake hadn't been the sharpest tool in the shed, but he'd deserved better.

"So what was the endgame?" Fern asked. "You kill Jake, torch the truck, and run off with Misti and Gloryanne like your own little harem? Or were you planning to ditch Gloryanne after she hauled all those stolen electronics around for you?" She tilted her head. "We saw what was in her trunk."

Victor's grinned. "Oh, sweetheart. I wasn't running off with anyone. Gloryanne has her fantasy and she had no idea what was ever in the back of her car. She didn't know a thing and would never question a good reason to be around Dave Baer." His grin sharpened. "And if she *had* known?" He gave a small, amused shrug. "She talks too much. Always has. If Gloryanne were in on anything, everyone in this town would have known by lunchtime." His eyes narrowed. "I figured if she ever did catch on, I'd have to deal with her. Permanently."

The last word hung there.

"But she never did," he went on lightly. "Why would she? A clerk for the Sheriff's Office, driving around town like a good little local. No one would ever suspect her of hauling anything worse than gossip." He rolled his shoulders. It was a small movement that made Bunny's skin prickle. "She's got plausible deniability. Misti has her trinkets. And me? I have a boat waiting and a new name already printed on my passport."

Bunny studied him for a moment. "So why are you still here? Slumming it with the coyotes?"

Victor's face twitched. Just for a second.

And Bunny saw it. "Oh... you need the insurance payout."

Victor's expression flattened. "It takes time."

"You mean, you *thought* it would take time. But I think something else happened." Bunny crossed her arms. "Tell me, Victor... why haven't you tried to leave? Why hole up in the gravel pit like a fugitive gopher?"

Victor didn't answer.

Bunny took a slow step sideways. "Because you know someone's looking for you, don't you?"

His eyes flicked to the darkness beyond the rocks. He didn't speak. "You two only found me by luck. No one ever comes down here."

Bunny felt his uncertainty. "But we did. And so will the man from New York. You know the one. Italian leather shoes? Very shiny. He's looking for you. What will he do when he finds you, Victor?"

Victor's jaw clenched.

"Just how many people *were* you betraying?"

Victor's eyes narrowed, calculating. "What man from New York?"

"I don't know him personally," Bunny said. "But I'll never forget those shoes."

Victor was quiet, until, "That's a bluff of some kind. He's not here."

Bunny shrugged. "Maybe not here-here. But close."

That hit. Victor's face tightened.

"Oh no!" Fern cried, her eyes wide and voice full of theatrical panic. "Look out behind you!"

Then she ran. Not a stumble or a stagger, but a full-on sprint, kicking up gravel behind her. She whipped past the truck and up the embankment, calling over her shoulder to Bunny, "You run, too!"

But Bunny was already gone, her legs jolted to life by pure adrenaline. She ignored her knees screaming in protest, her apron flapping like a cape, as she wove between darkened piles of rock and weed-strewn debris. Behind her, she could hear Victor, his breath heavy, his boots slamming against the uneven ground, curses flying. She turned sharply, veering toward a cluster of boulders, trying to make herself smaller and harder to follow. She fought the urge to look back, but when she finally glanced over her shoulder to see how close he was, her apron snagged on something, throwing her off balance. She landed hard on her hip with a grunt.

The pain hit fast and hot.

She tried to suppress a scream. *Of course.* Just like every scary movie, she thought, clenching her teeth, the woman looks back and trips like an idiot. She pressed herself up, gasping, trying not to cry out. The moon wasn't up yet and the dark was thick, but that worked both ways. He couldn't see her, either.

He was getting closer. "I see you! You can't hide forever!" he called behind her. But his voice wasn't so sure now. He was wheezing. Slowing.

Bunny moved, quieter now, hands groping along the side of a large boulder. Then, she felt it. Not stone. Not wind.

Fabric. Soft, luxurious fabric.

She looked down, heart thudding, at two wide, terrified eyes that met hers in the dark.

Misti. Her hair was tangled, her face streaked with grime and fear. She looked like she hadn't slept.

Bunny didn't speak. She just lifted one trembling finger to her lips. "Shhh."

Misti nodded and they crouched together behind the rocks, listening.

Victor was cursing louder, his voice wobbling at the edges. "You think you're clever? You think you're smarter than me? This is all going to come crashing down on—"

There was a sharp thud. The sound of sliding gravel. A yelp.

Then silence.

Bunny and Misti both held their breath.

Seconds passed. Then minutes.

Then, gently, Bunny reached out, took Misti's trembling hand in hers. and gave it a small, steadying squeeze. It was time to move. She winced as she rose, one hand still clutching Misti's whose shaking fingers gripped tightly around hers. They picked their way carefully up the embankment, feet slipping in the loose gravel. "It's not far," Bunny whispered.

Misti didn't speak, just followed, eyes wide and glistening. She hadn't let go of Bunny's hand once.

When they reached the road, the sound of footsteps and a low voice reached them first, followed by the unmistakable silhouette of Hoodoo, lantern in hand. Fern walked beside him, her face dirt-streaked and grinning with relief. There was also a third person with them. Bunny blinked several times to be sure, but there she was—Jerlene. Upright. Walking on her own two feet.

"Well, I'll be," Bunny breathed.

Fern broke into a jog toward her. "Thank heavens," she said. "You're alright!"

Hoodoo arrived seconds later, giving Bunny a once-over, then Misti. "Sheriff's on his way," he said. "If that snake is still down there, he won't be for long." He stopped and looked at Bunny. "Is he still down there?"

Bunny nodded.

He reached out, gently taking her elbow. "Come on. Let's get you both inside. You've had enough excitement for one lifetime."

Chapter Twenty

I nside Cran General, the old place smelled like warm leather and strong coffee. Bunny took it in, her heartbeat finally calming, while Hoodoo coaxed Misti to let go of Bunny's hand and guided her to a chair. "Warm barley tea," he said. "Not fancy, but kind on the stomach." He poured carefully. "You girls look like you've wrestled a bear."

Fern pulled up a stool beside Bunny and gave her a meaningful look. "I told him what happened," she said. "Jerlene was already here when I came tearing in like a banshee."

Bunny turned toward the woman leaning quietly against the counter, thick lenses obscuring her eyes. "Why?" Bunny asked softly. "How did you know?"

Jerlene adjusted her glasses. "I didn't know. I just guessed. After your visit, I was thinking... what you said about Mrs. Kettel and Misti..." She gave a half-smile. "I figured I owed you."

Bunny blinked at her. "You owe me?"

"Well," Jerlene said. "I owed your granny."

Fern sipped her tea, ears perked. "Granny Gene?"

Jerlene nodded slowly. "Years ago, I asked her for a remedy. I wanted something to keep my husband's attention where it belonged."

Fern blew over the rim of her cup. "A love potion? You wanted a love potion."

Jerlene chuckled, sad and low. "Yeah... I wanted a love potion. For my own husband."

Fern was rapt. "Did she give you one?"

"No." Jerlene shook her head. "She told me, 'One word... Honesty.' That was the remedy. She told me to speak the truth. To him. To myself. Most of all to myself." She paused. "I didn't listen."

Fern looked at Bunny, then back to Jerlene. "So, you think you're paying Granny Gene back for that."

"I should have listened to her. She was right. She was almost always right. I envied you, that, Bunny," Jerlene said.

For a moment, the room was quiet, broken only by the distant wail of sirens drawing nearer. Misti sat very still, her fingers tracing the edge of a tear in her cashmere cardigan. It may have been the pink one but it was a dirty gray now. Three buttons were missing. With a soft sigh, she pulled it from her shoulders, held it for a moment in her lap, then let it drop to the floor.

Feeling something dig into her side, Bunny reached into her apron pocket and pulled out the carpenter's pencil she'd found where Jake's truck had gone over the embankment. She placed it on the table with a sharp clack. No one said anything. She reached out and took Misti's hand again. Misti didn't look up. She just gripped back, holding tight, like someone trying not to slip under.

The sound of sirens was replaced by the low rumble of a cruiser pulling up outside.

Bunny stood slowly, knees aching all over again, as the front door creaked open and Sheriff Greenwood stepped in, his broad shoulders backlit by the porch light. Behind him, Rawlings entered, alert and scanning the room like he expected more trouble to come busting up through the floorboards.

"Evening," the sheriff said, his voice low.

"Evening, Sheriff," Hoodoo returned. "Kettle's still warm, if you want something."

Greenwood shook his head. "Blagg's taken over down at the gravel pit." His tone suggested exactly how he felt about that. "He considers Tew *his* bounty. He always did have a possessive streak."

"Good," Hoodoo said. "The snake is with the honey badger."

Fern looked at him quizzically.

"Honey badgers eat snakes," he explained.

"He can have him," Bunny said, under her breath.

Rawlings stepped around the sheriff and reached for the cup Hoodoo offered. He grinned, but glanced at the sheriff before adding, "He's welcome to the paperwork, too."

"Amen to *that*," Fern said.

Greenwood gave a small, tight smile. "Amen."

Fern crossed her arms. "So, they got him?"

The sheriff nodded. "Caught, cuffed, and loaded into the back of Blagg's Tahoe. I'm surprised he didn't want to tie him to the hood like a prize buck."

"Congratulations to him," Hoodoo said flatly. Then added, "Figured you might want the rundown. I can walk you through if you follow me outside, boys. Let's give the ladies a moment to decompress."

The sheriff nodded, but his eyes locked on Bunny, brow creased. Then he turned and walked back out onto the porch, Rawlings right behind.

Hoodoo winked at Bunny. "I'll keep it clean and simple. He'll want to talk to you anyway, but you just relax for now. Drink some tea."

She adjusted her apron, fingers grazing the tear left by the rock that had nearly taken her out. "You can tell him that I know we should've waited. I should've stayed out of it. But..."

"You did what you thought you had to," Hoodoo said. "I'll tell him."

Bunny breathed a sigh of relief, then leaned back in her chair, looking around. She caught Fern motioning toward the window with her chin and turned to see the sheriff looking through the glass at her. She couldn't make out everything that was said, but she heard, "Tell her to get on home. I'll want to see her…" Something muffled, then, "I'll get Misti to the station and then home."

Misti must have heard it, too, because she stood without argument. She was still silent, still pale, one arm held tightly across her middle as if bracing herself.

Rawlings opened the door for her, as if he heard her coming. The sheriff peered back inside. "I'd like to talk to you both tomorrow morning. At the station," he said to Fern and Bunny.

Fern nodded. "You got it."

Jerlene stood up and said, "What about me, Sheriff?"

There was no gushing this time.

He looked her up and down, his expression even, despite the discovery she wasn't in a wheelchair. "We'll be in touch. You'll most likely hear from Blagg's team."

Bunny opened her mouth, ready with an apology, but the sheriff was halfway to his cruiser before any sound came out.

Jerlene walked to the door. "I'll get on home now, then." She looked around, first to Hoodoo, then to Bunny. "I guess I have a lot of explaining to do."

Fern gave Bunny a tired smile.

When it was just the three of them, Hoodoo crossed his arms and looked at Bunny. "He's not mad, you know?" he said. "Not like you think."

She looked at him. "He looks mad."

"No," Fern said, "He looked like a man who thought he nearly lost something."

Bunny frowned. "You mean the case?"

Hoodoo shook his head and chuckled, but she didn't ask. The kettle let out a low hiss, just shy of a whistle, and Bunny moved to lift it before it made a fuss. She poured the water into ceramic mugs and set them on the table.

Fern wandered in from the guestroom wrapped in a quilt Bunny had pulled from the cedar chest, her short hair jutting out in all directions. "You have the coziest, most beautiful house on earth, did you know that?"

Bunny smiled faintly as she set a spoon beside Fern's cup. "It's drafty in the winter, and half the windows stick."

"It's perfect." Fern sank into the chair, pulling the quilt tighter. "The guestroom is so Santa Fe."

"Gigi was good friends with Georgia O'Keefe. Back in the 1970s, I think."

"Well, it's beautiful. Magical. I half expected the teacups to pour themselves. The light in the bathroom clicked on like it read my mind, and your fridge hums like it's keeping secrets."

Bunny gave her a slight smile.

Fern looked at her earnestly. "Are you sure you don't know how any of it works?"

Bunny glanced over the rim of her mug. "It's on my list."

Fern chuckled softly. "Of course, it is."

For a while, the only sound was the soft clink of spoons and the kettle's residual sputtering on the stove. Outside, the morning dew was drying here and there on green leaves and colorful petals.

Fern finally spoke again. "Now that things are going to calm down again, what are your plans?"

"I want to remember what Granny Didima told me..." Bunny rubbed her hip, still bruised and sore. "...to keep my eyes ahead of me. I want to get back to what I was creating," she said, looking out at the gardens. "I want to start going through rooms and boxes I've been avoiding."

"That should be exciting, actually," Fern said. "If you need any help, just let me know."

Bunny smiled at her. "First, I'll get things ready for the study group I was planning. Priscilla has agreed to teach for us, at least the first time."

"Ivy mentioned that you'd talked to her. You'll love Cilla. She does readings at the tea shop sometimes. Her bookshop is amazing." Fern sipped her tea.

"I want to spend more time there, when there *is* more time, that is," Bunny said. "Anyway, a lot has happened. I'll check in with G.Didi soon. I have a new word for her... 'Verisimilitude.'"

"What does that mean?"

"The appearance of being true or real."

"Good word."

"Yeah, she collects them. Then I will call my sister. She'll be happy to hear I'm branching out, becoming more a part of the community, instead of just keeping to myself."

"I'm happy about that, too." Fern smiled.

"But, I'll plan to keep my head down." She stirred her cup and looked back out at the gardens. The deep maroon color of her favorite roses, the spires of purple foxglove and blue delphinium, and masses of mahogany cosmos, all seemed to compliment each other.

Fern looked at her for a moment. She bit her lip, then sighed. "He looked at you like a man nearly undone, you know."

Bunny looked up. "Who?"

Fern gave her a flat look. "The sheriff. Cal Greenwood."

Bunny let the words hang in the air. She stared into her tea.

"I know that look," Fern added. "I've only seen it a few times, and never directed at me."

Bunny gave a half-laugh. "He's clearly someone who cares about the citizens of this holler. He cares about the people in his town. That's all."

Fern didn't answer. She took a sip and leaned back in her chair, watching Bunny quietly.

After a pause, Bunny said, "I hope he realizes I wasn't trying to be reckless. I just... someone had to help Misti. Someone had to do something."

"You did," Fern said.

Bunny looked up at her and smiled. "Thanks for your help, by the way."

Fern shrugged. "Anyway. We should probably get dressed and get it over with. I'm hoping Blagg is long gone, now that he got what he came for, and Friday is a busy day at the tea shop."

Chapter Twenty-One

The sheriff's office sat beneath the same eave of peeling white paint it had for fifty years, stoic and plain against the rising sun. Bunny parked out front and turned off the ignition with a sigh.

"I'll be right there with you," Fern said, one foot already on the ground. "I'm sure he may want to talk to each of us alone. I'll keep Rawlings company."

Bunny gave her a tired smile. "You're a good friend."

Fern winked. "You're lucky I didn't let Victor tie you to a train track just so I could rescue you and claim the glory."

Bunny gave a weak laugh and opened the door.

Inside, the air was cool and quiet, punctuated only by the distant hum of the overhead lights. Deputy Rawlings gave her a respectful nod from his desk and jerked a thumb toward the back. "He's waitin'." She nodded and walked slowly past the rows of worn filing cabinets, while Fern planted herself on Rawlings' desk. The sheriff's door stood ajar. He was standing by the window, arms crossed, staring out at the road that curved toward the hills.

"Sheriff?" Bunny said, her voice soft.

Greenwood turned. His expression was unreadable. "Come in, Miss Sparks. Sit down." He gestured to the chair opposite his desk, then took a seat himself. The chair creaked under his weight like it had a hundred times before, but the quiet between them was different. Dense. Waiting. "I want to start by saying thank you," he said.

Bunny didn't quite manage to hide her surprise, her mouth falling open before she could stop herself. She snapped it shut. "For what?"

"For getting to Misti before anyone else did. For not giving up. For keeping your head when you could've... well, lost a lot more than your footing."

She looked down at her hands. "I just..."

He leaned forward, resting his elbows on the desk. "You almost got yourself killed."

She nodded slowly. "I know."

"Victor Tew could've had a gun."

"I know."

He looked at her for a long moment. "So why'd you go down there?"

Bunny hesitated, then lifted her eyes. "Because it felt like I had to. Because Mrs. Kettel was so upset. Because it felt like so many secrets and lies were flying around like grackles, I had to see for myself."

He was silent for a moment, then gave a short nod, as if that was the only answer he needed. "You're not in any trouble," he said, more gently. "I want to be clear about that."

She exhaled.

"But," he continued, "you do something like that again, well, I won't be so generous."

She frowned.

He looked at her squarely. "I thought for sure you were dead, Bunny." He cleared his throat and stood. "Miss Sparks, I mean."

She swallowed, her throat dry. There was a quiet knock on the door as Fern peeked in. "Sorry to interrupt a potential slow-burn moment," she said, grinning at Bunny. "But Rawlings says if he has to pretend to like crossword puzzles for one more minute, he's going to report you for cruelty."

They both regarded her with mild confusion.

"What I mean is, he's trying to keep himself busy and he's growing impatient," Fern explained.

The sheriff cleared his throat and stood. "We're done here."

Bunny rose, and held out her hand. "Thank you, Sheriff."

He took her hand in his, then gently gave it a squeeze before releasing it and sitting back down behind his desk. "Did you give the deputy your statement, Miss Booher?"

Fern saluted. "As ordered, Cap'n."

He gave her a stern look and waved her off.

As Fern fell into step beside Bunny, she looked at her a little sideways. "You gonna tell me what he said?"

"Nope," Bunny said, drawing out the 'p' sound.

Chapter Twenty-Two

Priscilla smiled brightly as she stepped out of her car. "It's nice of you to host this, Bunny. It's a good way for some of the women in the holler to get to know each other better." Her eyes swept over Bunny's home, the barn, the herb gardens, the winding path into the woods that led up the hill to the graveyard, all before resting again on Bunny. "And a good way to get to know *you* better, too."

Bunny offered a gentle nod. "I hope so," she said. "It feels good to be building something here. Not just the house. Friends, too."

Priscilla hummed a soft note of agreement. "Looks amazing back here," she added. "I always figured there must be a big old Queen Anne hidden off this road."

Bunny smiled, heart swelling with pride for Gigi's house and her own quiet work. "My papaw built this house. My granny built the gardens."

"It's beautiful. And the weather, too. I thought we might get rain, but the sky is perfectly clear. It'll be a lovely night to see the constellations." Priscilla smiled broadly as she looked up at the cloudless sky. It was almost 7 o'clock and the evening would culminate with everyone getting a view through the telescope at the constellation Capricorn. "We may even get to catch a glimpse of the Perseid Meteor Shower!"

As more women began arriving, Bunny felt pleased with herself that she had stretched out of her comfort zone and accepted Priscilla's offer to guide the first study group. Ivy had recommended her so highly, it was easy to say yes. As if on cue, Ivy breezed into the barn with her skirts flowing and bangles jingling in the most endearing way. She gave Bunny a quick hug, looked around, and smiled. "Everything looks just lovely, Bunny," she said.

Following Ivy, Jerlene, walking without help or fanfare, held a cookie tin out to Bunny. "Here," she said. "I made these."

Bunny took them and smiled at her.

Fern brought Misti, who was wearing a plain summer dress and flats. Nothing sparkly. She dipped her head when they approached, cheeks pink. Fern wrapped an arm around her shoulders and guided her toward Bunny before entering the barn. "I..." Misti began.

Fern gave her shoulders a little squeeze.

"I..."

"It's okay," Fern said, "Tell her what you told me."

Misti looked up at Bunny, her eyes shiny. "I was told to do some things, Bunny. I didn't want to, but I did them."

Bunny patted her arm. "I know. It's okay."

Misti shook her head. "I buried a St. Joseph statue by your mailbox. Upside down. I was told that you were planning to move, and it would help. I was just going to give it to you, but when I didn't see you... I... I buried it for you." Her face went crimson.

Bunny gave her arm another pat. "I'm not moving."

Fern gave her another squeeze. "It's okay, hon," she said.

Misti wiped her nose with the back of her hand and sniffed. "I got a rash when I did it. On my hands. I told memaw, when I was coming clean about everything. She said it was my punishment."

"Did you bury the statue near the foxglove?" Bunny asked, gently.

Misti nodded.

"Don't worry, Misti." Bunny stepped aside and made room for them to pass. "Things are different now. Go on in. Just enjoy yourself tonight."

Fern gave Bunny a nod and a wink, then guided Misti into the barn. They settled around the wide table set with blank astrology charts and colored pens. Bunny brought out tea and cookies, sprigs of lavender brightening the old wood.

"Oooh," Misti breathed. "I've *always* wanted to peek inside this old barn." She waved toward the far end, where shelves of old books and lab glass shimmered in the warm light. "My memaw said magic happens in here."

"How is your memaw?" Bunny asked.

Misti's cheeks turned a deeper shade and she looked into her lap. "She says to tell you 'thank you, again,' Bunny. She won't stop telling me to tell you that. Forever."

Bunny laughed softly. Just then, Gloryanne swept in, deep purple chiffon clinging tightly. Fern's eyes widened, but Bunny stepped forward without ceremony. "Glad you could make it," she said, motioning to the remaining empty chair.

Priscilla stood and lifted her teacup toward the rafters. "To quote Paracelsus," she began. "The human body is vapor materialized by sunshine mixed with the life of the stars." A hush settled over the room, and the women leaned in. "Anyone familiar with planetary symbols?"

Bunny raised her hand. Several turned toward her, eyebrows raised. "I use them for planting," Bunny said. "It's all part of the rhythm."

Priscilla beamed. "Then you're ahead of the curve."

As the lesson on planetary glyphs got underway, the women focused on their pages, tongues poking out in concentration as they tried to replicate Leo's mane. Bunny saw at least one sketch that resembled broccoli with an antler before she felt a nudge at her elbow.

"Hey. What the heck *is* that?" Fern whispered, pointing toward the open barn doors.

Bunny looked in the direction Fern indicated at the squat figure outside, just off the path, tucked near a mossy log beneath the trees. "Oh. That hideous thing? It's been glaring at me for days."

"Looks like a maniacal rabbit with mange."

"I don't know if you can tell, but there are two of them out there. The one you see from here is the second one that came in a package I got," Bunny said. "No return address, no note. It sat on my porch for over a week before I finally opened it, there was so much going on."

Fern squinted at it. "Why'd you put it there?"

"I didn't know what to do with it, so I stuck it over there with the other one, hoping someone here tonight would see it and come clean."

Fern gave it a long, suspicious look. "That thing looks cursed."

While the women around the table chatted and compared their drawings, Fern pulled Bunny to the door so she could get a better look at the other ceramic rabbit statue. They stood just outside, staring at the unwanted gifts from a distance, when Jerlene's voice rang out inside the barn. "I was *already* at Hoodoo's, you know, when the whole gravel pit ordeal went down. That whole situation was practically handled by then. Honestly, I was the one who told Hoodoo what was really going on."

Fern and Bunny looked at each other.

"Anyway, practically handled. Then this stupid toad kept hopping in front of me," Jerlene added. "I was going to kick it out of my way, and Hoodoo plum near bit my head off. Heckfire. Crazy ol' coot."

Gloryanne bristled. "Why would you kick a little toad, anyway?" She reached for her fourth lemon-lavender cookie. "They're harmless, and everything else."

"Harmless? You shoulda seen it." Jerlene's voice rose. Then, in a rare show of restraint, she looked around and checked herself. "Oh, alright. Bad, Jer." She lightly smacked the back of her own hand and bent back over her drawing, giving it her full attention.

Fern gave Bunny a slow blink. "What is she talking about?"

Bunny whispered, "Toad, I think. I'll tell you later."

"Badger, you say?" Priscilla asked, in a sing-song voice that mesmerized the women. "Why, Misti, did you know your name is the genus of a lovely European badger?"

Misti brightened. "Meles?"

Priscilla nodded wisely and upbeat chatter once again ensued. Until Gloryanne insisted she wanted "sparemint" tea. From then on, she and Jerlene argued about the pronunciation of the word "spearmint."

Fern and Bunny were about to walk back inside to the table when the crunch of tires on gravel caught their attention. Fern turned her head and smiled slyly. "And *that* is my cue to go stir the tea."

Bunny watched as the sheriff's truck came to a stop just down the drive, behind the row of cars. The door creaked open and he stepped out lightly. After just a stride or two, he saw her. "I'm not interrupting, am I?" he asked.

Bunny hurried down to greet him. She hoped this wasn't a loose-end to tie up about gravel pits or car parts.

He walked around to the passenger side and opened the door. "I ran into someone earlier. Said she was on her way out of town, but asked if I could give you something."

Bunny tilted her head. "Who?

"Said her name was Parsy? A friend of G.Didi? I'm guessing that's Granny Didima, up the hill there?"

Bunny nodded, slightly startled.

"According to this Parsy, who had the greenest eyes I've ever seen in my life, if that helps... she said Granny Didima would say you needed this... and that she'd check on you later in the week." From the cab of the truck, he gently opened a small carrier and lifted out a tiny black kitten, its wide eyes, velvet fur, and the tiniest wisp of a meow pulled at Bunny's heart.

"Holy crocus."

He handed the kitten over carefully. "He's all yours. Unless you want me to take him to animal control..."

"You'll do no such thing," Bunny scolded, cupping the kitten to her chest. It smelled faintly of sandalwood.

He smiled. "Didn't think so." When his gaze drifted toward the path behind her, his eyes narrowed at the sight of the two ceramic rabbits glinting in the fading light. "What the heck are *those*?"

"You didn't send them either?" Bunny asked.

The sheriff raised his hands in mock surrender. "Not guilty."

Silence fell between them, broken only by the rhythmic purr of the kitten nuzzling Bunny's chin, as dusk softened the edges of the trees around them. A single cricket chirped happily in the hush. Somewhere in the trees, an owl offered a low, thoughtful hoot. Bunny cleared her throat. "What happened to the shiny New York guy?" The sheriff chuckled. "Turns out, he's a special agent, national security credentials and all. His team's been on the smuggling case too, just coming at it from the other end."

Bunny laughed. "Verisimilitude," she said, "something that appears real."

"That's a new one on me." He grinned. "Blagg was pretty peeved he wouldn't get that interstate crime ring bust for himself. I expect he had a special place already cleared in his office for a trophy."

"I'm glad things might be back to normal." She looked down at the dark fur in her hands and smiled. "Well, almost normal."

He looked beyond her, to the barn this time. "How's it going? Your party, I mean?"

Bunny looked back toward the barn herself, catching light sounds of laughter drifting through the door. She turned back to him. "It's more of a class, really. Jerlene came, walking as if nothing ever happened. Not one person has said a word."

Greenwood nodded, his expression unreadable. "Probably too scared."

"Gloryanne is also here." She waited for him to respond. When he didn't, she added, "She's also pretending nothing happened."

He nodded again, this time absently, staring at the kitten she cradled. They stood there a few moments longer, until he gave her one last look, soft and kind, then tipped his hat. "I'll leave you to your party, then."

As his truck rumbled away down the lane, Bunny watched, catching his eyes in the rearview mirror more than once. She was just about to head back toward the barn when headlights swung through the trees. The black sedan with the neon-lit license plate rolled up like a spaceship landing. "GT2GO." The door popped open just as Misti came prancing down the drive, radiant, her cheeks flushed with new confidence. She saw the kitten in Bunny's arms and said, "Oh, how cute." Her gaze didn't linger long, however. "I've met someone," she announced breezily. "Did you know?"

The man in shiny shoes and matching belt stepped out and offered her his arm.

"This is Angelo," Misti said. Then whispered, "Isn't he dreamy?"

Bunny stared between them. "You're leaving?"

"Yeah." She swayed, her dress swinging to and fro. "Astrology is fun and all…" She made a fluttery gesture toward the barn. "But Angelo is taking me to the movies in Morgan City."

"Your memaw knows?"

"She does. You can call her if you want. I told her everything. I promise." She hopped into the car as Angelo held the door for her.

He smiled shyly at Bunny as he helped Misti in before gallantly closing the door, then he stepped carefully over, extending his hand. "It's a pleasure to meet you," he said.

Bunny tucked the kitten into the crook of one elbow and shook his hand. "Same. But, I have to ask... your license plate. GT2GO? What does it mean?"

He looked toward the car. Misti waved to him from the passenger seat and he gave a little wave back, smiling broadly. "Got to go get the bad guys," he said.

Misti leaned over to call through the window. "We've got to go, or we'll miss the movie."

As he got back into his shiny sedan, Bunny held the kitten close and watched the taillights vanish into the twilight. Then, with a long breath, she looked up.

The stars had come out. Still and watchful.

Familiar now.

Like the hills.

Like her friends.

Like home.

If you enjoyed this story, I'd be grateful for your honest review wherever you like to talk about books.
It helps more than you know.

If you'd like to hear about upcoming releases, special updates, and the occasional behind-the-scenes treat, I'd love to welcome you to my newsletter. Subscribers receive a free bonus story, *The Case of the Tainted Tea*, featuring a young Gene Sparks, an even younger Cal Greenwood, and plenty of herbal intrigue.
You can join at: pruscott.com

Special Thanks

This book would not have been possible without the lovely people in my life who offered their time, keen eye, and expertise when needed.

Of course, I owe a debt of gratitude and heartfelt thanks to the two creative women in my writing group: Angie and Anna. Your insights, encouragement, and endless supply of support got me through every plot twist. Thank you for the many sprints to keep the words flowing!

I'm thankful to so many author-podcasters willing to share their knowledge and experience, especially Joanna, Sarra, Lindsay, Andrea and Jo. IYKYK

Thanks also to Becca Syme, who insisted I lean into my #1 Learner Strength. I had all kinds of theories about why I was stuck. She cut right to the chase and got me back on track!

Many more thanks go to Glenn Simon, for generously sharing part of his process with a stranger; to Denise of Stonelight Candle, whose beautiful creations made writing a sensory experience ("Nature Walk" was burning through every page); to my students, whose curiosity and enthusiasm kept me motivated to reach the finish line; and to my readers, in whom I hope to instill the same joy of curiosity that drives these stories. Your support means the world.

Lastly, but mostly, to my husband, whose patience was only exceeded by his generosity.

Summer in the garden

Pru Scott writes the *Bunny Sparks* cozy mystery series, where small towns have long memories and everyone has secrets. Set in the deep magic of the Appalachians, her cozies draw inspiration from the beauty of her favorite mountain landscapes, old family stories, and places where people know one another's business, whether they mean to or not.

Her books blend warm community ties and found family with eccentric locals, sharp-eyed heroines, and just enough danger to make things interesting, always threaded with a bit of folklore and a touch of mischief.

Pru currently lives among the city folk, where she keeps a small, stubborn garden and teaches all about herbs at a nearby institution. She loves her students, her plants, and a good mystery, especially one solved with quiet determination, a cup of medicinal tea, and a little practical wisdom.